Italian Rendezvous

JUNE PATRICK

FLORENCE & REYNOLDS

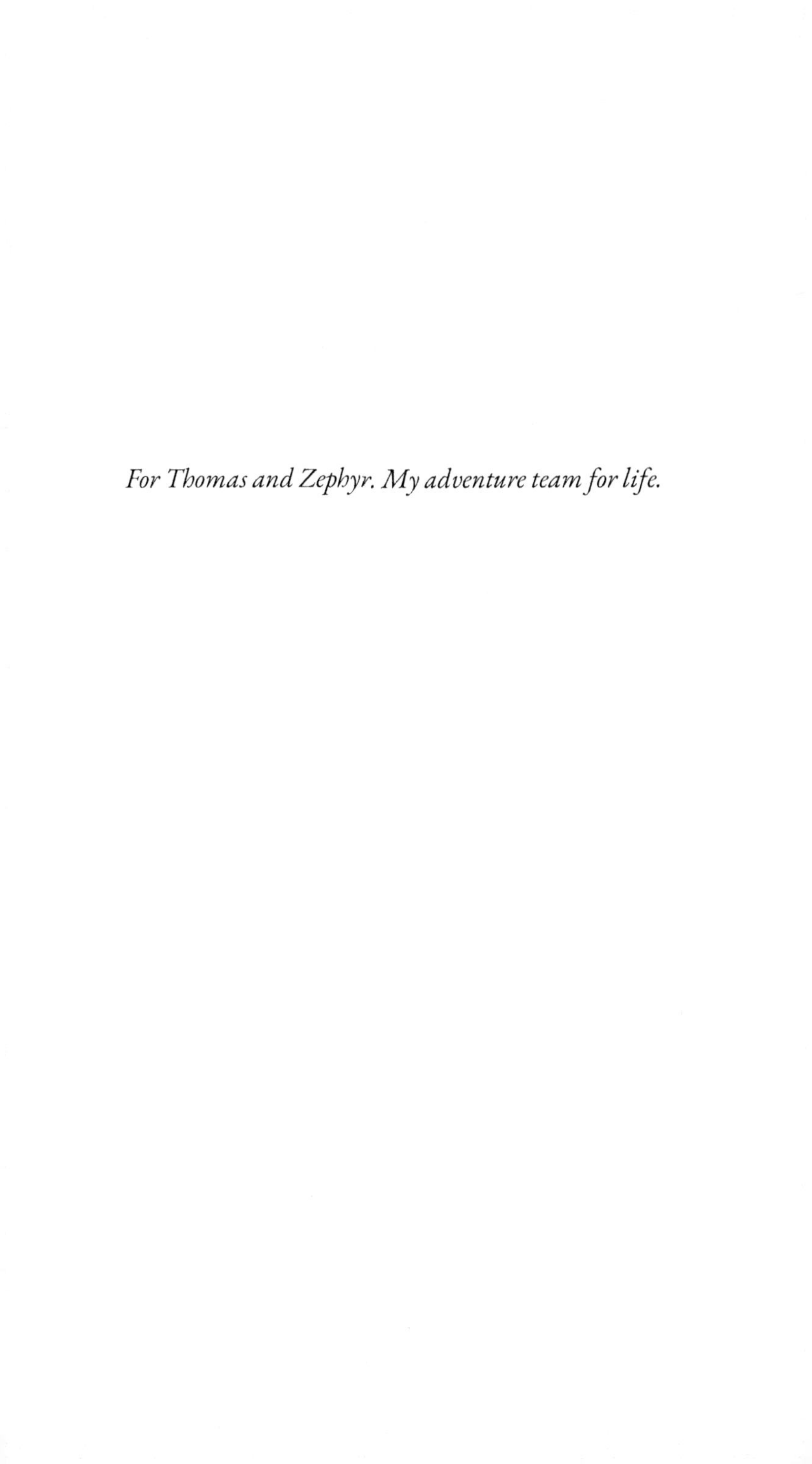

For Thomas and Zephyr. My adventure team for life.

Chapter One

Stepping off the rickety, overcrowded train on the outskirts of Mare Sereno—a small village hugging a curve of the Italian Riviera—I felt a peculiar cocktail of exhaustion and exhilaration. After two hours on a packed cattle car with sweaty patrons seeking coastal refuge from the inland Italian summer, I was practically gasping for air.

But after a whirlwind week touring every museum and historic site I could manage in bustling Milan and Genova, I, too, was dying for some ocean breeze. I'd been warned about the humidity in an Italian summer, and it was all too magnified by the crowded cities. Summer in Italy was not for the faint-of-heart traveler. Even if the San Franciscan in me secretly enjoyed the sensation of melting like an ice cream cone on a summer afternoon.

Before Milan and Genova, there was, of course, a non-stop twelve hours in a chair meant for someone half my size and a steady diet of romantic comedies to distract me from my crumbling life back home. By the time my SFO-Milan flight had landed, my slightly drunk, sleep-starved brain was wondering if life really was a series of meet-cutes and dramatic airport chases.

But here I was. Mare Sereno—the true reason for my trek across the world. My ancestral land. The very dream I'd concocted over years of second-hand armchair travels and nostalgic tales from Nonna. The little train station, with its freshly brewed espresso and baked bread, seemed to embrace me like a nonna. The symphony of unintelligible Italian conversations swirled around me like a thousand operas being performed all at once.

Armed only with a rented cottage address and a wallet full of colorful euros that felt a bit like Monopoly money, I stepped out into the coastal sunshine. Six more weeks of uncertainty stretched before me, offering either an opportunity for self-discovery and reflection or another six weeks of a downward spiral. As I filled my lungs with the fresh sea air, I pledged to make it the former.

Dragging my compact carry-on bag, which felt a bit like a petulant toddler unwilling to follow along the cobblestone, I started toward town. A pleasant warmth greeted me, a world away from the bone-chilling, gray drizzle I'd left behind in California.

I surveyed the quaint town and caught sight of a vintage Fiat taxi waiting nearby, as if summoned by my wide-eyed tourist aura. The driver, a short, rotund man with an unruly mop of dark hair, leaned leisurely against the taxi, smoking a cigarette.

As I approached, I offered him a timid wave, and he sprung to his feet, dropping his cigarette and snubbing it out with his shoe. He flashed me a wide grin accented by a bushy mustache. He made a grand hand gesture as if presenting a new car on a game show.

"*Buon pomeriggio, signora*!" he called out, rushing to take my meager luggage and shoving it haphazardly into the trunk of the car.

I couldn't help but laugh at his theatrics. "*Buon pomeriggio*," I replied, squeezing into the tiny backseat.

"Where are you going?" he asked in accented English.

I sputtered out directions to my rented cottage in my best Duolingo Italian. I hope Nonna wasn't listening to her butchered native tongue from above. I choked back a forming lump. Was grief supposed to go on this long? It had been nearly a year now, but the pain of her absence was still so raw that the mere thought of her laughter was like salt on an open wound. No wonder Ian wanted out. Despite my anger, part of me didn't blame him. I was a hot mess.

"*Bene. Bienvenuta a Mare Sereno*. I am Rio."

"Piacere, Rio. Isla."

"Isla! Bella name. Perfect for the seaside."

He started up the Fiat and flew out of the station with gusto. The short drive was an ocular feast, full of so many sights, smells, and colors that my senses seemed to be at a rock concert. Mare Sereno was like a scene out of a travel influencer's Instagram post — perfect cobblestone streets, buildings that looked like they'd been dipped in a pastel palette, and tiny piazzas filled with locals who seemed to have mastered the fine art of living *la dolce vita*.

Rio whizzed through the tiny streets and into the main piazza, where we dodged scooters and rogue children running amok in their summer freedom.

The Ligurian Sea, a glittering diamond-encrusted tapestry, was a sight to behold. It was so stunningly beautiful that, for a moment, I wondered if my senses were still pickled in the aftereffects of jet lag and tiny liquor bottles because, surely, no place could be this perfect.

A flashback of my grandmother's fairy-tale-like tales of her childhood in this little corner of paradise flitted across my mind. I had once begged my ex-fiancé, Ian, to whisk me here. The absurdity of that notion struck me—as if I needed him to travel anywhere. As if I couldn't just hop on a plane whenever I desired. It was a clear testament to how much I had allowed him to control our lives. But Ian and his control were now relics of the past. I was here, solo, on the precipice of a new, unscripted chapter of my life, savoring the sweet scent of freedom mixed with sea air.

Rio proved to be quite the talker as he regaled me with tales of his unsuccessful attempt to start a tomato garden this spring.

Mid-story, Rio abruptly pulled over to the side of the road, leaving me momentarily confused. "Un momento, signorina," he said, extracting a pouch of tobacco and rolling paper from his pocket. He began to hand-roll a cigarette with expertise that suggested years of practice.

"But anyway," Rio continued, not missing a beat as his fingers dexterously moved. His hands danced around the cigarette paper as he spoke, finally pinching the ends to seal it. "The thing about tomatoes is, they are like women, si? You give them too much water, they get spoiled. Too little? They leave you for a richer soil. And let me tell you, signorina, balancing their needs is an art."

I wasn't sure if he was serious or if it was the punchline.

"Are you allowed to smoke while you're driving?" I asked, trying to keep my amusement at bay.

Rio shrugged nonchalantly. "Who's gonna stop me, the tomato *polizia*? Anyway. Oh, look! A goat."

I whipped my head around to see a lonely goat chewing away on the side of the road.

"I rescued a goat once," Rio said.

"I'm sorry?" I said, uncertain I had heard him correctly.

Rio maneuvered the car around a sharp bend. "It was a stormy day, much unlike today. Dark clouds covered Mare

Sereno, and the sea roared louder than a lion. Not the best weather for a taxi driver, but I was brave."

He paused to take a long drag from his cigarette, and I was grateful he at least had the window rolled down.

"So, there I was," Rio continued. "Driving along these very streets, fighting the storm. Suddenly, I heard a noise. It was distant but desperate. A bleat, signorina, the saddest bleat I've ever heard. So, I pulled over."

I leaned forward in her seat, caught up in Rio's theatrical recounting despite the absurdity of the story.

"I got out of my Fiat, the rain lashing against my face, and walked towards the noise. There it was, a small goat, stranded on a ledge, trembling like a leaf. It had somehow managed to climb up but couldn't find its way down."

Rio paused, taking a deep puff of his cigarette before continuing.

"Seeing the fear in its eyes, I knew I had to act. I'm no firefighter, signorina, but in that moment, I felt like one. I started climbing, grabbing onto rocks, slippery and wet. And just when I was about to reach the goat, it lost its footing."

I gasped audibly, prompting Rio to glance back at me through the rearview mirror with a twinkle in his eye.

"But," he continued with a grin, "I caught it. Just in time. It bleated in my arms, probably thanking me in goat tongue. I climbed down with it, safe and sound. And that's how I, Rio, the humble taxi driver, became Rio, the goat savior." He patted his chest dramatically.

The taxi came to an abrupt stop, jolting me from the moment. "As far as I can go in car, si? The last part is too narrow. But it's just a little walk up that hill."

I laughed and reached for my wallet to pay the fare.

"Grazie, Rio. That was the most entertaining taxi ride I can remember."

I paid the fare and stepped out.

Navigating the cobblestone streets with my tiny suitcase, I silently thanked myself for packing sensibly. My suitcase contained nothing more than comfortable walking shoes and a few breezy dresses. I had hoped to shop locally and embrace the local vibe, but as I took in the quaint fishing village, I doubted I would find any fashionable boutiques here. Maybe I should have shopped in Milan when I had the chance.

Even though I was quickly drenched in sweat and anticipation, the journey up the small hill to my temporary home felt oddly cleansing. The air was ripe with the fragrance of the sea, sharp citrus, and the intoxicating sweetness of gelato. Even my sweat smelled like adventure.

I rang the door chime, a flutter of nerves stirring within me. The sound of approaching footsteps echoed, and the door swung open to reveal a petite woman with a cloud of untamed black curls. Her large, doe-like eyes sparkled with warmth, and her wiry arms seemed to emanate strength. She had the warm, welcoming eyes of someone who'd lived a sun-soaked Italian life and was eager to share it with everyone.

"Ciao!" She said enthusiastically. Her grand 'welcome' gesture would have put even the most enthusiastic Broadway performer to shame.

"Ciao, I'm Isla," I said, only to have her wave off my introduction as if I was stating the obvious.

"I have been expecting you. Come in, *per favore*. I am Maria."

The cottage smelled like fresh citrus, a scent that instantly whisked away any remaining anxiety. Piles of lemons and oranges adorned the counters, and through the back window, I could see a small grove of trees bearing vibrant fruit. The sight alone was enough to lift my spirits. A large black cat lounged lazily on the counter, one paw dangling over the edge and purring happily.

She looked me over, her gaze finally landing on my small

suitcase. "That's all you have?" she asked with a hint of surprise in her voice.

I felt a blush creep into my cheeks. "Yes, I pack light."

Her grin widened. "That's actually quite refreshing to see. I can't tell you how many travelers come and bring their entire wardrobe. Packing light is much more freeing. Come, let me show you to your room. We are so excited to have you here with us for the next six weeks."

Maria led me up two flights of stairs and finally opened the door to a breezy top-floor room.

"There is a little terrace and an ensuite bathroom with shower. There is no personal kitchen, but there is a small refrigerator as well as a little espresso machine in the corner."

The room was luminous and spacious, with sunlight pouring through the grand windows. The soft white walls lent it a bright and tranquil quality.

On one side, there was a small separate bedroom with a fluffy queen-sized bed graced with crisp white linens and an array of vibrant, patterned cushions. A beautifully woven throw blanket was casually draped over the foot of the bed, inviting me to snuggle up and unwind.

In the living space, a pair of French doors opened onto a petite private balcony, offering stunning views of the surrounding coastal scenery. There was also a cozy armchair facing the terrace—it practically begged me to curl up with a book.

"I serve a light breakfast every morning at nine," Maria was still going on, pointing out various features. I forced myself to pay attention.

The room was the sanctuary I needed.

"It's perfect," I said to Maria.

She beamed. "Bene. Well, I will let you get settled. Let me know if you need anything."

I made myself at home in my cozy room, and I felt my soul

slowly expanding. The tranquility of my surroundings was infectious, a healing balm on the still-raw wounds from my past life. As I gazed out onto the shimmering sea from my new sanctuary, I couldn't help but think, "Hello, fresh start. It's nice to finally meet you."

This was a reset button I was more than ready to press. I was going to spend the rest of the summer drowning in pesto and good wine.

Chapter Two

I set about unpacking and settling into my new digs.

Absorbing the charm of my temporary home, I felt a wave of tranquility and satisfaction wash over me.

I opened my modest suitcase, meticulously arranging my clothes in an antique wooden dresser and draping my favorite scarf on the coat rack near the entrance. I hung my two travel-approved dresses on a small hanging rack in the corner of the room and arranged my toiletries on the tiny bathroom shelf. It wasn't much, but it was sufficient.

Maybe I would take a hot shower and spend the day in that armchair.

My stomach grumbled in protest. Ok, maybe after some lunch. I rummaged through my bag for some airplane biscuits to tide me over until I could locate a local proper trattoria.

Pouring a glass of tap water, I stepped out onto the quaint stone terrace. The view stretched westward, and as far as I could see, the horizon was adorned with a stunning canvas of colors. I gazed out over the sea, wondering what my grandmother would have thought if she could see me now. Would she be proud of me? Or would she be disappointed with the mess I'd made of my life? I thought my life was on the right track. I thought I knew what I wanted. I had done everything right, hadn't I?

The thought of her brought a prickling sensation to my eyes again, but I didn't fight it in my private space. I let the small tears come. She had been more than a traditional grandmother to me—she had been like a mother. She had supported me through so much. Fought for me. Cheered me on. She had been my rock when my parents were too preoccupied to notice me—their patients were always the top priority. I couldn't imagine a life without her.

"I am always with you, silly girl," I could hear her saying now. She was a deeply spiritual woman, believing that you never truly leave this world. I hoped that was true. Because right now, I needed her. If she had known what Ian was about to do to me, I think she would have held on just a little bit longer. That was the kind of woman she was. But then again, would Ian have done it had I not been lost in grief?

I remember the day she first told me about the magical land of her birth. I was a little girl—maybe seven—sitting on the porch swing at her house in San Francisco, a blanket draped over our laps against the cool evening breeze rustling the leaves in the small backyard. The scent of freshly baked cookies filled the air, adding to the evening's sweetness.

Nonna Rosa held a small, weathered photo album filled with black-and-white photos, each one a frozen moment from her youth in Mare Sereno, Italy.

"See this one, Isla?" Nonna Rosa pointed at a picture of a young girl standing on a cobblestone street, the grand, shimmering sea forming the backdrop. "That was me, not much older than you are now. That was our town, Mare Sereno. It was a magical place."

Her voice was saturated with nostalgia as she described the quaint coastal town. She spoke of charming houses painted in vibrant colors, the lively piazza teeming with laughter and chatter, fragrant lemon groves, and the boundless, brilliant blue sea. Of the magic said to live in the sea.

She shared tales of her youthful adventures, darting through the narrow, winding streets with her friends, exhilarating scooter rides along the coastline, and joyous festivals that lit up the town with music, dance, and vibrant lights.

"And the food, oh, the food!" Nonna Rosa sighed, her eyes shimmering. "Freshly caught fish grilled to perfection, homemade pasta with Nonno's secret sauce, and the gelato... it was heavenly. Life in Mare Sereno was different." she gently patted my hand. "We knew how to live, truly live. We cherished family, friends, and the simple pleasures of life. It wasn't perfect, but it was home. And it was beautiful."

"Why did you leave, nonna?"

Longing flooded her eyes. "It was a hard time for Italy, *cara mia*. There had been a very bad war, and it was hard to find work anywhere. My mama and papa had some family who had come to San Francisco to make a better life, and they thought they could do the same."

I flubbed my lips. "Sounds like you already had a pretty good life."

Nonna chuckled and pulled me close. "The world is complicated like that."

After that day, my young heart filled with a longing to see this magical place myself one day. I couldn't believe it took me this long.

A single tear escaped as I whispered, "Well, Nonna, here we are. We finally made it. Let's do this."

A knock at the door jolted me from my thoughts. I quickly wiped away the tears and unconsciously smoothed my hair. Taking a deep breath, I opened the door with a smile.

Maria was standing there holding a small tray.

"I thought you might be famished after your journey," she

said. My eyes dropped to the tray, which held an assortment of tiny pastries, a carafe of coffee, and some biscotti. My stomach rumbled in agreement, and my mouth watered at the sight of the scrumptious spread.

"You read my mind. I am, indeed, starving. And I can think of no better welcome gift than pastries," I said.

She studied me briefly and then grinned. "Something tells me you don't usually indulge in pastries."

I shrugged. "Maybe not normally. But I am on vacation."

I stepped aside and gestured her in. "Please, come in."

"I hope you find everything here to your liking," Maria said as she placed the small tray on the table in the kitchen nook. She arranged everything meticulously, as though I were in a quaint seaside restaurant.

"Everything's perfect."

She studied me for a long moment, as if trying to decipher my hidden layers. I felt my defenses rise, and I forced a bright smile to mask the sadness that had overwhelmed me just moments ago.

"Well then, darling, I do hope your stay is restful. Whatever brought you here, I hope you leave it behind. You'll find peace here."

"I have a feeling I will. Just keep the pastries coming," I said, grinning.

Maria chuckled.

"Well, if you fancy a glass of wine later, do swing by the lounge. We always offer our guests a little afternoon refreshment."

"Thank you, that sounds lovely," I said, considering I might need a stiff drink a bit sooner than this afternoon after the journey I'd endured. "I was thinking of venturing into town to explore. Do you have any recommendations for good local food?"

Maria clicked her tongue, a hint of a smile playing on her

lips. "Well, I suppose I'm biased, but I believe everything in the town is delicious. We don't have an extensive variety, but what we do offer is quality. If you're in the mood for something traditional, stop by Trattoria Manoli. They do very good local fare. You won't be disappointed."

"Thank you. And thank you for everything."

Chapter Three

Feeling invigorated after a robust cup of coffee and a surge of sugar, I pulled myself together and strode out into the town, eager to explore my new temporary home. The instant my foot touched the narrow cobblestone streets, a sensory symphony unfurled before me.

The town was a stunning display of colors, with quaint houses painted in warm shades of ochre, salmon, and terra-cotta. Their facades were adorned with tumbling ivy and radiant geraniums springing from rustic pots. Wrought-iron balconies, embellished with climbing roses and bougainvillea in full bloom, lent an enchanting touch to the picturesque scenery.

For a sleepy village, it was surprisingly alive. I strode along, taking in the animated hum of conversation in rapid Italian all around me, punctuated by the sporadic tolling of distant church bells. The distinctive putter of Vespas whizzing by, combined with the chatter of vendors peddling their goods and the gentle rustle of the sea breeze rustling through the trees, created a uniquely Mare Sereno soundtrack.

I imagined the piazza coming alive at night with laughter

and music as locals and visitors flocked to lively cafes and cozy trattorias. I envisioned legendary sunsets, painting the sky with hues of pink, orange, and gold as the day drew to a close.

Yet, it was the tantalizing array of scents that truly captured my attention. Jasmine and citrus blossoms permeated the air, and freshly brewed espresso drifted out of sidewalk cafes, mingling with the sweet, yeasty scent of just-baked bread and buttery croissants. I spotted Trattoria Manoli tucked away in a little alley—so discreet it was easy to miss if you weren't looking for it. I couldn't help but notice a gleaming red Vespa leaning against the ancient building. It was such a clichéd yet charming emblem of Italian culture that it made me chuckle.

I stepped into the restaurant and sucked in a breath of pure garlic.

"*Benvenuta a Trattoria Manoli,*" a man at the front greeted me enthusiastically as I stepped up.

"*Ciao. Posso sedermi qui*?" I sputtered in broken Italian, gesturing toward a cluster of rustic tables with white tablecloths. He nodded and gestured toward a little table.

I slipped in and closed my eyes, feeling like I could just die content right then in a vat of oily garlic.

"Menu?" he asked. I nodded, and he slipped me a printed-out paper with a handful of daily dishes.

I had a simple house-made tomato basil fusilli and a small glass of chianti. The simplicity made it perfect, and I accepted I had been denying myself carbs for entirely too long. I followed up with a single shot of espresso and left the restaurant a happy—very full—tourist.

I strolled back to the town's historic center, taking my time admiring the immaculately preserved architecture and quaint shops teeming with both trinkets and necessities. Italy truly was a historian's dream. The town's waterfront peeked through the alleyways in a postcard-perfect backdrop of sandy beaches and sailboats contrasted against the rugged cliffs and verdant hills.

I passed a hole-the-wall cafe where a group of locals was clustered around the counter, sipping espressos and engaged in animated conversation. It was a quintessential Italian scene, straight out of an old-timey travel poster.

And then I saw him. In the center of the conversation, broad shoulders and dark, unruly hair stood out. He was immersed in a lively debate with an older gentleman, his hands gesturing dramatically as he spoke. His laughter was infectious, and there was a wicked glint in his eyes. I actually stopped in my tracks and stared. There was just something about him. He was ridiculously handsome, sure. But there was something more. A gentle devilishness that ensnared me.

He turned toward me and hi eyes locked on me. Oops. Caught in the act. He flashed a knowing smile, his dimples betraying his mischief and flirtation. He raised his espresso cup in a silent toast, and I felt a blush creeping up my cheeks. I quickly averted my gaze, suddenly awash with embarrassment. I hastened in the opposite direction and ducked into a small boutique. Once the door closed behind me, I burst into laughter. Was I possibly losing my mind? I caught my breath and righted myself.

Looking around, I realized I had stepped into a quaint shop stocked with local wares. Perfect. I was instantly enveloped by a cool, earthy scent. The shop was a charming blend of old and new. Antique wooden shelves lined the walls, groaning under the weight of various trinkets, produce, and handwoven textiles. Glass jars filled with colorful candies sat alongside rustic ceramics, and an array of olive oils gleamed under the warm glow of the overhead lights.

The center of the shop was dominated by a large wooden counter, its surface worn smooth by countless transactions.

Behind it stood the shopkeeper, a petite woman with a crown of silver curls.

She greeted me with a broad smile, her Italian-accented English wrapping around me like a warm embrace.

"*Buongiorno, bella*! How can I help?" she asked in English. My foreignness was clearly obvious. Her hands were already busily rearranging various items on the counter. Her large brown eyes twinkled with a lively energy that belied her age.

"Buongiorno. You have a lovely shop."

She beamed. "Grazie. Please, look around. I can help if you needs."

As I browsed around the shop, I felt the pulse of this place. The history, the charm. The eclectic personality I was starting to see unfold all around me in this little town.

I stopped in front of a shelf brimming with intricately painted pottery, each one a tiny allegory.

"These are beautiful," I said.

The shopkeeper slid in beside me and eyed the wares. "Ah, yes. They are all handmade here in Mare Sereno. Each piece narrates a story of our town, you see."

I picked up a beautifully painted bowl. Its vibrant colors and intricate patterns were mesmerizing. I traced over the design with one finger.

"What story does this one tell?"

She carefully took the bowl from my hands, a far-off look in her eyes as she cradled the ceramic piece.

"This one," she began, her voice softening, "is a story of love. The two birds on the branch represent two lovers. The blooming flowers around them symbolize the blossoming of their love, while the sun above is the universe bestowing its blessings upon them."

"That's lovely."

"It is said, by bringing the art into your home, you help

the stories live on and bring their magic into your home. And who does not need a little more love in their home, si?"

I smiled lightly, thinking of the loveless gray cloud in my own home.

I looked at the bowl again, this time with newfound appreciation. The woman's words had brought the piece to life in my hands.

"I'll take it," I declared, meeting the shopkeeper's warm gaze. "You're right. I could use a little more love."

"Bene. I shall wrap it for you."

I strolled through the bustling piazza full of pasta and hope. Hope for what? I wasn't exactly sure. But being here with a piece of local pottery in my bag made me feel as though I at least was doing something—anything—to propel my life out of the dark hole I'd been in. The warm sun cast a cheerful glow as I navigated the surprisingly lively streets. A delightful blend of sights, sounds, and scents enveloped me. Shopkeepers called out to potential customers, friends greeted each other with affectionate kisses on the cheek, and the mouthwatering aroma of freshly baked pastries wafted through the air. Children's laughter echoed in the distance, mingling with the gentle lapping of the ocean against the coastal rocks. The tantalizing scent of gelato lingered in the air, teasing my senses.

In the center of the piazza, I stopped before a fountain. I gazed into the glittering water, admiring a beautifully carved statue of a mermaid breast feeding an infant mermaid. It was bizarre and beautiful all at once. The aesthetic charm of Europe captivated me, where even a simple park bench was a work of art.

Lost in thought, I turned and stepped back onto the road. Suddenly, the loud, impatient honk of a horn jolted me. A bright red blur barreled toward me, then swerved to avoid a collision. It skidded to a halt, stopping inches away from my thudding heart. I stumbled back, my coffee splattering down the front of my dress, my hand emptying of the newly purchased vase, which shattered on the ground. The rider leaped from the red blur, which I now realized was a shiny red Vespa. "What the hell! Asshole!" I shrieked, reaching for the broken pieces.

He whipped his helmet off, and my heart skipped a beat. There stood my little brief obsession from the cafe earlier.

"*Mi dispiace. Sei ferito*?" The man asked, concern etched across his face.

I blinked, trying to decipher his words. Gathering from his pained expression and outstretched hand, he was inquiring about my well-being.

"I'm fine," I responded, then repeated in Italian, "*Sto bene*."

His face softened into a cheeky grin. He reached for my hand, and I allowed him to help me to my feet. I looked down at my ruined dress and groaned.

"Not Italian, I see," he observed.

"Ah, you speak English."

He winked. "If I must. Americana?"

I forced a small smile. "How did you guess?"

"Well, if it wasn't for your accent, I would've known by the fact that you were carrying around a takeaway coffee the size of your head," he retorted, a playful glint in his eyes.

"Well, I was. No thanks to you. Now my dress is carrying it."

"I'm sorry! I was lost in thought. I didn't see you there. But in my defense, you weren't exactly paying attention, either. You wandered right into the road with your head in the clouds."

"It's a tourist town. Aren't you used to people wandering around aimlessly?"

He chuckled. "It's a tourist town for Italians. We don't get many Americans. We're not used to the way they... *passo lento.*"

I raised my brow.

"How do you say? Walk without a purpose. *Ambio*?"

"Ah. Amble. Right. We do that sometimes."

He eyed me up and down. "Oh, your dress. Mi dispiace. It's so beautiful."

I rolled my eyes at his apparent mockery. Sensing my annoyance, he raised his hands defensively. "I am being genuine. It looks lovely on you, coffee stains and all. But let me make it up to you."

"Do you have a spare dress in your Vespa?" I retorted.

He smirked.

"It's fine. Bene," I conceded, sighing. "My one-of-a-kind vase, not so much."

He leaned down and inspected the broken pottery. "Oh no, I am so sorry. But never fear, it can be replaced."

I eyed him suspiciously.

"You got this from Senora DiAna, si? In that shop?" he said.

I followed his eyes and nodded. "Yes, she said—"

He chuckled. "Si, I know. She told you how rare it was and how it was a tale of love or magic or something. Don't listen to her. She is a... storyteller. Very good at convincing tourists to happily buy her products."

My cheeks reddened with embarrassment.

"Oh, don't be embarrassed. One of a kind or not, it was still a lovely vase, and I am sorry. I will replace it."

I sighed. "It's fine. Lost its charm now anyway."

A wicked glint flashed in his eyes, but then he shook his head. "You know, it's difficult to be upset when you have a glass of wine in your hand."

I chuckled and folded my arms. "That does seem logical."

"Allow me to escort you to Enoteca Serena. They have the best local wines. My treat?"

I hesitated for a moment. The hardened city girl in me was always wary of strangers. But I looked around. I imagined the biggest threat about a glass of wine in the middle of the day in this idyllic Italian town was his dreamy smile.

"I do suppose it's the least you could do," I said. "I'm Isla, by the way."

"Enzo. It's a pleasure to meet you."

Enzo escorted his Vespa to the sidewalk and parked it in a designated area for scooters and bikes. He took the keys, then led the way down the block to the most charming café I had ever seen. He gestured toward a seat on the patio.

"Please, have a seat. Do you prefer red or white?"

"Well, red, really, but it's such a hot day. Should I order white?"

Enzo chuckled. "You are not supposed to do anything. You're simply supposed to do what you feel. Americans love rules so much."

"I don't know, I think we're the land of do whatever you want."

He chuckled again. "You think that, don't you? I love your lack of self-awareness."

He was smiling, but I couldn't tell if he was genuinely making fun of me or not.

"I'm not sure I'm the only one who lacks self-awareness," I said.

"Sorry, too blunt?"

"Red then. I prefer red."

Enzo grinned and nodded. He entered the café, then re-emerged a moment later with an open bottle and two rustic glasses. He splashed a bit into both glasses and settled in next to me. He raised his glass to mine.

"*Cin Cin.*"

I clinked my glass against his and took a sip. The palate was simple. Ripe berries, fresh. Refreshing light. It danced across my tongue.

"I think that is some of the best wine I've ever had," I said.

He smiled. "The beauty of Italian wines is even our simple table wines are made with love. The land is tended well, the grapes are worshiped. The farmers are taken care of."

"You know a lot about wine, then?"

He shook his head. "No, sadly. Only a great deal about how to drink it."

I laughed. "Then you and I have that in common. I'm a connoisseur of nothing more than how to make it go down."

"I think you and I shall get along just fine, Isla."

"So, Enzo, where were you going in such a hurry that you nearly cut my vacation short?"

He sipped and stared into his glass as though thinking through the answer. Finally, he shook his head. "Nowhere. I was just out for a ride."

"Do you always race through the town like that?"

"But of course. Vespas were made for letting go."

I chuckled. "Can't say I've ever been on one."

His face fell in mock horror. "That is truly a crime. We must remedy that."

"Maybe someday I'll ride along the coast like a movie starlet."

"So, what brings an American like you to our sleepy little town? We're not exactly in the Rick Steves book."

"You know Rick Steves?"

He smirked. "Every Americana I've ever met has that blue book." He eyed my tote bag. "I bet you've got one."

I laughed. "Ok, guilty. But it's on ebook." I took a long sip of my wine and savored it before swallowing it and answering. "It's a long story. Mostly, I just needed to get away from my life for a little while."

He nodded thoughtfully. "That's why most people come here, I suppose. To get away. And what is it that you do back in America?"

"I work at a university in San Francisco. I'm a professor."

His eyebrows went up. "A smart woman, then."

I laughed. "Well, an educated one, that's for sure. I don't know about smart. Doesn't seem like I'm making very smart decisions these days."

"Oh, I see there is a story." He refilled both our glasses.

"There is a story," I said with a small laugh. "But I'm not sure I want to share it just now."

He nodded. "Fair enough. Perhaps after the second bottle."

I laughed and covered my glass playfully. "I think I'll stick with just the one for today. I still have some things to do."

He looked around. "Things to do? Like what? Like stroll along the sidewalks aimlessly? Stare into fountains? Read books and drink wine and eat pasta?"

He had a point. I didn't actually have anything to do. Why couldn't I get a little drunk in the middle of the day with a handsome stranger? I looked Enzo over. He was handsome. No doubt there.

"Is this your first time in Italy, then?" He asked.

I nodded, feeling somewhat embarrassed. My lack of world travel was a sore spot for me. As a young person, I'd always dreamed I would be traveling the world in my 20s, having adventures. But I had spent the better part of a decade in school. My nose in a book, always thinking about the future. Trying to build the right kind of life. The kind of life I was supposed to have. Success and stability always at the forefront.

"I'm afraid it is."

"What brings you here, then? I mean, most people usually

hit the big three their first time in Italy. You know Venice, Florence, Rome."

I smiled. "Well, I do hope I'll get down there someday. I saw Milan and Genova before I got here. But, well, this town has some family meaning for me." I swallowed, the lump feeling stuck in my throat as I thought about it. "My grandmother was actually born here."

Enzo's face lit up. "Is that so? Then we are basically family."

I laughed. "She left when she was about twelve. After the war. They emigrated to San Francisco. It's a long shot, but I was just thinking there might be people here who might have known who she is. Or at least I can walk some of the same streets she might've walked. She recently died. And we were really close. I mean, really close. It's a long story, but she was like a mother to me." The wine and the company were loosening my tongue in a way I hadn't anticipated.

Enzo's hand reached out and gently touched mine.

"I am so very sorry for your loss. There is no pain worse than that. But how great to have had her so long?"

"Thank you, that means a lot to me," I responded, my voice thick with emotion. "So, anyway, things got a little complicated back home, and I needed an escape. I've always wanted to come here, and now more than ever, it just felt right. It's as if I needed to be here, to feel close to her again. Maybe a bit of her spirit has found its way back home. That sounds silly, doesn't it?"

Enzo's expression softened. "Not at all. We are a spiritual bunch here in Mare Sereno. I believe her soul may well have found its way home. Perhaps you even carried it with you on your journey."

I felt a warm sensation spread within me at his words. "I love that idea. Thank you. That's a very kind thing to say. I needed to hear something like that." I sipped my wine and tried to regain my lost composure. "Are you from here, then?"

"Si. Well, mostly. I was born here. I moved away for a bit. Went to school in Genova. But I like it here. It's peaceful, easy-going. *La dolce vita*, no?"

"How did you learn English? I mean, you speak it really well."

"Grazie. In school, mostly. But my parents were fluent because of their work, and they knew it would be important. I'm grateful for their foresight in that. Most people around here have tried to learn, seeing the importance of it."

"Wish I knew Italian. I feel like such an idiot bumbling around."

"You can learn. Just spend a bit more time with the locals." He winked, coaxing a sheepish smile from me. Leaning back, Enzo sipped his wine thoughtfully, his eyes reflecting an idea brewing in his mind. "You know what you need to do? See the coastline."

I laughed and wiped away a rogue tear. "Yes, I definitely think I should."

He waved his hand dismissively. "None of that tour bus nonsense. Not even a car. No, what you need to do is see it the way the Sea Gods intended. On a Vespa, like a true Italian."

I half laughed and started to protest when he interrupted me. "Probably how your grandmother would have."

I mock glared. "Unfair ammunition."

He grinned.

I bit my lip, trying to decipher if he was just teasing me. "I don't know how to ride a Vespa," I finally admitted, my cheeks flushing.

He shrugged nonchalantly. "That's not a problem. Luckily for you, I happen to be an expert."

"But you almost ran me over with yours. Not sure I trust your driving skills."

"Just because I'm an expert rider does not mean you're an expert pedestrian," he retorted.

I chuckled. "I suppose you have a point."

"Then it's settled. You'll join me tomorrow for a ride up the coast. I need to head out that way, anyway."

I felt my jaw drop slightly. Shaking my head, I protested, "I can't just go on a Vespa ride with you."

"And why not? Do you have other plans?" he queried, a playful smirk on his face.

I hesitated. "I... I... No, not exactly, but..."

"Then I see no problem. I'll pick you up first thing in the morning. Let's say, 10 o'clock?"

I laughed. "10 o'clock is your idea of first thing in the morning?"

"In the summer? Absolutely. It's all relative to when the sun rises and sets, isn't it?"

I tilted my head, considering his logic. "I've never really thought about it that way. I tend to follow time the conventional way."

He smirked at me. "Ten it is, then."

"I don't think I've agreed to anything. I don't even know you."

He shrugged. "Ok. I am Enzo Allegretto, son of Enrico and Alessia of Mare Sereno. I love art and pesto but prefer the sea and the open coastal road to the city. Piacere."

He said it with such theatrics I nearly spit wine.

"I suppose anyone with that stellar CV couldn't possibly be dangerous."

He stood, a wide grin on his face. "I recommend comfortable shoes and a hat. Ciao, Bella."

"I did not say yes!" I called out, but he chose to ignore me, the infuriating, charming Italian.

I found myself stealing glances at his well-sculpted backside as he sauntered back to his gleaming Vespa. He swung his long legs over it, fired it up, and sent me a casual wave as he disappeared down the street.

Shaking my head in disbelief, I drained the last traces of wine and packed up my things. With a small smile, I thought of the stories I could tell back home about my encounter with an impulsive Italian on a Vespa.

Chapter Four

Enzo left me feeling flustered, annoyed, and admittedly a little intrigued. Despite his overt charm, his arrogance was hard to ignore. He was likely accustomed to American tourists swooning over his velvety accent and stereotypical Italian allure. After all, he rode a cherry red Vespa through an Italian beach town. Could it be more cliché? Yet, the way he looked at me... I brushed off the thought. I refused to let his charm ensnare me on the very first day. I had an entire summer ahead.

I stood to go, then noticed Enoteca Serena was attached to a small wine shop. Now, that was something I could immerse myself in, learning more about Italian wine. I decided to pick up something to enjoy later on my little terrace.

I pushed open the door, triggering a soft chime from the small bells hanging overhead. Inside was a cozy, dimly lit space that seemed to transport you to another era. The shop carried a faint smell reminiscent of a cellar, but it was neither unpleasant nor damp. Instead, it was fresh, like Napa during harvest season, with an undercurrent of acidity and the scent of fresh leaves. I closed my eyes, inhaling deeply.

The shop was lined with shelves from floor to ceiling, each

one bearing an impressive collection of wines from various regions of Italy and beyond. Each bottle was meticulously arranged with its label facing outward, inviting you to take a closer look.

In the center of the shop stood a large, rugged wooden table, surrounded by mismatched chairs, and I hoped it was an invitation to taste. Above it, a rustic chandelier crafted from old wine bottles bathed the space in a soft, warm glow.

"*Buongiorno! Benvenuta.*" A woman popped in from around the corner. She was probably a little older than me, with short curly red hair and wide green eyes. If it wasn't for the golden skin, she could have been Scottish.

"*Buongiorno. Parla inglese*?" I asked shyly.

She grinned. "Si, I do. Sorry, I was helping in La Enoteca. Welcome to La Botega del Serena."

"Oh, is it part of this shop? The enoteca?"

"Ah. Si. They are both mine. A place to buy and a place to sit." She smiled warmly. "I am Gianna, the owner. What brings you in today?"

"I was just having a glass next door, and I wanted to pop in and see what else I could find. The wines here are so good."

She smiled bashfully as though she was responsible for all the grapes in Italy. "Please, look around. Take your time. Let me know if you need any assistance."

"Grazie."

I meandered through the shop, eyes grazing over each label. I knew practically nothing about Italian wine, but every label seemed to tell a unique narrative, and I was utterly enchanted by the assortment of labels and vintages. Sensing my keen interest, Gianna approached me.

"You seem to have a discerning eye for wine. Are you a connoisseur?" Gianna asked.

I chuckled, gently shaking my head. "Not in the least. I

know basically nothing about the wines here other than that they are delicious."

"That's the most important part."

"It's the stories behind different types of wine that fascinate me." Gianna shot me a questioning look, and I clarified. "I'm a history professor. And I'm always looking for a story."

Gianna's eyes sparkled with enthusiasm. "Then you've landed in the perfect place. If it's about Italian wine, I assure you I am your Google."

I grinned, appreciating her self-assurance, which, in her case, seemed endearing rather than presumptuous.

"I'm all ears, then. What would you recommend?"

A knowing smile played on Gianna's lips, as though my question was the one she had been anticipating.

"Well. Understanding Italian wines can be a lot at first. There are vast varieties and regions." She picked up a bottle of red from the shelf and handed it to me. "We'll commence with one of the most renowned Italian wines, Chianti. You've probably had it, si?"

"I think I've had an $8 bottle from a Trader Joe's."

She smiled. "For eight euros, you can have a pretty nice Chianti here. It comes from the Tuscany region and is primarily concocted with the Sangiovese grape. It is a versatile wine, very easy to drink. This one here has cherry, plum, and a subtle hint of earth. This one is reasonably priced. Six euros."

"You've sold me."

She chuckled. "Bene. If you want something more complex, I recommend Brunello di Montalcino. It's also crafted from Sangiovese grapes, but the flavor profile is significantly more intense."

"I'd love to try them both."

"Wonderful. You want anything white?"

I shrugged. "Why not. I'm in a buying mood."

She flashed me a playful look. "I'll try not to take advantage." She plucked another bottle from the shelf. "This is a vermentino, a delightful white from the coastal regions of Tuscany and Sardinia. It boasts a tangy, citrusy flavor with a whisper of almond and an agreeable minerality."

I passed Gianna eighteen euros for three bottles and cradled the bag to my chest.

"Grazie. I can't wait to try them all," I said.

Gianna's smile radiated. "It was my pleasure, Isla. Thank you for coming in. The best way to learn about Italian wines is to keep tasting and exploring. In fact," she opened the desk drawer and pulled out a small flyer. "I host wine tastings here in the shop once a month. And there is one this Friday. You should come. It's a wonderful opportunity to taste some exceptional wines and learn more about them. And you will meet some local faces as well." She handed me the paper.

"That sounds lovely. But—"

She smiled. "We can translate to English, don't you worry. All are welcome."

I smiled and tucked the flyer into the bag. "Thank you. I can't wait."

"Thanks for coming in. Enjoy your day and Benvenuta a Mare Sereno."

* * *

The piazza was taking on a lazy afternoon lull as I walked back to my rental. A feeling of warmth washed over me, as if a comforting hand had been placed on my shoulder. I closed my eyes, letting the feeling linger. I realized that I was not alone on this journey. My grandmother was with me, her spirit guiding me, encouraging me to embrace the unexpected, to live a little. And so, I decided that's exactly what I would do.

I passed back by the fountain at the center of the piazza

and eyed the scene of the crime, spotting a few pieces of broken "one-of-a-kind" pottery lingering on the ground.

Smiling, I left it there as a symbol of my unexpected encounter. Maybe it would bring luck to future visitors.

That evening found me unanchored, with no particular plan or itinerary in mind. This style of aimless wandering was uncharted territory for me, as I was accustomed to a more structured approach to life. Nevertheless, as the sun set and a chilly ocean breeze swept across the shore, I made a conscious effort to slow my pace, to let each new sensation seep into my very core. Just as I was becoming one with my surroundings, my stomach issued a timely protest. It was then that I realized the quaint trattorias were devoid of patrons. Still adjusting to local dining customs, I found myself at odds with the Italian meal schedule.

But who says I need to follow the rules? I mused, a smirk playing at the corners of my mouth. I could always have a glass of wine to kill time.

Scattered along the water's edge were a handful of tiny restaurants displaying signs for Aperitivo—7 euros. I'd seen those signs in the cities, too, and it seemed like a version of Happy Hour. I'd been tempted by the crowds of young professionals clutching bright orange goblets, but I'd always felt too shy to join in with the fast-talking, chic Italians in sharp suits and deadly heels.

I chose a small restaurant with a terrace and slid into a vacant table with an unobstructed view of the sun sinking into the Mediterranean's azure depths. The Italian Riviera, with its pastel-hued houses clinging to sheer cliffs, was a sight to behold.

The small restaurant was bursting with local chatter and activity—all of it bordering on intimidating. I wasn't exactly sure how things operated here. But soon, a vivacious young server approached, rattling off in Italian.

"*Buonasera. Benvenuta a Ristorante Marina.*"

I mustered up my limited vocabulary to ask for the menu, only to falter. Recognizing my struggle, he smoothly transitioned into English.

"Americana?" He queried.

"Si. I'm beginning to see it's quite obvious."

He waved away my concern. "Is no problem. We don't have a menu right now. Is apertivo now."

"Oh, bene. Like a happy hour, si?"

He bobbed his head. "Si. It is..but it is more than just a cheap drink." He winked at me. "Is a way to whet your appetite. Encourage your senses to open. To bring your day to a halt and enjoy."

"Sign me up," I said. "What's on offer?"

He grinned. "You like an Aperol Spritz?"

His suggestion piqued my interest. I noticed that a majority of the patrons were savoring a vibrant, peach-hued cocktail. Acknowledging his recommendation with a nod, I decided to give it a shot. "I've never had one, but it looks perfect."

"And something to eat?" Caught off guard, I hesitated. He chuckled. "Is part of the whole thing. I'll be right back."

Within minutes, my attentive server returned bearing a stunningly colorful cocktail and a platter of delectable morsels. He presented the food and drink with a flourish, explaining the spread before me.

"This is an aperitivo. You have prosciutto, cheese, fruit. You always have something to eat with your drink. Keeps the head light, no?"

"Looks amazing. Grazie."

He dismissed my concern with a laugh, explaining that food was an integral part of the Italian drinking experience.

"Will you be expecting company, signorina?"

"No, it's just me."

His eyebrows shot up. "Alone? A shame. A woman like you shouldn't be alone."

I chose to ignore the faint hint of patriarchal sentiment, accepting it as a well-intentioned compliment.

"Thank you. But I'm actually quite enjoying my own company."

With a nod, he acknowledged my position. "As you wish. If you need anything, don't hesitate to ask. My name is Ricardo."

"Grazie, Ricardo."

Ricardo receded into the restaurant's warm interior, leaving me to my solitary enjoyment. I inhaled the fragrant aroma of the cocktail before taking a sip. Its crisp, tangy flavor took me by surprise, refreshing in its understated sophistication. Not wanting to completely pig out in public, I carefully ladled generous helpings of prosciutto onto slices of crostini drizzled in fragrant olive oil. The combined flavors burst in my mouth, a symphony of taste so delightful it bordered on sinful.

Before I realized it, my plate was bare, and my glass stood empty. Ricardo reappeared, a teasing smirk playing on his lips as he surveyed the aftermath of my gastronomic adventure. "Did you enjoy your meal?" he asked, his eyes twinkling.

I dabbed my mouth with a napkin, grinning sheepishly. "Yes, I enjoyed it immensely, as you can tell. And the drink too."

"Another drink?"

"Most definitely."

His smile broadened as he disappeared, returning shortly with a fresh spritz. This time, however, he lingered beside my table. The silence stretched on, becoming awkward. Finally, I asked, "Did you need something else?"

He seemed hesitant. "Actually, I had a question."

"Yes?"

"Why are you here alone?"

I was taken aback and laughed awkwardly. "What do you mean?"

"Why are you dining alone?"

His question, though simple, struck me as odd. Back home, I frequently dined alone, went to bars alone. I even went to the occasional movie alone. No one had ever questioned my solitary activities.

"Well, I'm traveling alone. I don't have anyone to dine with at the moment."

His expression registered shock. "You have no one to dine with?"

"Really, it's not a problem. I chose to travel solo."

Despite my reassurances, he seemed to see me as a lone, pitiful figure. "Ah, an independent spirit," he said, though his tone bordered on condescending.

Choosing to ignore the slight, I sipped my drink. "Something like that."

"Ah, I didn't mean to offend you!" he exclaimed, flustered. "I didn't doubt your ability to travel alone. It's just that this place is inherently romantic, best enjoyed with loved ones."

"Well, I suppose I'm out of luck then," I retorted lightly.

Laughing, he asked, "Where are you from, bella?"

Resigned to the fact that he wouldn't leave me alone, I replied, "California."

"A long way from home. But I've heard that California is much like Italy."

I chuckled, "Yes, Northern California does share some resemblance to this region. We have some rolling vineyards as well."

"And what brings you to our humble corner of Italy?"

A wave of fatigue washed over me at his question, but I merely shrugged. “I’ve always wanted to see it.”

He seemed to catch my unspoken signal and didn’t probe further. “Well, do enjoy your stay. And if you’ve no other plans, you might consider staying for dinner.”

Pondering over the generous spread of antipasti I had just devoured, the thought of more food seemed overwhelming. “Thank you. What time would that be?”

“About nine,” he answered.

I stifled a laugh. Eating so late would certainly disrupt my usual schedule. But I shrugged it off, reminding myself *When in Rome.*

As the nine o’clock hour drew near, the little restaurant began to hum with life. Families trickled in, filling up the previously empty tables. Wicker baskets brimming with bread were served, and wine was generously poured. The ambiance transformed from a relaxed seaside café to a bustling, cozy Italian ristorante. Spotting Ricardo, I called out, “I think I’d like to see your dinner menu after all.”

His face lit up as he theatrically slid a small paper menu in front of me. “Our menu is simple but always fresh and seasonal. Our pescatore delivers to us daily, and our chef prepares everything from scratch. I assure you, no matter what you choose, you won’t be disappointed.”

I scanned the menu, my eyes roving over the enticing options: Fritto Misto, salads, fresh fish, and homemade pasta. “I’m tempted to order one of everything.”

He laughed heartily. “We’d be delighted to keep you here all night. And if you can’t manage the walk back, you’re welcome to sleep out back. However, I highly recommend our pesto—it’s a local specialty.”

“What would the chef recommend?”

Ricardo’s eyes sparkled mischievously.

“*Un momento*,” he said, disappearing into the restaurant.

Soon, a genial man with a sun-tanned face and sauce-stained chef's whites emerged from the kitchen. He greeted me warmly, "*Buona sera, signorina*. I'm Salvatore, the chef. Ricardo tells me you have questions."

I grinned, loving every moment of this scene plucked right from a campy Netflix comedy. "Si. I was just wondering what you'd recommend to a first-time patron."

"Bene. The trofie al pesto is, of course, a staple. A hand-made pasta twists smothered in fresh basil pesto. But I think today's fresh tuna is divine. Light herbs and olive oil with Myer lemon." He made a kissing noise. "Simple but will melt on your tongue."

I literally felt drool forming at the corners of my mouth.

"I'll take your recommendation," I said. "And maybe a wine to go with it?"

I could get used to this service, I thought. A chef at a popular restaurant in San Francisco wouldn't give me the time of day.

"Of course! I think tonight bring signorina a bottle of the Domenico Pinot Nero."

"With fish?" I asked, brow furrowed.

"Don't you trust me?" There was a glint in Salvatore's eyes that made me grin.

"With my dinner."

He bowed theatrically and nodded to Ricardo.

"I'll be back for la dulce." Salvatore winked and scurried off.

* * *

As the night deepened, the cafe began to empty out, families making their way home and the clinking of glasses and cutlery fading into the gentle hum of the ocean. The once-lively ristorante had returned to a serene state, illuminated by the soft glow of lanterns hanging haphazardly from the ceiling. The air was still warm, carrying the remnants of the day's heat and the salty tang of the sea.

Finishing off the last of my house-made strawberry gelato and Sciacchetrà dessert wine, I looked out over the darkened waters, the moon casting a silver glow over the undulating surface. The waves, the wine, and the lingering taste of pesto and fresh seafood brought a sense of satisfaction and peace I hadn't known I was searching for when I embarked on this solo adventure.

Ricardo, with his tray tucked under his arm, approached the table, a gentle smile playing on his lips. "Did you enjoy your meal?"

"Immensely," I replied, patting my now protruding belly. "Grazie, Ricardo. And please extend my compliments to Salvatore. It was all simply divine."

"I'm glad to hear that," he said, looking genuinely pleased. "I hope this means we'll be seeing you again?"

"I wouldn't miss it," I assured him, already looking forward to my next culinary adventure in this charming place.

With a final wave, I rose from the table, wrapping my shawl around my shoulders. As I meandered along the cobblestone path back to my rental, I felt a sense of fullness—not just from food and wine, but from the experience of being fully immersed in the Italian way of life, if only for an evening.

The soft glow of the moonlight illuminated the piazza as I got home, casting long shadows on the cobblestone streets. The town had settled into a quiet slumber, and all was calm and peaceful.

Lying in bed that night, my thoughts drifted back to Enzo, who I'd nearly forgotten about. I almost couldn't believe I'd agreed—well, sort of agreed by not refusing—to go up the coast with someone I literally just met. But something about Enzo's reckless spontaneity was intriguing. And wasn't that why I had come here? To break free from the structured monotony of my life, to experience something different, something unpredictable?

I fell asleep to the lapping waves and the budding feeling of freedom.

Chapter Five

The next morning, I woke with the crow of a rooster, who I'm pretty certain had made himself at home right on my windowsill. I rolled over sleepily, enjoying the feel of the rising sun on my face. If this was a Riviera alarm clock, I'd take it. I checked the clock. Five a.m. I'm sure it was partly due to jet lag and partly because I've been an early riser my whole life. But what did it matter? I could wake or sleep at my leisure all summer long.

Then my memory came back to me in a flood, and I sat up with a jolt. Had I actually agreed to go on a Vespa tour today with Enzo? I hadn't exactly said yes, but he sure acted like I had. Nerves started stockpiling in my gut.

I fixed myself some coffee using the little espresso maker on the stand. Nervously staring out the window, I threw it back in one sip. Although the taste was incredible, I still hadn't gotten used to not having a super-sized cup of strong black coffee in the morning. I opened the window and stepped out onto the tiny veranda. Bursting lemon trees welcomed me with birdsong, and the glittering sea waved in the distance. Everything was vibrant and alive—a world in Technicolor.

After a second shot of espresso, I showered and headed down to the main room in search of the included breakfast, secretly hoping for pastries. For too long, I subsisted on strong black coffee and green smoothies in the morning. During my past week touring Milan and Genova, I'd had my share of treats, but the constant walking and climbing of ancient towers had kept any holiday weight gain in check. Now that I found myself in my lazy beach days, I was slightly concerned about what all these decadent carbs were going to do to my hard-earned waistline. But not nearly concerned enough to resist the decadent display of croissants, chocolates, fruit, and cheese laid out. My taste buds started salivating at the sight of all the deliciousness. After all, I was on vacation, right?

I settled in and plucked a decidedly delicious croissant, and filled my plate with fresh fruit. I closed my eyes and savored every bite.

"Buongiorno!" a chipper voice said. I looked up and saw Maria coming in. She had a tray carrying a French press, percolating the sweet scent of rich coffee. Next to it was a cup decidedly larger than an espresso.

"You're up early," Maria said.

"Couldn't resist the smell," I responded, laughing slightly.

"I know Americans like their coffee. We Italians, too. Do you take it with any sugar or cream? I'm terribly sorry I forgot to ask."

I shook my head. "No, I am a strong black drinker all the way."

She nodded softly and then filled a little cup with the thick black liquid. She set it down in front of me, and it was everything I could do not to just slam it back in one go. Instead, I picked it up and sipped it slowly, just as I was trying to do with everything in my new experience.

I glanced over at the dining table and noticed two unfamiliar faces. A couple, I assumed—probably a bit older than I was. They looked up and shared polite smiles.

"Ah, let me introduce you," Maria said, noticing my glance. "Isla, meet Lucas and Ava. They're also staying here for a while."

Lucas was tall with a sandy hair color that mirrored the tones of the Italian beaches. His eyes were a friendly blue, and he offered a warm smile as he stood and extended a hand. "Nice to meet you, Isla."

He was also decidedly British.

Ava was petite, with a cascade of curly red hair and bright green eyes. She flashed a warm smile that held a twinkle of mischief. "Pleasure to meet you, Isla."

"Likewise," I replied, returning their smiles. "Are you two on vacation?"

"I think it's more of a culinary adventure," Ava said, eying the spread on the table.

"I think you've come to the right place," I said.

Maria, looking flattered, gave me a playful nudge. "Go on now. Sit, sit. Breakfast is fresh and hot."

Lucas poured a cup of steaming coffee and slid it across the table to me. "Thank you," I said, cradling the cup in my hands, relishing the warmth seeping into my fingers. "Hard to subside on espresso shots, no matter how delicious."

"Cheers to that," Lucas said. "So what brings you to Mare Sereno? Seems an unlikely vacation spot for a solo American."

I sipped my coffee—gut-punching robust and just what the doctor ordered. "My family is from here. Generations ago, but I always wanted to visit, and I had the time off, so I came for the summer." I shrugged.

"Brilliant!" Ava said, clapping her hands gently. "Isn't it marvelous here? I honestly fell in love at first sight. It's our first time here as well. We usually hit up the usual traps like Rome and Milan, but this place is just magic."

"I agree," I said, smiling.

"And what do you do that you had the summer off?"

"Oh, I'm a college professor."

"How fascinating!" Ava exclaimed. "What do you teach?"

"History. With a focus on the Renaissance and medieval periods, actually. Random, I know."

"Brilliant," Lucas chimed in. "You could probably show us a thing or two about the local sites then."

I blushed. "Happy to, although I'm learning right along with you, I'm afraid. Are you two working while you're here or just enjoying the food?"

"A bit of both," Ava said. "We hail from Hampstead, outside of London. But we both work remotely. Lucas is a software engineer, and I'm a freelance illustrator. But the food..." Her eyes lit up at the thought, "the food is a significant part of why we're here."

Lucas laughed, taking Ava's hand in his. "She wants to start a food blog. So we decided, why not start where the food is best?"

I smiled, admiring the ability to live life on your own terms, to take a risk.

"How's everything?" Maria came back into the room.

"This is all wonderful, thank you. One of the best breakfasts I've had in a long time," I said.

"Divine, as every day," Ava agreed.

Lucas checked his watch—a flashy gold and leather thing that caught the morning light. "Oh! I'm afraid we must be off, Ava. We have that lunch."

She dabbed her mouth with her cloth napkin, then stood. She was tall and graceful in a cream jumpsuit and, in my opinion, looked like the exact person who should be spending the summer on the Italian Riviera.

"Lovely to meet you, Isla. Perhaps we'll see you again for tea?"

Not knowing if she meant actual tea or some kind of British afternoon ritual or simply dinner—I never could quite keep it straight—I just nodded enthusiastically.

"And what will you be doing today, Isla?" Maria said as she gathered Lucas and Ava's dishes.

I sipped my coffee thoughtfully before answering. I don't know why I felt so embarrassed, but it just felt terribly reckless to be going off on a rendezvous with someone I literally just met. He could be a serial killer, for all I know. Did they have serial killers in Italy?

"Well, I am actually going on a little sightseeing tour."

Maria's face lit up. "Oh! How wonderful. Did you book a tour guide? Is it Lorenzo's bus? He's a cousin of mine, you know. Second cousin, really. At least, I think that's how it goes."

I chewed my lip. She'd given me the opening, so I took it. "Yes, actually. Well, not Lorenzo, but someone I met in town. I suppose that seems a little unsafe, but—"

She waved away my concerns. "Unsafe? Nonsense. This is the safest place in the world. The only thing you're in danger of is your own stupidity. We've had more than one tourist fall off a cliff after too many Aperols."

I chuckled.

"So just don't drink too much wine and fall into the sea, and you'll be fine. Who is your guide, might I ask?"

"Oh," I said, buying myself time. I was sure she would know who Enzo was. And I suppose that could be to my advantage. Maybe I could find out a bit more about him.

"His name is Enzo." I hesitated when I realized I didn't know his last name. We hadn't exchanged such formalities.

"Enzo. Do you, by any chance, have any more details? It's a fairly common name."

"Right, he's young, probably my age, and he drives a bright red Vespa," I said, trying to smooth my nerves.

She smiled. "Oh, Enzo Biagioni. Si, I know Enzo. That sounds like a wonderful afternoon. You're going to have a great time."

I fidgeted with a lock of my hair and picked up my croissant nervously. "Do you... do you know Enzo well, then?"

She shrugged. "Well enough. I know everybody in this town. There aren't that many of us to know, you know?" She laughed.

I wanted to ask more, but I didn't want to sound too eager. "Is he safe to go out on a tour with?" My voice was nervous and creaky.

She left. "Safe? Sure. I assume he's taking you out on a Vespa? That's sort of his thing, you know?"

"Yes, that was his proposal. I'm a little nervous, I guess. I suppose I don't trust people all that easily, and it seems reckless."

She nodded sympathetically. "Yes, I can understand that. But you are a long way from San Francisco. We are all family here, do not worry. Enzo is a fabulous driver. Just... be careful, okay?"

"Careful?"

She just smiled. "Wear your helmet, si?"

"Oh, right. Ok."

After a moment, she turned back to me and said, "I assume you know he's not actually a tour guide."

My face reddened. "I do know. Well, I guess I was lying a little bit."

She chuckled. "Oh, I get it. You're embarrassed. No need to be. You're on vacation. You're supposed to meet handsome strangers and go off on adventures. It's the very nature of an Italian vacation."

"That's what I keep telling myself. Live and let live and all that," I said it more to myself than anything.

. . .

An hour later, I found myself staring into the mirror, admiring my flowing white linen dress dotted with a colorful motif—a sundress I hoped would make me look less like a scholar on sabbatical and more like an adventurous woman in her prime. Well, "adventurous" was a relative term. I had once eaten Fugu blowfish sushi in L.A.'s Japan town — that was pretty damn adventurous. Did you know they can kill you? Fugu blowfish, I mean.

I paired the dress with soft Italian leather sandals I thought would work well riding a scooter along the Ligurian Sea. Did I look the part? I thought so. I'd spent a lot of years looking the part with Ian. I should be a pro by now.

I pulled my hair back into a messy twist, noticing that my chocolate hue was already getting streaks of gold from my days beneath the summer sun. Nature's highlights beat my over-priced salon any day.

I checked the time and realized I still had an entire hour before Enzo was supposed to arrive. I needed more coffee. Story of my life—more coffee.

I popped into the kitchen and poured another cup of coffee, then made my way out to the little bench outside the cottage. The day was already hot, but the sea breeze kept it comfortable.

A couple strolled by hand-in-hand, and my thoughts drifted to Ian again. I tried to toss them out on their ass, but the wound of his betrayal was still so gaping. We'd always talked about coming here. Once grad school was over. Once he'd made partner. Once I'd made tenure. Once we were married. Once, once, once... It seemed we'd spent the last decade kicking our dreams down the road. I wondered if he'd come here with sexy baby Miranda now.

Grr...I shoved all thoughts of Ian out and locked the door.

I glanced down at my phone and realized I hadn't noticed the phantom ticking of the minutes going by. It was now 10:20.

Still no Enzo. As the minutes slipped by unnoticed, I found myself growing increasingly irked by Enzo's lack of punctuality. Every second that passed felt like a tiny prick to my well-honed sense of time management. I was a creature of precision, thriving on exactness and timely execution. To me, tardiness was the epitome of rudeness — a blatant disregard for someone else's time and commitments. I was a professor, after all. If I expected my students to show up on time, I better develop the same habit.

Now, here I was, sitting outside a charmingly rustic Italian cottage, staring at a phone that refused to ring. Waiting for a man named Enzo. Who names their kid Enzo, anyway? Ferrari fanatics? I supposed maybe it was common in Italy, but still—

In a state of increasing agitation, I began to pace restlessly outside the cottage, my eyes frequently darting to my phone. A storm of annoyance brewed within me as I thought of an entire day's plans derailed. What were those plans? I had no idea. But surely, they were something that relied on a schedule. Because normal, sane people kept to schedules, right? I plopped back down on the bench, wondering if I was still too wound up to accept random Vespa rendezvous with Italian strangers.

Suddenly, I was struck by the sheer absurdity of the situation. What in the world was I doing here? I was supposed to be at home, deep in summer research, enjoying over-priced nut milk lattes and not trying to blend into the scenery like a misplaced garden gnome.

What would I say if my students could see me now? "Yes, I am still Professor Amante. The one who is a stickler about late papers and tardies...Yes, well, I'm currently waiting on a ridiculously bright red Vespa to whisk me off into the unknown with a man I barely know."

This was supposed to be a break, a chance to unwind from the rigors of the academic world, from my crumbling life. But who was I kidding? The only unwinding happening was the winding up of my stress levels. The sun was just getting started. My patience was smoldering down to a nub, and Enzo was still nowhere in sight.

If my life were a sitcom, I'd definitely be the lovable yet snarky protagonist in a constant state of existential crisis. Cue the laugh track.

Oh well, when life gives you lemons, make limoncello, right? Or when in Rome... or, you know, the Italian Riviera.

This is the adventure you've been waiting for, Isla. So sit tight, enjoy the scenery, and for God's sake, stop talking to yourself. You're a respected scholar, not a character in a rom-com.

There, that's the spirit. Now, if only Enzo would arrive before I started referring to myself in the third person...

The purr of a motor pulled me from my absurd inner monologue spiral. I spotted him in the distance — a leisurely figure cruising along on his ridiculous bright red scooter as if plucked right out of a Pixar movie. A broad smile lit up his face. As he pulled up, he shook off his helmet, revealing a mane of black hair tousled by the wind. My fingers itched to tousle it more.

"Ciao, Isla!" he greeted me, his voice ringing with carefree joy. "Ready to embark on another splendid day in Italy?" The theatrics in his voice made me cringe.

"You're late."

He blinked earnestly for a moment, then snickered. "School is out for the summer, Professoressa. Relax."

His flippant tone felt like a hot iron to my present irritation.

He laughed and raised his hands apologetically. "Don't look at me like that! *Mi dispiace*. In Italy, especially in summer, we tend to adopt a somewhat... casual approach to timekeeping. Punctuality isn't exactly our forte. It's one of the many stereotypes we happily own."

Exhaling a breath I hadn't realized I was holding, I responded, a hint of frostiness creeping into my voice, "I just wouldn't want our plans to get disrupted, that's all."

Enzo's smile remained unwavering, his gaze steady and warm. "What plans are those? A leisurely ride along the sea needs no plan. Please, come." He extended a helmet toward me.

"And are you a poet in addition to a—what are you exactly?"

"A man of the world."

I rolled my eyes and took the helmet.

"Here, let me help." Enzo fitted the helmet to my head, then adjusted the chin straps. His fingers brushed my cheek, and I noted the slight callouses. He smelled like sea air and something slightly metallic.

"I assure you, we won't miss out on anything. The best way to enjoy the Riviera is by loosening your grip."

"My grip on what?"

He lowered his voice to practically a whisper. "On everything."

His infectious smile and casual attitude began to thaw my annoyance. I was indeed in a different world, where life moved at a leisurely rhythm. The relentless, fast-paced lifestyle I was accustomed to back home had no place here.

I involuntarily laughed. "All right, let's seize the day."

"Bene. That's the spirit. Now, climb aboard, and let's uncover the magic of Mare Sereno without a glance at the clock, si?"

He slid onto his sleek little machine, and I hesitated. I suddenly realized I was going to snuggle up back-to-front with a man I didn't know as we barreled along a winding — surely treacherous — road at high-octane speeds. I'm not going to say I always make great decisions in life, but this had to be up there with a less-than-stellar one.

"What's the matter?" Enzo asked.

I bit my bottom lip. "Um...I'm just. I feel..."

"You're scared?" He teased.

I rolled my eyes. "No. I just—well, how do I stay on? I've never been on a scooter motorcycle thingy deal."

Enzo caressed the shiny handles and leaned in and whispered loudly. "She doesn't mean what she says, *cara mia.* You are not a thingy deal." He looked up with a cheeky smile. I folded my arms.

"You know, romantic feelings toward inanimate objects is considered a psychological disorder."

"Clearly, you don't understand the depths a man can feel for his vehicle. Especially not a Vespa 946 special edition."

"Do you enjoy being a cliche?"

He made a show of thinking about it and then nodded. "Si. Very much. Now, just relax, Isla. Climb on back and hold on to me. I won't let you fall off. Promise. If you jump, that's on you."

"Hold on to you?" I swallowed, the idea making my insides twirl about like Cirque du Soleil.

"As tight as you like," he winked and slipped on his helmet.

I took a deep breath and nodded curtly. I slipped one leg over and straddled the seat, now feeling incredibly stupid for having chosen a dress. I held my breath as I slipped my arms around Enzo's waist and leaned in. I did my absolute best not to sniff him.

As we set off north, the sun above us and the wind in our hair, the breathtaking coastline unfurled before us. I felt a sense of liberation, a release from my usual constraints. I was relinquishing my hold on control, surrendering to the unpredictable allure of the present.

The Ligurian Sea, a vibrant canvas of turquoise, stretched out to the horizon, its surface dancing with the reflection of sunlight. To our right, the cliffs towered majestically, their harsh edges softened by a verdant cloak of vegetation. Groves of olive trees, lemon orchards, and vineyards punctuated the landscape. The scent of the sea intermingled with the heady aroma of wildflowers and the earthy undertones of the fertile soil. Everything was alive and pulsing.

The Vespa's soft purr harmonized with the distant rhythm of waves meeting the shore. The morning air, crisp and tinged with salt, brushed against my cheeks as I held onto Enzo. As we sped along serpentine roads, weaving through verdant vineyards and ancient olive groves, my heart pounded with exhilaration.

As we journeyed, Enzo shouted out random facts about the sites rushing by. A family vineyard he knew, a restaurant he'd been to. A villa with a tragic past. As we slowed around a corner, he gestured toward the ruins of a clearly Roman structure, its silhouette etched against a distant hill, the weathered stones whispering tales from a bygone era.

"People don't often associate this part of the world with the Romans, but battles once raged, and empires rose and fell along these shores," he said.

I laughed at his dramatic telling, but the history nerd in me was hanging on every word of his narrative. He would make a great professor.

"It's amazing how even in my lifetime, these little villages have become bustling tourist towns," he continued.

"That has to be a good thing for the area. Financially anyway."

I felt his shoulders shrug against me. "Depends on who you ask, I suppose. With tourism comes money but also its own set of problems. There are a lot of ancient ruins and precious landscapes around here. It's a delicate ecosystem."

"I get it. You have to balance the integrity of it all with the revenue."

We zipped along in silence for a while, hugging the mesmerizing coastline. We dipped in and out of charming towns and past relics of ancient civilizations. It all began to feel like a voyage through time.

"Pit stop?" he asked over his shoulder.

"Sure!" I shouted back over the roar of the engine.

He pulled the Vespa off the road and onto a little overlook. He parked, and we slid off. I wobbled a little to be back on solid ground.

"It takes some getting used to. Kind of like sea legs," Enzo said.

"Vespa legs. Got it."

He chuckled. "Water? Something stronger?"

I laughed lightly. "Just water for now, thanks."

He nodded and plucked two bottles from his pack. He handed one to me and we both drank greedily.

Hydrated and steady on my feet, I finally took in the view. Breathtaking was a clichéd phrase, but the vast expanse of sea and curving coast did, in fact, steal every last ounce of my remaining breath.

"Pretty incredible, si?" Enzo said, following my gaze.

"Si," I said. "You know you have a picture in your mind of what it will be. But you just can't ever really know what it feels like to be here."

He smiled lightly and nodded.

We admired the view in relative silence before Enzo tapped his knee and stood. "All right. Moving along? I have a place I'd like to show you."

I tilted my head and shot him an inquisitive look, but he only replied with a snarky smile. I rolled my eyes and climbed back onto the Vespa.

Chapter Six

After a short journey down a steep trail, the trail broadened, unfolding into a stunning beach tucked away beneath a rocky overhang. The secret cove was enveloped by towering limestone cliffs, softened by trailing ivy and bright wildflowers. The sun kissed the sandy shore, causing it to shimmer, while the translucent turquoise sea beckoned enticingly.

"Where are we?" I said, feeling as though we'd stepped through a portal to a secret world.

"Just a little hidden place I know. Perfect for deep thoughts. Come on. The best place is just down this path here."

As we descended the beach, I had to resist the urge to take his hand. There was something about him that made me want to cling to him, as though he were a lifeline for my turbulent life. I stepped away slightly. No, I was getting too caught up in the Italian summer fantasy to make rational decisions. The last thing I needed was to get involved with some Riviera Playboy. Because, really? That had to be his angle here. Whether he owned it or not, he was one giant walking marketing poster.

"Is this the kind of beach you find in San Francisco?" Enzo asked.

I chuckled at the contrast. "Not even close. Our beaches are freezing, and the only thing you can do there is watch surfers in wetsuits with a death wish. Northern California is notoriously brisk."

"Si? I thought it was all palm trees and bikinis."

I snorted. "Southern California. But it's basically a different country to us. It's a big state."

"Ah, well. Here you have plenty of warm sand, clear water, and, of course, the pleasure of my company," he added with a grin. I couldn't help but smile.

"Oh, of course, the real highlight of this trip—Enzo Biagioni's unparalleled company."

Enzo's smirk grew wider. "You say that with such sarcasm, but deep down, I know you're secretly enamored with my charming ways."

I rolled my eyes. "Enamored, huh? Maybe I'm just enjoying the change of scenery. You know, the beach, the sun, the..." I trailed off, realizing I couldn't deny the fact that his company wasn't so bad either.

"*Aspettate*—how did you know my last name?"

My cheeks reddened. "I...mighta asked around."

His brow went up with amusement. "Did you now?"

I shrugged. "I mean, I was about to ride off into the unknown with a total stranger. I had to do my due diligence."

He tapped his nose. "Can't pull one over on me. There go my evil kidnapping plans."

"Sorry to disappoint you."

I let the words tail off and started to walk ahead, but I was stopped short by the unfolding scene.

"What is this place?" I said almost in a whisper as my eyes drank in the seemingly untouched beauty of the cove.

"Ah. My favorite spot on this beach. My nonno used to

bring me here when I was a kid. It's always been our little secret," Enzo shared, his smile beaming almost childlike as he opened up this special corner of his world to me. "There are some unique fishes and plants you can only find right here. You see those darker stripes in the water?" He pointed out into the sea. "Mediterranean Red Coral. Indigenous to this area. It has this brilliant blood-red color. People have been using it in jewelry since ancient times."

"Is that ethical?"

He shrugged. "Possibly not now. This whole area has been over-fished, over-polluted. Locals are pushing for more protections."

I shook my head. "It's sad."

Enzo sighed. "As the world goes. Hard to protect your integrity once the world knows your secrets. Anyway, Nonno always said in the old days, this little bit of coast was seen by the rest of Europe as a heavenly garden."

"Sounds magical," I said.

"Nonno was a man of nature. He loved the sea and the marine life. The plants."

"Is he gone now? Your nonno?"

Enzo sighed. "Si. It's been a long time now. He got cancer young. Too many cigarettes."

"I'm sorry to hear that."

He smiled thinly. "Anyway. I always find my creative muse down here."

I tilted my head. "And what do you need a creative muse for?"

He snickered but didn't answer.

As we ambled along the shore, we stumbled upon a small rock pool teeming with a kaleidoscope of fish and other marine life.

"Oh, look!" I squealed like a child seeing gelato for the first time.

Enzo watched me, a spark of admiration in his eyes. "Don't eat them."

I flashed him a look that made him grin.

"Do you know much about the fish here?" I asked.

"Are you a fisherwoman?"

I laughed shyly. "No. Just curious. Have to have some sort of intelligent dinner conversation in the event I meet anyone interesting here."

"We get a lot of tuna. Popular for fishing, of course. Then the octopus is all over. And, of course, you have to watch out for Barracuda. They'll eat your face right off." He shuddered.

"Ok, now you're telling lies again."

He pressed a hand to his heart. "Would I lie to you?"

I tapped my finger against my lip. "Yes. I think you would."

He laughed. "Possibly. But on this, I'm not lying. There really are Barracuda in there. Ok, fair, they probably won't eat your face—unless you have an exceptionally delicious face—but they are deadly predators to the local ecosystem."

"I'll be sure to give a wide birth should I see one."

Our exploration of the cove led us over rocks and through the cool, refreshing water. Eventually, we found a shady retreat under a rocky overhang.

"You want to sit for a bit? I have a blanket in my pack."

I nodded, not wanting to admit how perfect this all was.

He slipped his small pack off and unrolled a compact blanket that unfolded to at least quadruple its size.

"That's handy," I said.

"I'm always prepared. Hungry? I have a few snacks."

"You've thought of everything. Are you sure you're not a professional guide?" I said teasingly.

He smirked and passed me a little snack box with olives and crackers.

"At least I know I have a backup plan should I need it," he said.

"What exactly is it you do? Besides carelessly gallivanting up and down the coast."

Enzo popped an olive in his mouth and chewed thoughtfully before answering. "I own a little shop. We restore rare cars and scooters and such."

I said nothing for a moment.

"What?" Enzo asked.

"Nothing."

"You have a funny look on your face."

I smiled sheepishly. "I was just wondering how a business like that stays afloat in such a small town."

He smiled and nodded. "Ah. Fair question. We have a bit of a following in Europe. We are very specialized, so we can work on some of the rarer beauties. I have some clients from Germany and even the U.K."

"That's impressive."

He shrugged. "And admittedly, we have a shop in Genova that does more day-to-day business. My shop here is more specialized work. Long-term projects commissioned well in advance."

"So Vespas aren't just your hobby."

He flashed me that mock, affronted look. "They are not my hobby—they are my one true love."

"How did you fall into that?"

He leaned back against a smooth boulder. "*Non lo so.* I always had a mechanical inclination as a child. I used to go up to Genova to visit my uncle a bunch, and he was always tinkering with something or another. He had a little side business repairing cars. When I was at University in Genova, I would help him out on the weekends. One day, this man from Monaco comes in with a vintage 1959 Piaggo. He needed an emergency tire repair. I swear, I fell in love right there in that old garage."

"Why Vespas over cars?" I asked. I could picture him in a vintage roadster, hugging the curving coastline.

He tilted his head in consideration. "Don't get me wrong, I love a sports car as much as anyone. Don't tell anyone, but I do actually have a little vintage Alpha Romeo in Papa's garage. I take it out to play sometimes. But I love the feel of the Vespa on the open road. It's more...real, I guess. You feel everything. The wind. The smells. The bugs," he chuckled.

I laughed too. "That's really cool. That you've made a living doing something you love."

"I feel lucky, it's true. They used to be just little scooters to get you around, but there is a huge luxury market now. We do a lot of business with them. Every day is fun."

"That's the key, isn't it? Find a passion."

He shrugged. "I suppose. Not always easy, though, is it?"

"Definitely not," I agreed.

"But you have yours, yes? Teaching history?"

I sighed. "Supposedly. Don't get me wrong, I do love it. I could geek out on history all day. It's just that American universities can just be—complicated. The politics can zap the fun right out."

"Why history?"

"I guess—I guess I just love stories. I love thinking about how far we've come as a civilization. I love that, despite the fact that the globe is huge and people all over the world started from different places with different resources, in so many ways, we evolved the same way." I turned toward Enzo. "It's kind of magical, isn't it?"

He thoughtfully bit into a cracker. "I've never really thought about it that way."

My professor's brain roared to life, and I sat up straighter. "Think about it. We all had to develop methods of transportation, clothing, ways to cook our food safely. And while, of course, there are some variations, civilizations figured out the same things. Fire, boiling water. How to preserve meats."

"I suppose the trade routes helped."

I nodded. "Yes, there's some truth to that. But if you look at even the way structures were built, long before trade routes ever came into play—there are so many similarities. The human mind just instinctively knew how to put various things together, no matter where that person was born. It's fascinating, really."

"So, you're not so much a historian as an anthropologist." A small smile tugged at Enzo's lips.

I laughed. "A little bit, I suppose. I guess it all kind of goes together, doesn't it? The study of cultures, whether it be in the past or now."

"I think all observers of the human condition are anthropologists at heart."

"That's very poetic, Enzo." I flashed him a wry smile.

"So, what kind of history do you like best?" Enzo asked.

"Well, I teach medieval and Renaissance history, actually."

His eyebrows went up. "Really?"

"Does that surprise you?"

He shrugged. "Not necessarily. It's just sort of an unusual interest, for an American, anyway. I sort of thought all of you were more interested in the Civil War, World War II—things like that."

I flashed him a double-edged look. "What do you know about American history?"

"You know, we do learn about your history, too, in other countries."

I considered that. "I guess I know that academically, but I never really thought about it."

"Do you think we're all ignorant?"

I laughed and shook my head. "No, not at all. I just figured it wouldn't be very interesting to you."

"Why is that?"

"You have medieval torture and conquered kingdoms to learn about. There's not a lot of 'there' there to the U.S., you know? We haven't been around that long."

"And look how fast you dominated the world," Enzo said with a dramatic flair.

I chuckled. "Dominated, destroying."

He raised his hands defensively. "Hey, you said it, not me. What about that time interests you? The medieval and Renaissance."

"Why the twenty questions?"

"Can't I just take an interest in my new friend's life?"

"Friends now, are we?" I said.

"Just humor me."

I tilted my head and thought about it. "I saw Romeo and Juliet as a kid, and I guess I fell in love."

"Ahh, yes. Nothing like the double suicide of two teenagers to spark a passion." He held up a dramatic fist.

"It left a mark. That play is taught to every freshman high school class in America."

"To warn them off eloping with your enemy?" Enzo said with a straight face.

I bobbed my head. "Think it has more to do with relatable young love."

"I think my idea is better."

I smirked and went on. "It was just such a transformative time, you know? The things that happened during those decades changed the world forever."

"You could say that about many decades."

"Yes, but there's something about the revolution of art and architecture and just society in general. The way people came out of such an old way of thinking, a way of treating people, into a new age. Granted, there was a long way to go as far as humanity was concerned, but leaps and bounds were made. Separation of church and state, and all that."

Enzo hung his head. "Oh, that traitor Henry the Eighth. We have never forgiven him."

I chuckled. "Exactly. Hey, somebody had to shake things up in the Holy See."

"You know your stuff then," Enzo said with a grin.

I blushed. "Yes, I'm a nerd."

"No! I like it. It's sexy to be brainy. Sexy professor."

And then I blushed even harder. "Like the plot of a porn," I said without thinking. This time Enzo's cheeks went crimson.

"So, you teach it. Do you have a lot of students interested in the subject?" He said, moving on from whatever rabbit hole we were about to tumble down.

I bobbed my head from side to side. "Some are as passionate as I am—the really nerdy ones. Americans have a strange obsession with European history."

"It's not that strange when you think about it."

"Yeah?"

"Well, it's the homeland for a lot of you, no?"

"True. There are so many of us who are still only a few generations deep. We want to know where we came from. Have some deeper roots. I guess in that vein the Renaissance is my ancient family history."

"I knew we were kindred spirits."

I sputtered a laugh. "The truth is most of my students take my seminars just to fulfill an interesting elective. I teach some more general history too. Like, I have a sort of seminar on the world as well."

He raised his eyebrows. "On the entire world? You must have a lot of information in that small head of yours."

"It's not that small."

He tilted his head and examined me. "I think you have a pretty tiny head."

"In some countries, that's considered very desirable," I said, turning away.

"Yeah? Which countries?"

"You've never heard of them."

He chuckled. "How long were you in school for all that learning?"

I looked to the sky, thinking back on all those years. "The better part of a decade. Let's see, four years of undergrad and another five for the Ph.D. And then I suppose another year for my dissertation."

His eyebrows went up. "Maybe math isn't your strong suit, but that's not the better part. That's a full decade."

I laughed. "Kind of depressing when you say it."

"Do you regret it?"

"No, regret isn't the word I'd use. Sometimes I just think I hid from life by disappearing into the past. It's easy not to think about the real world happening around you when you can lose yourself in what the Medicis are doing to the Albizzis."

"You really are a nerd," Enzo said with mock disgust.

"Sometimes I think I wasted my potential." As my father had put it, I recalled bitterly.

Enzo was quiet for a moment, as though letting that sink in. Almost as though he could relate. "Don't say that. Isn't that the beauty of history? It's not just about the past—it's about understanding the present and shaping the future. It's about learning from our mistakes and appreciating the complexities of human nature."

I looked at him, surprised by the depth of his insight. "Deep, Enzo." He grinned. "History does have a way of repeating itself, doesn't it?"

He nodded. "Si. That's why it's essential for people like

you to teach it, to make sure that we don't forget the lessons of the past. You're not hiding from the real world. You're helping to shape it."

His words pricked a nerve deep within me, bringing a sting to my eyes. I blinked it away.

"Thank you. The validation of strangers is always appreciated."

He chuckled. "I get it. I've done well enough with it but tinkering with cars and Vespas wasn't exactly my parents' dream for me."

"What do your parents do?"

He hesitated for a moment. "They have a little family shipping business, and they hoped I'd be more involved. But, *così è la vita*. That's life."

I smiled and, in that moment, time seemed to slow, the rest of the world fading into insignificance. It was just me and Enzo, tucked away in this secret paradise, encased in the spellbinding beauty of the hidden beach along the Italian coast, exposing ourselves. Above us, the sky was a canvas of deep cerulean, dotted with a scattering of marshmallow clouds.

But then thunder sounded above, snapping us both back to the reality of the moment.

"Damn. Looks like a storm coming over the sea," Enzo said, eyeing the sky warily. "We should head back before the sky opens. It comes on quickly here."

I nodded as I watched the thick gray clouds move in, but I was secretly disappointed. For a few moments there on the beach, I was actually starting to forget who I was.

We made our way back up the cliff and loaded back onto the Vespa. My eyes cast out at the incredible horizon, and I felt a pang of grief as though it might be the last time I would see her.

"She will wait for you here," Enzo said, his gaze heavy on me. "Don't worry."

I blushed and turned away. We loaded back onto the scooter and slipped our helmets in place. Enzo started her up, then spoke over his shoulder.

"How about a limoncino?"

"A what?"

"A limoncino? It's a lemon liqueur to sip."

"Is that the same as a limoncello?" I asked.

"Ah, si. What we call it in the North."

"That's a random suggestion."

"Is it? No. It always cures what ails you. We can sit and watch the storm from the safety of a little cafe."

I shook my head and waved my hand. "I don't know. I don't really like limoncello. Or limoncino."

Enzo's eyes almost bulged out of his head. "Do not say such sacrilegious things to me, signorina. I might just pass out and die," he pressed a hand dramatically to his chest.

I laughed lightly. "I just don't really like the saccharine sweet stuff. It gives me a headache. I prefer to just stick with wine."

He shook his head and clicked his tongue. "You have just not had a proper one. I imagine what you had came in some pre-made bottle and served in a little shot glass or some kind of test tube. Am I right?"

I blushed a little. "Maybe. I feel like I've had it in some pretty good establishments. You know, I am from California. We do Italian food right."

He shook his head. Then he waved a finger at me. "No, I'm afraid you have not. Let me at least show you. Indulge me, *per favore*?"

I laughed incredulously. "Fine, fine. If I get drunk and make a fool of myself, though, or get sick in the bushes, you've been fairly warned."

He wiggled his eyebrows, shaking his helmet. "Oh, but you have foiled my plan."

Chapter Seven

We drove back down the coast in silence, both of us drinking in the fading afternoon, Enzo focusing on getting us back to town before the sky erupted.

The sky suddenly darkened ominously. The clouds rolled in, and I felt a twinge of unease. Just as we slipped into Mare Sereno, the first large, cold drops splashed against my skin. I clung to him, my heart pounding, as we navigated the slippery path, the Vespa's headlight barely cutting through the deluge. The rain was relentless, drenching us, reducing visibility to almost zero.

"*Merda*!" Enzo expertly steered the Vespa into a little parking spot on the piazza.

"Are you okay?" He asked as we dismounted and huddled under an overhang.

"I'm soaked," I replied, laughing a little despite myself, "But I'm okay."

We removed our helmets, our clothes sticking to our skin, our hair plastered to our heads. Enzo's white shirt was almost transparent, and I could see the outline of his muscular torso through it. I blushed and quickly averted my gaze.

"That seemed much faster on the way back," I said.

"You just didn't realize how fast I was going." He winked. "But if anyone has any doubts, your hair gives it away." He tousled my tangled locks playfully. I swatted his hand away.

"Come on. Let's go into that place there. Right around the corner, see?"

I eyed the stormy sky. "I'll race you," I said before taking off.

The cafe, tucked away in a narrow alleyway just off the main piazza, was as unassuming as it was enchanting. One could easily stroll past its antiquated facade without giving it a second glance. The centuries-old stonework of the exterior told tales of a different era. A tiny, scrolled sign saying Osteria Marco was the only indication of the hidden gem within. The dark wooden door was adorned with an elaborate iron knocker in the shape of a lemon, adding a whimsical touch.

Stepping through the threshold was like stepping back in time. The walls were adorned with faded frescoes and vintage photographs of Mare Sereno, the small, intimate space filled with the aroma of fresh coffee, baking bread, and, of course, lemons. There were a handful of tables that had the appearance of reclaimed wood, surrounded by mismatched chairs. The worn terracotta tiles underfoot were uneven, bearing the imprints of countless visitors over the years. A couple of stools were tucked beneath a small window that opened to an enchanting view of the winding cobblestone street and pastel buildings beyond.

"This is not a real place," I said, looking around. The clink of cups, the low murmur of conversation, and an old Italian ballad softly playing on a vintage radio infused the cafe with a sense of infectious conviviality. It was like a cocoon, insulating its patrons from the world outside.

Enzo grinned. "Settle in wherever. Be right back."

. . .

I slipped into a window-side table with a perfect view of the stormy sky. Enzo made his way to a tiny countertop where an elderly man with a weathered face and twinkling eyes held court with a few likely locals. The shelves behind him were lined with various liquors and concoctions that I couldn't identify, all in bottles that could double as art pieces.

A moment later, Enzo returned carrying two slender glasses filled with vibrant yellow liquid. But there was nothing neon or artificial about the shade. They were a perfect summer yellow. I was already a little tipsy just looking at it.

"*Cin cin*," he said, raising his glass to mine. We clinked our tiny glasses and sipped. My whole mouth came alive with flavor, and the buzz went right to my head.

"Don't shoot it. Sip slowly," Enzo said.

I obeyed, taking tiny little sips, savoring every sensation.

"Well? Is it saccharine sweet and disgusting like you feared?" Enzo said.

I shook my head and laughed. "Okay, I stand corrected. It's divine. It's like somebody harnessed summer and put it in a glass."

"Very poetic, Isla. I'm glad you enjoy. It's more popular in the south, like Sicily. But everyone here knows how to make a good limoncino. In fact, there's a reason it's actually kind of hard to find out at *tavernas*. Everyone has perfected their own recipe at home, and no one thinks anyone does it as well as they do. Or as well as their mama or nonna or zia. You know what I mean."

I smiled. "I do. But this is really good."

"You should taste the one my mama does. I think she will put this one to shame. But I can't say that too loudly around here, you know?"

"And do you make your own?"

"I would, if I had my own trees. There's something about your own lemon trees that just makes the best limoncino.

Store-bought lemons—I don't know. My mama says they don't have the same character. That they're lacking a little bit of soul because they've lost it during the transportation."

I sipped my yellow drink and smiled. "I think I like your mama."

"I think that she maybe would like you too," Enzo said with a wily grin.

We lingered over our drink, then Enzo talked me into a second as we waited for the storm to clear.

I was admittedly feeling a little lightheaded as we walked back up toward my cottage. The rain had come with abandon, then given us a break, leaving the night smooth and sultry.

I swayed a little as my feet caught on the cobblestone, and Enzo leaned in to help me stay steady.

"I'm okay," I said, grasping for balance.

"You weren't kidding about how the limoncino goes right to your head," he teased, tapping his temple.

"It's just the uneven streets," I said. I pushed him away playfully, but he wasn't entirely wrong. My head did feel a little foggy. But it was a nice fog—a pleasant haze, like a lazy summer day. I could feel his body heat radiating, and I could smell his sweet, earthy scent. I wanted to lean into him. I wanted to feel his warmth against me. Just a friendly hug, a gentle embrace. I just wanted to be hugged, I thought suddenly. A little sadness came over me at that thought. It had been too long since I had a good old hug.

"Well, here we are," Enzo said. I lingered for a moment at the door, my fingers brushing the knob. I didn't really know what to make of this afternoon. I mean, it wasn't exactly a date, was it? Did he expect anything?

I shook my head. I was overthinking things again. Apparently, a very American trait. Or a very Isla Amante trait.

"Thank you. Today was lovely. Honestly, it was even better than I anticipated," I said.

He smiled. "Grazie for joining me. It was such a pleasure to share my little slice of the world with you." He hesitated for a moment, and for a second, I had a terrifying thought that he might try to kiss me. I took an instinctive step back.

But he did not. "Enjoy your night, Isla. Maybe I will see you around? Be sure to say ciao."

With that, he turned and left, his back fading into the summer evening. For a moment, I stood stupefied on the doorstep. He hadn't even tried to make a move? No doubt, I was a little too boring for his taste. He had his pick of all the sultry women of the Mediterranean. I couldn't imagine a buttoned-up American professor had any kind of appeal—especially not one who was currently sopping up the mess of her life. I smiled anyway, though. At least I was just one Vespa ride closer to being the free spirit I deep down wished I was.

Chapter Eight

The quiet calm of my morning—coffee, the lap of the ocean, a bird singing me a wake-up tune—was abruptly interrupted by the ding of my phone. Glancing at the screen, my heart leaped at the sight of my best friend Luna's name. I swiped to accept the video call, and her familiar face filled the screen.

"Luna!" I exclaimed, unable to keep the excitement from my voice.

"Isla!" She echoed back, her wide grin mirroring mine. Her dark hair was pulled up into a messy bun, paint smears dotted her cheeks, and her glasses were slightly askew—the quintessential image of an art professor in the midst of creation.

"What time is it there?" I asked, glancing at the clock and trying to do the math to San Francisco time.

"6:30. PM. Just doing a little pre-dinner work."

"Good for you. Apologies for my hot mess aesthetic. Just waking up here."

"It suits you. Soooo, tell me everything." She leaned closer to the screen as if she could physically pull the stories from me.

"I want to know all about Italy, and don't you dare leave out any juicy details."

I laughed and sat upright. "Hold on, here." I turned my phone so she could see the stunning view from my bedroom—the vibrant lemon trees and the shimmering sea. Luna's eyes widened at the sight, a sigh of envy escaping her.

"It's even more beautiful than the pictures," she admitted, sounding slightly wistful.

"It's incredible, Luna," I confessed. "The sights, the food, the people..." I trailed off, a certain local popping into my mind.

"Is it helping? I mean, I know you haven't even been there a week, but how do you feel?"

I pulled myself from bed and popped an espresso pod into the machine.

"I feel—I do feel lighter. It's like I've been holding so much inside for so long, and I'm finally shedding it. I mean, my time in Milan and Genova was great. But I kept myself so busy with every museum I could find, I wasn't really processing anything. Does that make sense?"

I settled into the armchair in the sitting area and tucked my knees up. I positioned the phone on its stand and sipped my coffee.

"Makes all the sense. Meeting anyone interesting?" Luna asked.

Her question felt like a probe right into the center of me. I hesitated.

"Isla?" Luna prodded, her eyes narrowing suspiciously.

"I... might have met... someone," I slowly admitted, my cheeks flushing.

Luna squealed, clapping her hands excitedly. "I knew it! You've got that look! Quick work, woman. So, who is he? Tell me everything."

I rolled my eyes at her enthusiasm, but I couldn't help the

smile that tugged at my lips. "It's nothing. I shouldn't even think of it in that way, you know?"

"Shut it and dish it."

"Ok, ok. His name is Enzo."

"Like Ferrari?"

"Basically. He's a local here, and he's been showing me around. He's... different."

"Different good, or different bad?" Luna asked, her tone serious now.

"Different... good. I think. I don't know. He's charming, funny, and kind. But—"

"Unattractive?"

"God, no. He's like—like an Italian GQ model or something. But like one with callouses and muscles because he's been working outside."

She gasped. "Oh my God, Isla, he sounds horrible. Run AWAY."

I chuckled. "I know. I sound insane."

"Slightly."

"He's just like this giant poster child for the perfect 'man you meet on an Italian vacation.' All swagger and charm. And I mean, c'mon, he rides a Vespa. It's too right not to be all wrong."

Luna giggled. "That's like vacationing on a Wyoming ranch and being skeptical of meeting a rugged cowboy in a 4x4."

"Fair point. But it's... it's complicated. My situation is complicated."

"Only because you make it that way."

I stiffened. "What's that supposed to mean?"

Luna's face softened. "I just think sometimes you cling to your complications as a way to keep people at a distance. Especially since Nonna Rosa died. But you know, sometimes, it's the complicated things in life that turn out to be the most beautiful. Just like in art."

"Have you been drinking?"

She bobbed her head from side to side. "Only the normal amount."

I brushed my hair back. "Anyway, it's nothing. He was fun to look at for an afternoon, but I'm not jumping into some summer fling three days in. I have other things to worry about right now."

Luna rolled her eyes. "You are too pragmatic for your own good."

"Someone in this world needs to be."

Luna was silent for a moment, her eyes studying me. "Isla, you sound... happy."

I couldn't contain a smile. "I am," I admitted, a warm feeling spreading through me. "At least happier than I've been in a long time. But I mean, c'mon, look at the view. I'd have to be a psychopath not to be happy right now."

"Enjoy the moments," Luna smiled at me, her eyes soft. "Now, tell me more about this charming Italian. Does he have a brother?"

I rolled my eyes and pretended to hang up. Luna laughed. "Ok, sorry, sorry."

Luna was quiet for a moment, her playful demeanor softening as she asked, "And have you talked to... Ian?"

I sighed, staring at the tile beneath my feet. "Um, no. We haven't talked. Not since it all went down. I don't know. I know we'll have some things to sort out with the condo and all that, but I figured we had time. Right now, I'm still processing."

Luna nodded. "It's going to take time. He pulled the rug out from under you. You don't just bounce back from that right away."

"But being here... it's helping."

Luna's eyes filled with sympathy in a way that made me want to look away. I didn't want to be pitied.

"I'm sorry, Isla. Ian was an ass for letting you go. But you know what? He didn't deserve you. You deserve someone who knows what they want, someone who appreciates you and wants to be with you."

"When did you become a self-help guru?" I asked, brushing away the annoying emotions flooding my body.

"Just enjoy the ride, Isla," Luna said, her eyes twinkling. "And remember, if you ever need to talk or vent, I'm just a FaceTime away."

Smiling, I said, "I know, Luna. Thanks. For being there through the shit show of the past year."

Luna winked at me. "What are best friends for? Oh, hey, I have to run. I have a meetup tonight with that gallery owner I'm trying to woo. There's this *Women Wave Makers* exhibition coming up, and I'm dying to showcase some pieces."

"Go get 'em, Lun. You deserve to be on that wall."

"You have to say that. You're biased."

"Makes it easy to be biased when it's true."

"Talk soon. Love you!"

"Love you," I said softly as I clicked END.

Chapter Nine

I didn't know what to expect from an authentic Italian wine-tasting event. Although I'd experienced Napa's finest over the years, this felt different. I knew how to swirl and sip (and sip some more), but admittedly, I didn't know much about wine. I'd savored some fancy wines, especially during dinners with Ian's clients, but I was no connoisseur. Those wines tended to be overpriced Napa varieties or something extravagant from France that I don't think anyone fully understood. I had never really explored Italian wines, and I couldn't wait.

Stepping into Gianna's wine shop, the rich, velvety scent of fermented grapes wrapped around me like a warm embrace. The vibrant buzz of conversation, punctuated by the occasional clink of glasses, dispelled any lingering trepidation. The shop was beautifully decorated, with wine-tasting setups adorning rustic high-top tables. Juicy bouquets of grapes and lemons sat as decorative centerpieces.

Gianna weaved through the crowd with the grace of a seasoned dancer. Spotting me, she waved enthusiastically.

"Ciao, Isla!"

I smiled warmly and waved back. "Ciao, Gianna. This looks amazing."

Gianna came toward me, and we exchanged cheek kisses.

She looked around the room and nodded satisfactorily at her handiwork. "Grazie! I love these events so much. It's fun to share my passion. Maybe it seems like a small thing."

"Not at all. I think it's wonderful. And I am personally excited to learn a thing or two. I admittedly know a lot about drinking wine, but that's about it."

Gianna grinned. "That is the best part. Wine is meant to be enjoyed. It may sound strange, given that I sell expensive wines, but I've never understood the point of collecting wine and just keeping it in the cellar. It seems a shame, you know? Good wine, even the very expensive and rare, is meant to be enjoyed."

"I couldn't agree more." Already, I was drooling at the sight of an open bottle of red on the table.

"Here, let me get you situated," Gianna said, gesturing toward a table with a tasting setup. "I hope you're not too shy. You'll be sharing a table with some of my regulars. *Carlo, Paulo, questa è Isla. Lei non parla italiano.*"

Carlo and Paulo nodded at me with friendly smiles, but I got the impression they didn't speak much English. It should make for an interesting pairing.

"*Ciao, buonasera,*" I said in my best Italian accent. They both smiled a little wider.

"*Buonasera, signorina* Isla. I am Carlo," he said with a thick accent, his twinkling blue eyes and chiseled tan face hinting at long, leisurely days on a boat. "My partner, Paulo."

"Piacere, Isla," Paulo said. "Where are you from?"

"San Francisco."

Both their faces lit up. "Ah, bene. We love your Little Italy."

I beamed. Before I could say more, the sound of a utensil tapping a glass silenced the room.

"*Buonasera!*" A middle-aged man in a trim summer suit with jet-black hair stepped to the front of the room, a full glass of bright white wine in his hand. "*Benvenuti nell'enoteca di Gianna. Sono il Maestro Lorenzo DiMarco, sommelier. Sono entusiasta di insegnarti una cosa o due!*"

If he was going to speak in rapid-fire Italian all night, I feared I wouldn't learn much. As if reading my thoughts, his eyes landed on me, and he grinned.

"*Stasera abbiamo con noi un visitatore dall'America, quindi tradurrò anche in inglese*. I will translate for you, signorina. Don't worry." He raised his glass to toast me from across the room, and I exhaled with relief.

As the class commenced, his initial lesson left me floundering in his linguistic wake.

Maestro Lorenzo, his eyes ablaze with the fervor of a true connoisseur, held up a glass of red wine as if it were a sacred relic. "*Sapete, il vino è una poesia*," he began, ensuring each participant had a glass in hand.

Despite grasping a word here and there, most of his sentences flew past me like exotic birds, their beauty lost in their speed. As an overly educated history professor back home, it was almost comical how I couldn't decipher this basic Italian wine tasting.

Then he came over to my table and repeated his instructions in English.

"Wine is poetry. It speaks to us, tells us its story, if only we know how to listen."

With a flourish, he showcased the wine in his glass. "*Questo vino* is a Barolo, hailing from the Piedmont region in the north. Made from the Nebbiolo grape, a variety as temperamental as it is rewarding."

"The color," he continued, glass held up to the light, "is a deep garnet. And if you look closely, you'll notice an orange tint at the edge, indicative of its age. A Barolo must spend at least two years in oak, and another year in the bottle before it can be released."

Swirling the wine, he asked, "*E il profumo*? The aroma? Breathe deeply." I leaned in to sniff. "Can you detect the roses? The cherries? Perhaps a hint of truffle, a touch of leather. These are the hallmarks of a Barolo."

"Smells delicious."

Finally, he sipped the wine, eyes closed in appreciation. "*E il sapore.* The taste. A Barolo is powerful, full-bodied, yet elegant. The tannins are present but balanced by the wine's natural acidity. And the finish... it lingers like a whispered secret. Go on. Taste."

I obeyed and wanted to climb right into the glass.

As the evening progressed, I found myself relying less on translations and more on my senses—the mesmerizing dance of the wine in the glass, the allure of its deep hues, the symphony of aromas, and, of course, *il sapore*.

Despite the language barrier, I even traded a few quips and laughter with Carlo, Paulo, and even Maestro Lorenzo. The barrier became less formidable by the moment. My cheeks flushed. A delightful warmth spread through me—a product of both the wine and the joy of the evening. Even though I couldn't understand every word spoken, I felt a sense of belonging. After all, good wine, like good company, needed no translation.

In that moment, a wave of contentment washed over me. I was here, in Italy, in a quaint little wine shop, learning about wine, about life, about myself. It didn't get much better.

Chapter Ten

After the official class concluded, Maestro Lorenzo worked the room, providing tidbits of information and answering questions. Eventually, he made his way to our table, his eyes sparkling with enthusiasm.

"Isla, how do you like our wines, then?" Lorenzo asked, his accent a charming melody.

"I love them, especially this Barolo. It's so... full-bodied," I responded, desperately trying to remember wine terminology. My head was a little cloudy from all the said Barolo.

"Ah, sì, full-bodied, indeed." He extended the bottle and refilled my depleted glass. "And how about the tannins? Do you find them strong?" he asked, swirling his own glass.

"Yes. Sì."

He chuckled. "Tannins, signorina, are what give the wine its dryness. They come from the skins, seeds, and stems of the grape."

"Right, the dryness, I knew that," I bluffed, offering a sheepish grin. I really had been trying to pay attention.

"Do you detect the truffle, the leather?" he continued, clearly trying not to laugh.

"Oh, absolutely. It's very... leathery," I said, teasing.

Maestro Lorenzo burst into laughter. "Leathery, you say? I must tell my friend who makes this Barolo that his wine smells like an old armchair."

I shrugged and raised my glass. "I think I've had a little too much leather to make a more poetic description."

Lorenzo grinned. "Bene." He clinked his glass against mine. "In the end, that's the most important part. I'm glad you joined us today. I'll be back at the end of the summer for a final tasting. I hope to see you again."

"I wouldn't miss it. Hopefully, my Italian won't be so embarrassing by then."

He bowed theatrically and moved on to the next table.

With the rich, earthy scent of aged wines surrounding me, I was contemplating which bottle to bring home when a familiar accent caught my attention.

Turning towards the sound, I spotted Ava and Lucas, the British couple from my rental cottage, engaged in a conversation with Gianna near the back of the shop. A smile spread across my face as I made my way over to them.

"Ava, Lucas!" I called out, causing them to turn in surprise. "What a coincidence seeing you here!"

Ava's face lit up with recognition. "Isla! Wasn't that a wonderful class?"

"Amazing. Even if I didn't understand a quarter of what Master Lorenzo was saying."

Ava chuckled. "I know! Us either. We were just getting some post-tasting advice from Gianna. Can't speak for you, but I'm going to be fat and perpetually tipsy by the time the summer is over."

"I think I'm right behind you," I said with a laugh.

"We're off. See you back at the cottage, then," Lucas said.

"Have a good night," I said. "I should probably as well—" My words trailed off as I spotted another familiar figure leaning against the counter, a wineglass in his hand. His eyes met mine, a playful smile spreading across his face. I hesitated, unsure how to react to the unexpected encounter.

Ava and Lucas flashed me a knowing look and artfully stepped away.

"Isla," Enzo greeted, pushing off the counter and making his way toward me. "What a pleasant surprise."

"Enzo," I responded, trying to match his ease but finding it challenging. "I didn't realize you were here."

He shrugged, that charming smile never leaving his face. "I came in a little late, so I slipped into a back table. I couldn't resist the chance to taste some of Gianna's new selections. Plus, I heard a rumor there would be a very interesting American lady in attendance."

I felt my cheeks warm under his flirtatious gaze. "Is that so?" I asked, trying to keep my voice steady.

"Sì," he said, leaning in closer. That devilish glint flashed in Enzo's eyes—eyes that, in the amber glow of the bodega, looked like honey. "I was hoping you would be here. I wanted to see you again." His boldness caught me off guard, but I couldn't help but smile back at him.

The air between us became charged, his words hanging in the air. I was at a loss for words. Enzo's bold flirtatiousness was disarming, and I was unsure how to respond.

"So, how was it for you?" Enzo asked, swirling his glass.

"I made a proper ass of myself, if that's what you're asking."

His laugh echoed in the small shop, causing a few patrons to glance over curiously. The sound was warm, like the wine I held in my hand. I wanted to hear it again. I also wanted more wine. I could get used to good wine and charming Italian men.

"That wasn't what I was asking, but good to know."

"As it turns out, I know nothing about wine."

"Ahh, but you know how to drink it with the best of us.

That's all that matters. Who cares about tannins and mouthfeel?"

I laughed sheepishly. I averted my gaze and aimlessly glanced around the room.

Just then, Gianna swooped in with a fresh bottle of wine in her hand. "Ah, Enzo, always the charmer," she teased, pouring us each a new glass. "You mustn't scare our guest away."

Enzo held up his hands in mock surrender. "I wouldn't dream of it," he said, still looking at me. His gaze was challenging, as if daring me to step into the ring with him.

Gianna winked and moved on to clear some empty bottles.

The crowd had thinned a bit now. I turned my head back to Enzo. I was both fascinated and wary of him. He was charming, yes, but there was a boldness to him that felt like a challenge—an invitation to step out of my comfort zone. I wasn't sure if I was ready for that yet, but the prospect was undeniably enticing.

"I should probably get home. Or back to my cottage, I mean. I'm pretty tired."

"Can I walk you home?" Enzo asked, his eyes had the slightest glossy sheen.

"I think I can find my way."

"You know, not all kindness is a reflection of your ability. Sometimes a man just wants to be polite."

"Didn't you know chivalry is dead?" I said. Both my head and mood were light.

"There are a few of us knights fighting for survival."

I tapped my nail against my chin. "In that case, I will give you a fighting chance." I extended my crooked arm, and he took it with a cheeky grin.

As we walked back to my cottage under the moonlit sky, the streets of Mare Sereno seemed to take on a new life. The vibrant colors of the buildings, once illuminated by the sun, were now bathed in the soft, romantic glow of moonlight. The cobblestones beneath my feet, still warm from the day's heat, seemed to hum with the day's leftover energy.

We passed through the main piazza, where a group of locals were gathered, their laughter and animated conversations echoing down the narrow, twisting corridors. A few strummed on their guitars, their fingers dancing effortlessly over the strings, and the beautiful melodies filled the night. I found myself swaying to the rhythm.

Enzo laughed.

"What?" I asked.

He shook his head, smiling. "Nothing. It's just nice to see you...unwind."

I tilted my head. "I can be unwind—unwound."

He laughed. "With enough wine, I see that."

I waved my hand. "Stop ruining my party, Enzo."

He laughed and slipped his arm around my waist. I stiffened, then instantly melted into his touch. He leaned in closer. "I'm just waiting for an invitation to the party."

Uh oh, was all my wine-addled brain could think.

We reached the cottage, the scent of the citrus grove wafting through the open window, and I paused to take it all in.

"It's a lovely little place. I've always admired Maria's lemon trees," Enzo said.

"It is. Thanks for walking me home. It was fun to see you again."

"Let me take you out again tomorrow," Enzo said, his hand slipping through mine. I didn't protest. The wine and the festivities had broken down my barriers—at least for the night.

"I would, but I'm supposed to go to this historic site. It's been on my list, and I really wanted to see it."

He looked mildly disappointed but recovered quickly. "Ah. Another time then. Which site?"

"Um, the *Pareti di Mare*. I'm going on tour."

He tsked, tsked, and it made me laugh. "Amazing site, si. But a group tour? With some cheesy guide? No."

"Be careful. He's Maria's cousin."

Enzo rolled his eyes. "Lorenzo's Bus? Definitely no. I cannot let you do that."

"You know a better tour guide, then?"

He shrugged casually. "I might."

"I can't imagine touring an ancient Roman site is on your to-do list for the day."

"Who me? I love history. Let me take you. You can still listen to Lorenzo prattle on, but I'll take you up on the Vespa. It will be a beautiful day. We can cruise along the coast, and you can see more of the area than you ever thought. Way more comfortable than a crowded tour bus full of sweaty Germans."

"What makes you say they're Germans?"

He shrugged. "Just a hunch. I'm usually right about these things."

I laughed and reluctantly agreed.

"Ok, but remember, this is my excursion. Don't go taking over. This is my agenda."

He raised his arm. "On my honor."

"And we leave early," I said, holding up a stern finger. "Like actually early. Not Italian early."

"How early?" He raised an eyebrow comically.

"Eight. Sharp."

He sucked in a dramatic breath but smiled. "I'll bring the croissants."

"The Italian Riviera, also known as the Ligurian Riviera, is famous for its stunning landscapes and colorful fishing villages. The history of this beautiful stretch of coast, however, dates back to prehistoric times, with evidence of human settlements dating back to the Paleolithic era. The region was inhabited by various Ligurian tribes before being conquered by the Roman Republic in the second century BCE. The Romans left a lasting impact on the region; many cities such as Genova, La Spezia, and Ventimiglia boast Roman ruins and artifacts."

Lorenzo went on in heavily accented English but with unparalleled enthusiasm. As the small group listened intently, my legs started to ache from hiking around the crumbling city. Despite the fascinating glimpse into the past, including nearly intact structures such as a basilica, temples, and a forum, my mind was starting to burn out on information. And that was saying something coming from an academic like me.

Not that I would ever admit it.

"You could read this in your guidebook," Enzo whispered in my ear. I swatted him away.

"Shh. I'm listening."

He pinched my side, and I gently elbowed him, much to his amusement.

"Following the fall of the Roman Empire, the region experienced a period of instability due to various barbarian invasions and the rise of feudalism. During the Middle Ages, the Italian Riviera was divided among several powerful maritime republics, such as Genova and Pisa, which competed for control over trade and territory in the Mediterranean. The city of Genova, in particular, rose to prominence as a major center of trade, finance, and maritime power."

"Are you taking good notes?" Enzo asked.

"Shh!" I snapped. The tour guide paused and stared at us, as did everyone else.

Forcing an embarrassed smile, I said, "Mi scusi. Go on. It's so interesting."

Lorenzo, his smile tinged with annoyance, continued, his hand gestures flowing theatrically.

"During the Renaissance period, the region flourished culturally and economically. The Italian Riviera became known for its art, architecture, and intellectual life, with Genova and other cities commissioning works from renowned artists such as Rubens and Van Dyck. Additionally, the famous explorer, Christopher Columbus, was born in Genova during this period."

"In the nineteenth and twentieth centuries, the Italian Riviera became a popular destination for tourists and the European aristocracy, who were drawn to its mild climate, beautiful landscapes, and charming seaside towns. The region also played a significant role in the unification of Italy, with figures such as Giuseppe Garibaldi and Giuseppe Mazzini having strong connections to Liguria. Now, we will see some of the best-preserved ruins from these times. Come, let's break for lunch in the amphitheater."

He gestured for us to follow him deeper into the ruins.

"Finally," Enzo said, his voice laced with sarcasm. "I might need to give Lorenzo a lesson in brevity."

"You're ruining my good time," I countered.

"I need to teach you what a good time is, then."

I rolled my eyes. "I happen to like it. Remember, I'm a history teacher."

Enzo laughed. "Ever the professor."

"I can't help who I am."

"A giant nerd?"

I raised my finger. "A professional nerd, thank you very much. I happen to be paid for my nerdiness."

"I can't argue with that."

Despite the supposed lunch break, Lorenzo had moved on to another site and was waxing lyrical about the ruins. But I had secretly lost a little interest in his lecture. I wanted to take everything in for a moment without explanation. It was like that with art sometimes—I didn't necessarily want to know every detail about the artist's thought process. I just wanted to feel and imagine.

From a distance, I could hear him speak. "A strong earthquake destroyed the city towards the end of the fourth century AD. It was then rebuilt on the ruins of the ancient settlement. The area was frequented until the ninth century when the population, tired of the Saracen incursions, finally abandoned it."

The midday sun had hit its crescendo, and suddenly I felt as if I might pass out. My stomach grumbled, but I wasn't in the mood to sit with the group and listen to any more history.

"Had enough?" Enzo asked.

"Of crumbling ruins? Never."

"I know a place nearby that's even better."

I looked at him skeptically. "Better than one of the most famous crumbling cities in Italy?"

He shrugged. "It's better because no one goes there. Come on. Let's ditch this baking tourist trap."

I rolled my eyes, but I was too intrigued not to follow. I was a sucker for anything unknown, even if it was likely to get me murdered someday.

* * *

The ancient castle stared down at us with crumbling majesty. Overgrown with moss and ivy, the stone structure was a perfect blend of natural beauty and man-made grandeur. Its towers reached for the sky, and the crumbling walls whispered tales of past glory.

"Wow," I said, looking up at the parapet, shielding my eyes from the glaring sun.

"Thought you might like it," Enzo said beside me.

"Do you know when this was built?" I asked.

"Not exactly, but I believe 14th century."

I nodded, eyeing the slab-sided stonework. "I would say that's probably correct."

"How did you find this?"

He smiled. "A long time ago, I discovered a map of this place among my grandfather's things. He was also a lover of history and an avid explorer. There's probably not a hidden castle in Italy he didn't know about."

"And let me guess. There are legends abound."

He chuckled. "Who knows? Probably. I've made up a few on my own."

I laughed. "Let's hear one."

He tilted his head and made a show of scratching his chin.

"There was once a princess locked in its tower—"

I shook my head. "No way. That's far too much of a fairy tale cliché. You can do better."

He raised his eyebrows. "You raised the stakes without my knowledge?"

I shrugged. "Consider it a challenge to your talents."

He rubbed his chin. "I see. Tough crowd. *Allora*." Enzo's eyes scanned the old castle, and his gaze finally landed on a peculiar, crumbling statue. It was the figure of a dignified man, the stone masterfully sculpted, but the mouth and nose had crumbled off, whether by design or erosion, it was unclear.

"Do you see that?" he asked me, pointing at the statue with a roguish grin.

I glanced at the statue and then back at him, my brows furrowed in confusion. "See what? The unfortunate man with no mouth?"

"No, no, signorina," Enzo replied, playfully wagging his finger. "That unfortunate man is King Enrico the Hirsute, better known as the Mustache King."

"The Mustache King?" I echoed, stifling a snicker.

"Si, si," Enzo confirmed, nodding solemnly. "It all began when King Enrico was just a boy prince. He sported this tiny, sorry excuse for a mustache. But a traveling bard told him a prophecy: 'As long as your mustache grows, so will your power.' Prince Enrico took those words to heart."

"Do traveling bards know secret prophecy then?"

Enzo maintained his serious facade. "In my story, si. Don't interrupt. So, upon becoming king, Enrico decreed that his mustache should never be cut. He was convinced that his authority, nay, the destiny of the entire kingdom, hinged on his facial hair."

With mock seriousness, I said, "However did he eat? Or drink? Wouldn't his mustache get in the way?"

"Oh, it did. His royal meals were a spectacle. He had a specific servant whose only job was to hold his mustache aside while he ate. And drinking wine? That was another show altogether. They had to create a special funnel made from a barracuda's tail."

"Um, why a barr—"

"Don't interrupt."

"I bet he wasn't popular at 'kiss the king' contests," I quipped.

"Ah, well, you'd be surprised. His Queen adored that mustache. It's said that she used it as her personal knitting yarn holder."

"Such romance." I batted my eyes.

"And now, comes the tragic part," Enzo continued, adopting a mock mournful expression, "One windy day, King Enrico was standing atop that tower over there," he pointed at a ruined tower, "flaunting his magnificent mustache for the kingdom to see. But a forceful gust of wind wrapped his mustache around the tower, and well...yanked him off."

"No!" I cried out theatrically, clutching my chest.

"Si!" Enzo affirmed, "And hence, the reign of the Mustache King met a premature end, just as his barber had always warned. 'Sire,' he used to say, 'one day, that mustache will be the end of you.'"

I tilted my head. "And what year was this?"

Enzo bobbed his head in mock seriousness. "Oh, many years ago indeed. No one knows for sure."

I laughed from deep in my belly. "Thank you. That is a piece of lore I shall take with me forever."

He offered me an exaggerated theatrical bow.

Our laughter reverberated through the abandoned castle, a sound that I bet hadn't echoed in those walls for ages. For a fleeting moment, I fancied that the spirits of the past were laughing along with us, the legend of the Mustache King living on in our mirth.

"Should we go inside?" I asked.

"Why not? Watch your step. This place doesn't see many visitors."

"That's a shame. The poor Mustache King living in eternity alone." I flashed him a cheeky look.

We moved into the castle, marveling at the remnants of lavish frescoes, intricate stone carvings, and grand halls now reclaimed by nature. We discovered hidden rooms filled with forgotten, crumbling artifacts and secret passages leading to breathtaking views of the surrounding landscape.

I couldn't help flashing him rogue looks. I had thought he might be humoring my fascination with the past, but he seemed just as curious and engaged as I was.

"Isla, come look."

"What?" I scrambled over, nearly breathless. With excitement about the whole place, my historian mind was in overdrive.

"May I present the ballroom?"

We stepped into an old room that was indeed vast, but now decorated with overgrown vines. Any grandeur had long been removed, but I could envision it filled with rich tapestries and flowing wine.

"Was it really the ballroom?" I asked.

He shrugged. "You're the historian, you tell me."

I looked around the room and took in every detail. The peeling frescoes, the broken windows.

"It's hard to say without a deep dive into the carvings, but it's definitely possible. It has the right layout."

"Care for a dance, my lady?" He bowed in a playful gesture.

I rolled my eyes. "Darn. I forgot my dancing shoes. Maybe later."

I started to walk further into the room, but he grabbed my hand and pulled me back.

"Enzo!" I protested. But I couldn't contain a laugh as he

began twirling me around the vast, crumbling room, the birds and the breeze acting as our soundtrack.

"You have some moves," I said.

"I practiced. I knew one day I would have to impress an American historian in an abandoned castle."

"And here I thought I planned ahead."

We danced around the hall, the echoes of our laughter bringing the room back to life. My heart thumped in my chest with a mix of elation and a twinge of longing. I couldn't shake off the feeling that I was part of something much bigger, something transcending time and space, as if I had been here before, dancing in a castle ballroom.

Suddenly, a gust of wind whistled through the broken windows, causing us to shiver and bring our merry dance to a stop. It was as if the castle had whispered something to us, reminding us of the passage of time.

"It's getting late. Maybe we should head back," Enzo said.

My cheeks flushed with heat as if to protest, but my arms prickled. "Yes. We should."

As we left the ballroom, I glanced back one last time, imagining King Enrico with his mustache wound around the tower and his queen knitting beside him. Somehow, even in its ruined state, the castle didn't seem so lonely anymore.

Chapter Twelve

The sun was indeed beginning its descent as we emerged from the ancient castle and in response my stomach grumbled—apparently loud enough to garner Enzo's attention.

"Hungry?" Enzo asked, noticing my reaction.

"Is it that obvious?"

He grinned. "Your stomach has a strong singing voice. And it seems like you're always hungry."

I playfully nudged him. "Who can resist this food? It's amazing you're not all 1,000 pounds."

"Our pesto has been the downfall of kingdoms, it's true. Who knows, maybe it was actually the pesto that took down our poor mustache king." He pressed a hand to his heart.

"May he rest in peace," I said.

"I know a place we should stop."

"What kind of place?"

He leaned in, and I felt his warm breath on me. "Trust me."

"Sounds perfect," I murmured so quietly that there was no way he could've heard me. But I'm pretty sure I felt him lean in a little closer.

We loaded back into the Vespa, and I sleepily leaned into him as we rode back down the winding coast. Enzo pulled the Vespa off the road and down a small path to a cliff side overlooking the vast expanse of the sea. A small, quaint, yet well-kept building sat on the very edge, with a row of tables circling the outside. Before we even got off the Vespa, I could smell the succulent scents of garlic, fresh fish, and herbs. Music hummed low in the background, too soft to be fully audible, but I could still tell it was something jazzy. Enzo killed the engine and helped me step off the Vespa. My legs wobbled as they hit solid ground again.

"I hope you're hungry," Enzo said. "Giovanni will whip up the best food you've ever had in your life. I swear on my mother and Jesus Christ." Enzo made the sign of the cross over his heart.

"That sets very high expectations," I said. "Does Giovanni know the pedestal you've put him on?"

"Giovanni has put himself there, I assure you."

The little restaurant was quiet this time of day, and I imagined that no one was eating dinner at this hour but lost tourists. A couple of people crowded around a tiny bar, small glasses of red wine in their hands. The music was a little louder inside, a soft Italian melody that was the perfect soundtrack for a tiny ristorante on the coast.

"Enzo!" A portly middle-aged man in a white chef's uniform burst from the back, his expression beaming as he hustled over to Enzo. His hands were covered in flour, and his cheeks were red.

"*Ciao! Cosa stai facendo qui*?"

Enzo extended his arms toward who I assumed was Giovanni and gave him a big embrace. He pulled away, hands still resting on Giovanni's shoulders.

"Ciao, Giovanni. It has been way too long. This is Isla.

She's a friend from America. I wanted her to experience the best food on the Ligurian Sea."

Giovanni looked utterly affronted, his expression falling. "Only on the Ligurian Sea? You insult me." He turned toward me and, with a very aggressive hand gesture, said, "Signorina, this is the best food in the entire country of Italy. Probably even all of Europe, if you ask me."

I couldn't help but grin. He was like a cartoon character, perfectly cast.

"Enzo might have sung your high praises. I'm definitely starving, so you'll have to serve me a little bit of your finest of everything," I said.

Giovanni grinned. "You don't look big enough to eat all the food, but I will give you the benefit of the doubt. Do you have any dietary restrictions, signora?"

"No. Only that I don't like food that doesn't taste good," I said.

Giovanni chuckled. "I like this girl, Enzo. She's funny. Better than most Americans we get in here, right?"

"When was the last time you got an American here?" Enzo asked.

"Exactly. They all ignore poor Giovanni."

"Yes, poor Giovanni, indeed," Enzo said.

Giovanni gestured toward a table in the back next to the window. It had an expansive view of the rocky coastline and the sea. "My best table for you. Please, have a seat. Wine?"

"Most definitely," Enzo said.

We made our way over and settled into the table that was perfectly set for the day. The waves lapped gently outside. A few coastal birds sang an afternoon song. As we took our seats, I couldn't help but feel a touch of skepticism. Was this all a performance to impress me?

"What did I tell you?" Enzo said.

"Well, you said nothing about the incredible view and the

atmosphere. You only talked up the food. So you're either underselling or trying to make up for the fact that the food won't actually be any good."

Enzo glared at me playfully. "Watch what you say. Giovanni is very sensitive."

I smiled. Moments later, a pretty server hustled out with an open bottle and two glasses. She set them down and then poured a serving.

"From Giovanni, Enzo. It's so good to see you again."

Enzo beamed up at the young woman, who was quite lovely with inky black hair pulled into a tight bun and big, deep-brown eyes. Perfectly olive Mediterranean skin. I felt a tiny prick of jealousy, completely unwarranted as Enzo and I were barely friends, let alone romantically involved. But still. He definitely seemed to catch every wandering eye.

"Anna, this is Isla. She has come to us all the way from San Francisco."

"Nice to meet you, Isla. It's a long journey. Did you miss the train to Rome?" Anna teased with a wry smile.

"I'll get there, eventually. But it was important that I came here. It's a long story."

"She has family in the area," Enzo added.

"Ahh, molto bene. You are one of us then," Anna said. "Please, enjoy your wine. Giovanni will be out with more food than you could possibly eat in a lifetime."

"Grazie, Anna," Enzo said. He turned to me and raised his glass. "Salute."

"Salute."

Giovanni emerged from the kitchen momentarily, arms teetering under the weight of the feast he'd prepared. A seductive scent wafted toward us, the aromatic preview of the upcoming indulgence stoking my anticipation. He unveiled each dish with a performer's flair, and my stomach responded with a growl of approval.

"*L'antipasto*," Giovanni said.

He set down the small platter of artfully arranged cheeses and delicately folded prosciutto while an assortment of olives and marinated vegetables lent a pop of color and texture.

"This is just the warm-up?" I asked with a laugh.

"It's worth every calorie, trust me," Enzo said.

Before I had time to truly appreciate the antipasto, a loaf of focaccia was introduced to our table. The bread was warm, the surface dusted with sea salt and scattered rosemary catching the evening light. Tearing off a piece, its soft, yielding interior called to me.

Giovanni emerged again, this time with a bowl of pasta.

"Linguine alle vongole," he said.

"Make it stop," I whispered playfully.

Despite my expanding belly, I twirled my pasta around my fork and slipped it into my mouth. I closed my eyes. The pasta was al dente, the clams subtly sweetness, all harmoniously brought together with a whisper of garlic and white wine.

"You look like you're having an orgasmic experience," Enzo said.

I nodded, not opening my eyes. I whispered, "I am. I really think I am. Don't disturb me."

Enzo smirked. "If I knew all it took was pasta—"

I opened my eyes and flicked a piece of bread at him.

"I hope you're a seafood lover," Enzo said as the branzino made its debut. The whole sea bass, perfectly grilled and skillfully deboned, was bathed in a dressing of fresh lemon and herbs.

"I think this might actually be a symphony in my mouth," I said. "But God, I am full. I hope he does to-go boxes."

Enzo cocked an eyebrow at the expression.

"Err—takeaway boxes."

"Ah. He might be offended, but I'm sure he'll oblige."

"How is everything?" Anna asked, returning to collect our empty plates.

"I think you're trying to kill me with food. Death by culinary ecstasy," I said.

Anna flashed Enzo a look.

"She gets poetic when she's in a food coma," Enzo said.

"Ah. Well, I hope you have a little room left for il dolce."

I held up a hand. "No, I don't think I could—"

"She doesn't think she could stop now," Enzo interjected. I glared at him. "Oh, come on. We're almost at the finish line."

I laughed but capitulated. "Il dolce."

Anna grinned.

Our culinary tour ended on a sweet note as Anna placed espresso and cannoli on the table. The cannoli, a delightful balance of crispy pastry shell and sweet, creamy ricotta filling, officially tipped me over the edge.

"Does il dolce come with a wheelchair?" I asked.

"He probably has a barrel out back I could toss you in."

"Yes, please."

"So, was Giovanni right? Was this the best meal in Italy or even Europe?"

With a contented sigh, I had to admit, "This wasn't just a meal. It was an experience. And yes, it might just be the best I've ever had. And now I think I'm dead. Congratulations. You've killed me."

Enzo chuckled, a warm, infectious laugh that echoed in the quiet restaurant. "A fitting way to go, isn't it? But at least you died happy."

I held on for dear life as we navigated the Vespa back into Mare Sereno, certain I was going to fall off in my food stupor. Street lamps cast a cozy glow on the cobblestone streets, and an evening breeze danced with the trees lining our path.

"I'm not sure I can eat again for the rest of the summer," I said as we walked up the steps toward my cottage.

Enzo's grin spread wide, as if he'd been the mastermind behind my indulgence.

"Don't be so self-congratulatory," I said.

His laughter rang out, full and rich. "Apologies. I merely relish knowing you've enjoyed our little adventure."

I bobbed my head. "That I have. You've been a stellar guide."

His gaze lingered on me, something flickering within. "Just your guide?" he asked, voice low.

My cheeks heated as a butterfly fluttered in my stomach. "We seem to make good friends, too, don't we?"

His chuckle rumbled. "Friends. A small upgrade from tour guide, I suppose."

Nervously, I tucked a loose strand of hair behind my ear. "I don't know, Enzo. What are we? Does anyone ever know?" I said with a nervous titter.

My gaze drifted to the panoramic view of the Italian coastline, stretched out like an artist's dream.

"Join me this weekend."

I swiveled to him, taken aback. "What?"

"Escape with me for the weekend. We can go inland. To the mountains. Or up to the city."

Laughing nervously, I replied, "A vacation within a vacation?"

His grin was infectious. "I'm not the one vacationing, am I? This is my reality."

"Sure, rub it in."

"I'm sure you want to see more of the area than just Mare Sereno."

"I suppose," I said hesitantly.

"So, will you come?"

Unease prickled beneath my skin—the cobblestones underfoot felt unsettlingly sharp. "I'm not sure about that."

"Why not?"

How could I articulate the warning bell ringing within me, urging me to bolt?

"We barely know each other, Enzo."

He scoffed. "What do you think I am, a serial killer? Why are Americans so paranoid?"

"I can't help it. It's been drilled into me. Don't talk to strangers. Definitely don't accept their candy. And never disappear for the weekend with a man you barely know."

He smirked. "That says more about your country's men than mine."

Despite his teasing, I shook my head. "Jokes aside, I'm not ready for something like that."

"I'm a gentleman, Isla. We can have separate rooms."

I shook my head. "It's not that." Wasn't it? Who knew? "It's just the whole thing. I—"

I could see the disappointment in his eyes, but he nodded. "It's okay. No pressure. I just thought..." He shook his head. "Forget it."

"It's not personal, Enzo. It's just—"

"You're afraid."

Defensiveness crept up my spine. "What?"

"I get it. It's a scary thing."

"You think just because I won't run away with you, I'm afraid? Afraid of what, living my life?"

I may have snapped a bit, but I didn't feel remorseful. I shouldn't have to prove myself by escaping for a romantic weekend with a charming Italian I barely knew. Even if he was very, very nice to look at.

He threw his hands up defensively. "I didn't say that. Why are you so defensive?"

I crossed my arms, "I'm not defensive, I'm just—"

"Did I offend you in some way?"

"I… No, not really. It's just…" I struggled to articulate my thoughts.

"Speak freely, Isla. Don't tiptoe for my benefit."

I sighed and forced myself to face him. "You make everything seem so simple. A Vespa ride, a bottle of wine, and life is perfect."

He looked at me, expecting a punchline. When I didn't deliver, he half-laughed, "Why can't life be that simple? Why all the seriousness?"

Frustration clawed at my throat. "Who even are you? You can't possibly be in earnest. Life is not a vacation. It has real problems, bills, responsibilities."

He shrugged. "Your definition of life sounds more like a prison to me."

"Life often is a prison, at least for most of us," I said, deflated. "This—" I gestured out to the town, the sea, "is not real life."

"It's real life to me. You need to relax. Constant tension isn't healthy," he said.

His nonchalance stirred my anger. "Well, I guess we can't all live a nonstop dolce vita, Enzo. Some of us need to plan for our future."

He bristled. "You make me sound like an aimless wanderer."

"That's not what I said. You just act as if life is a breeze, and things will naturally fall into place. But life isn't like that!" I countered.

He raised an eyebrow, surprised. "I think you're confusing a carefree spirit with recklessness. All I want is for you to experience Italy without carrying around your bundle of stress. And I'm not going to apologize for finding some contentment in my life. I am happy. So alert the polizia."

I sighed deeply. "You're just coming on a little strong for

me." I averted my eyes for a moment before speaking again. "I think we need to slow down. Let's take a break, okay?"

Enzo smirked. "A break? We're not children. Fine. If you don't want to see me, don't. We won't cross paths unless we want to."

His dismissive tone stung more than I expected, and it inflamed the irritation already simmering within me. Our heated words hung in the silence between us.

"I just—I need some space. This is moving too fast."

His lips thinned, but he refrained from arguing. He nodded curtly. "So you said. Fine. If you change your mind, you know how to reach me."

With that, he swung onto his Vespa and roared into the evening, leaving me alone under the night's sky.

Chapter Thirteen

I took a hot shower, then fixed myself a cup of mint tea. Settling into my new favorite armchair (I really needed to get one of these), I stared out at the night. What was my problem? Why had I jerked away from Enzo like that? Was I really so scared of a little adventure and no-strings-attached romance?

My thoughts whirled in the silence. Enzo, with his easy charm and infectious laughter, embodied the spirit of this captivating coastal town. His zeal for life was magnetic, but it was also the very thing that had pushed me to retreat.

I was a person of structure, a stickler for well-laid plans and meticulously calculated decisions. It wasn't fear that guided me, but a firm belief in control and the importance of self-determination. I liked knowing where I was going and, more importantly, that I was doing it on my own terms.

Enzo was the antithesis of that, wasn't he? He was the embodiment of a free spirit, embracing each day as it came without a thought for what lay ahead. His invitation to an impromptu weekend getaway was exciting—but utterly overwhelming. You couldn't build a life on that—could you?

The distant toll of the town's church bell interrupted my

musings. Was this all still about Ian? Six months ago, everything about my life had made sense. I had more education than anyone needed. I had a coveted tenure position at a university. I even had a handsome fiancé doing quite well in the tech space. I admit relationships had never been my strong suit—romance is complicated when you spend the better part of a decade in school—but we were on the right track. We had even bought a condo in one of the hottest housing markets in the country. Ian and Isla. We were all the things.

Then the news broke. He was calling off the engagement. He had met someone new. I was not his happily-ever-after.

Miranda.

Miranda, the public relations specialist who was consulting at his company. What other job could a woman named Miranda have? I tried not to let my anger consume me. I, a detail-oriented observer of human nature, an intelligent and educated woman, couldn't fathom how I had missed the signs. They had carried on right under my nose, and I hadn't noticed. I must have been naïve, optimistic, or perhaps a complete fool. There were so many red flags that I had ignored. So many offhand remarks and sly hints that I had dismissed. He was always the kind of man who was never satisfied, always seeking something better, brighter. I should have known. He was always acquiring new toys, losing interest in things that had captivated him just a week before. I should have known that the same would happen to me. If he was never satisfied with his things or himself, he could never be satisfied with just one woman.

Shouldn't I have known that a man like him would have a meltdown over choosing bedding? That was how it started. We were doing what engaged couples do—planning our future, our home. I thought it was special and symbolic to pick out new bedding for our marital bed. Regardless of the fact that we were already living together, I wanted something fresh and new to represent our significant step into matrimony. But then he had a meltdown. Why was I trying to change everything? How was he supposed to commit to bedding?

His reaction had baffled me, and I'd figured, hey, I guess all men get cold feet. Maybe he was hungry.

But when he uttered, "I've met someone else," it was like being pushed off a cliff without warning. I stood there, numb, in the linen section of Neiman Marcus.

"It wasn't like I was trying to. I'm not that kind of guy," he defended himself. But it wasn't the defense that kindled my anger—it was the insensitivity. The blatant betrayal.

"You met someone?" I snapped out the words. His meaning was finally sinking in. Truly sinking in. "Who did you meet? Who?" My voice was climbing.

"Can you keep your voice down, Isla? You're making a scene," Ian said.

"Oh, I'm making a scene? I'm making a scene, everyone!" I yelled at the top of my lungs over 1500 thread count.

He grabbed my hands and pulled me close to him. "Stop this. Don't act like a toddler."

Red rage simmered at my core. Did he think always-controlled, level-headed Isla would react well to this news?

"Oh, yeah? I haven't even begun to act like a toddler. Do you want to see a tantrum?"

He sighed and let go of my arms. "Can we just talk like adults here for a second?"

I folded my arms over my chest and glared. "Fine, you have thirty seconds to explain yourself."

"Can we go somewhere? Somewhere not in the middle of the fucking linen aisle?"

"Are you kidding me? So what, I can't embarrass you? God forbid one of us would embarrass the other person. Let me remind you that you're the one who just dropped the bomb in Neiman Marcus!"

I picked up a pile of Egyptian cotton and flung them into his face. The next thing I knew, security was politely escorting me out.

Miranda. Miranda who works in PR and talks like a sexy baby and overdoes it on lip injections, had taken my place. It wasn't fair. Life was not fair. That was the harsh reality I was coming to terms with.

"So, how are things going with Enzo?" Gianna asked, topping off my prosecco.

I focused on the tiny bubbles in my glass and pretended I didn't hear her. Even though I had only known Gianna for two weeks, we'd already formed a fast friendship. I'd found myself wandering into her shop daily for a little chat and a glass of something cold.

Gianna snorted. "Ah. I see."

I forced myself to look up at her. "What makes you think there's anything going on with Enzo?"

She smirked. "Oh, because everyone can see it. We all saw you at the wine tasting the other night. Undressing each other with your eyes." She wiggled her eyebrows.

I forced an uncomfortable laugh. "It's not really like that."

Gianna's cat eyes narrowed in on me. "And what is it not like? That you two are having a steamy summer fling?" She shimmied her shoulders.

"I'm not a college student, Gianna. I'm a grown woman." I felt every year of it, too.

She snorted. "And grown women can't have sex? I've been sorely misinformed."

For some reason, I blushed. I wasn't a prude, not really. Yes, I was a little tightly wound these days, but I liked sex just as much as anyone. I believed in loving freely and openly. In pursuing passion.

I shook my head. "No, obviously, I know." My voice was wobbly and nervous. "It's just not like that with Enzo. We're having some fun. He's playing the tour guide. But that's it. We're really just friends."

Gianna tilted her head and studied me. "Why the hesitation?"

"Why the assumptions? Just because two people are spending time together doesn't mean they have to jump into bed."

She smiled understandingly and shrugged. "It's not fair to deny attraction its due."

I glanced away, avoiding her gaze. Finally, I looked back at her. "Honestly? I guess I'm just not ready."

She waved away my argument. "It's a little summer flirtation, not a marriage proposal."

I laughed half-heartedly. "I know—I'm just feeling a little raw from everything." I'd filled her in on my tragic home life during our last wine chat. "And while I believe a casual summer fling can be just that, I'm not sure I'm in the headspace for it. Besides, he seems...I don't know—" I let my words trail off.

Gianna waited patiently for me to continue. I sighed.

"I get the feeling that he's sort of a playboy."

She laughed wholeheartedly. "As are all Italian men on the Riviera. Were you expecting anything else? Some dull, good Catholic boy?"

I chuckled. "No, I guess he does live up to the reputation.

I just don't really have any interest in being the point of gossip for the rest of the summer."

"And why do you care what other people think?"

"I don't," I retorted defensively. "But it feels like every time we turn a corner we run into one of his ex-lovers. From every waitress to barista, the girls are all googly eyes for him and daggers for me."

Gianna nodded thoughtfully, although I could tell her full lips were tightly containing amusement. For a moment, I had to wonder if they, too, had shared a tryst in the night. We were all about the same age, after all.

"Isla, I'll level with you. That's the saying, correct? Yes, Enzo has a reputation. He grew up here and has probably had a romantic dalliance with many of the women here. He has broken a lot of hearts, I won't lie. That's part of his charm, I think. He's a free thinker. A wild soul. But that doesn't make him a bad person. It doesn't mean he's not capable of love and commitment if that's what you're seeking."

I shook my head fervently. "No! I'm not looking for love and commitment. The exact opposite."

She threw up her hands exasperatedly. "Then I don't see the problem! You're going around in circles. You're just looking for an excuse not to be happy."

Her words stung like a slap. I searched for a counterargument. Was Gianna right? Was I looking for excuses?

"Well, I—" I stuttered.

She shook her head and reached for a bottle of Sangiovese. She artfully plucked out the cork and filled up two balloon glasses. She slid one to me. "What do you think of this one? The winemaker from Tuscany wants me to sell it."

I picked up the glass and stared at the deep red liquid. "I'm not really the right person to ask."

"Stop overthinking everything. Not every decision is life or death. Just tell me what you think."

I sighed and sipped. I swirled the wine around in my mouth, letting its slightly bitter flavor sink in. "It's—dry. But not in a bad way. A little—maybe a little smoky?"

Gianna nodded and sipped. She swirled the wine around as well, her eyes going up as if contemplating. "Si, I agree. What else?"

I sipped again. "There is something spicy about it. Like dark fruit. I've had Sangiovese before, but I feel like it was much lighter than this."

"Si. Sometimes they can be a more seductive grape, depending on the soil. The wine has a lot of nuances, even within the same varietal. A lot like people."

I nodded. I sniffed the glass. "I like it. I'd drink it."

Gianna smiled and picked up the bottle. "*Bene*. See? Sometimes, you can just be in the moment. Say what you feel right now."

I laughed. "You sound a bit like Enzo."

She shrugged unapologetically. "Well, maybe there's something all of us Italians have in common. We live our lives. Not every decision is a cause for anxiety. We don't just sit around worrying about the next bill to pay, or the next responsibility, or our retirement accounts."

I rolled my eyes playfully. "Yes, because you have a system that provides for you. We have to worry about those things. We're on our own in America. It is the land of dog-eat-dog. You can be anything and everything you want to be but be prepared to do it on your own."

Gianna sighed. "It is a shame, isn't it? I think America is a lovely place, and I admire much of your ethos. And I'm eternally grateful for the iPhone. But it seems sometimes you are living counter to how people are supposed to live. There's no sense of community, no taking care of your neighbor."

I sighed. "It's true. There are a lot of good things we do, but also a lot that could take a page from Mare Sereno."

"*Il dolce far niente.*"

"Hmm?"

"It's a saying we have here. *Il dolce far niente.* It means basically 'the sweetness of doing nothing.' It's about the beauty of slowing down, enjoying the present, and seeing the loveliness of life."

I smiled. "Yes, that's something we could definitely use more of."

She raised her glass. "Perhaps take a little back with you at the end of the summer." She sipped and nodded. "Si, I like this very much as well. You have a lot of things that we will never have here. Like electric dryers. God, I know I'm not supposed to say it, but can we please make that the normal here in Italy? I am so sick of damp, wrinkly clothes all summer."

I chuckled. "Maybe I'll have one sent over for you."

We smiled and sipped our drinks.

* * *

The next morning, as I strolled the piazza in search of sustenance and charm, I tried to think of other things. However, Gianna's words echoed in my ears. I couldn't help but chew on the bitter truth. Had that been what I'd been doing for so long? Denying myself a chance to be happy? If that was the truth, how could I change it? Did I need a little more il dolce far niente? Pff, who didn't, really?

I settled into a sidewalk table and ordered a glass of Vermentino. I could get really used to this wine in the middle of the day thing.

I thought I was doing all the things that would make me happy in life. I had pursued the passions I wanted. I wanted to research and teach at a higher level, to live the life a professor's career could provide—ample time off to travel and research, lifelong education, and being surrounded by a culture of learning and growth. I had pursued it with gusto. I loved my job, or at least I used to. If I were being very honest with myself, it hadn't quite lived up to my expectations. I had believed that working at a university would be fulfilling, and in many ways, it was. Each day was a quest for knowledge and truth. I had eager students and exciting research. However, soon enough, I found myself buried in bureaucracy and tangled in red tape. The politics of the university system were as intricate as those in Washington. The "publish or perish" mentality was taking a toll on me. The pressure to secure tenure was immense, and slowly, the joy I once felt for my work was dwindling. I assumed everyone faced a similar struggle at some point in their career. After all, the pressures of any job could erode passion and joy over time. Perhaps even professional athletes, actors, and artists who earned a living doing what they love sometimes feel like throwing in the towel.

I had spent my entire life pursuing this career. With almost a decade of education and corresponding debt to my name, this was my life. And Ian had always supported it, hadn't he? Or had he merely supported a very narrow version of it? Through the lens of time, it was becoming harder to tell what was reality. It was becoming more difficult to discern what I had actually done for myself and what I had done because I thought I was supposed to. Everything seemed cloudy now, blurry. Or maybe it was just the wine. I eyed my glass and decided the wine couldn't possibly be to blame. I took a heavy swallow, savoring the full notes and tannins. No, the wine was definitely not to blame.

I stared down at my phone, eyeing the WhatsApp messenger, trying to decide if the wine had made me brave enough to apologize—for what? For being so neurotic, I guess. But before I could make a decision, my eyes landed on the one thing I both did and didn't want to see—Enzo, sitting at an outside cafe table a few doors down.

He was sipping an espresso and reading a book, a little Italian cliche, and I had to resist snapping a photo. He was so lost in thought, his eyes buried in the book, his other hand tentatively fingering the tiny ceramic espresso cup. I didn't want to disturb him, but I needed to tackle this. I needed to live. I took a deep breath and found my courage. I finished my wine and walked slowly toward him, my dress swinging in the breeze, my sandals slapping slightly against the cobblestones. His eyes floated up casually, and when he saw me, for a second, he just stared. For a moment, I had a panic that I had misread the whole thing. Maybe I was wrong. Maybe I was too much for Enzo. If he was just looking for casual fun-in-the-sun, some tightly wound, overworked American with an Airbus A380 full of baggage was probably the last thing he wanted. I sucked in a breath and almost turned around when he flashed me a high-beam smile.

"Isla," he said so softly that I barely heard it.

"Enzo, hi!" The words came out high-pitched as though I, too, had just spotted him.

"Sit?" He gestured to his little table.

I smiled and nodded, slipping into the seat opposite him, grateful for the invitation. A server came around, and I ordered a single shot of espresso.

"I'm glad to see you," Enzo said.

I nervously fiddled with a sugar packet.

"Me too."

The server set down my tiny cup, and I eagerly sipped.

"Are you ok?" Enzo asked.

I stared at the black liquid a moment before setting down the glass. I looked up at him. "Yes. I'm fine. I just—I think I owe you an apology."

His brow went up. "Apology? What for?"

I shook my head. "I get so worked up about everything. I know that. I know I need to relax, to enjoy myself. I flew halfway around the world to find a little peace, and I still can't. And I'm sorry. I don't know what's wrong with me. It's just my personality."

He waited a moment before saying anything. The sounds of the day filled the void—the lapping waves, the zoom of a scooter, laughter, and chatter.

"You have nothing to be sorry for. You don't lie when you say you need to relax. Si, you have come to one of the most beautiful places in the world. This is a place that was made for tranquility."

"*Il dolce far niente*," I said. He laughed. "It's something Gianna taught me."

"Si, it's a good saying to live by. But we are all subject to stress. Life is hard. It is true. It's hard for everyone, even here. I get stressed too."

"Why do I find that hard to believe?"

He smirked. "You don't think running a small business can be stressful? It's okay if you need more time to unwind. You went through a lot, I understand. And I get it if carousing around with me, just letting everything go—I get if you're not ready for that. And there's no judgment there. I'm not angry at you. I can't force you into something you're not ready for. Maybe I'm the one who's pushing you too hard when you need some time to yourself to just wander the streets and read good books."

My cheeks warmed. "Thank you. I suppose I needed a little validation. But the thing is, though, I might not be ready, but I know it's what I need. I have control over me. Yes, I'm going to grieve the loss of my Nonna for a very long time, probably for the rest of my life. But I know she wouldn't want me to come to her hometown and just simply wallow and refuse to live. And Ian," I shook my head, almost cringing at the sound of his name on my tongue. He didn't belong here in this beautiful place. "I can't let Ian have any control over me any longer. The truth is, what he did to me was the greatest gift he could've given me. It freed me from a life I thought I wanted, but I now know was all wrong for me."

"I'm glad to hear that. Does this mean I can see more of you before you leave?" He flashed me a knowing little smile. Its infectious nature pulled at my own lips.

"Yes, I think I would like that. I think I would like that very much."

He tapped the table lightly. "Bene. Come to dinner tomorrow night at my family's."

I laughed incredulously to myself. He was persistent—I'd give him that.

"Ok, whoa, not what I expected. Definitely not taking things slowly then."

"No, no. Nothing like what you're thinking. There will be tons of people. No pressure. My mama hosts big family dinners a few times a month. All my *cugini* and *zin* come. Some family friends. Lots of fun."

"I'll think about it."

"*Il dolce far niente*, remember?"

I glared. "Cheater."

He grinned. "*Bene*. We serve drinks at five."

Chapter Fifteen

I found myself questioning my sanity for agreeing to this. Had the Italian sun and too much wine caused me to lose my mind? Meeting his *family*? I barely even knew Enzo. Surely one didn't meet someone's family after only two weeks. Yet, he insisted it was different—his family would be delighted to meet me. His assurance left me puzzled. Did he bring random girls home all the time? It seemed too easy for him. If the situation were reversed, I'd be a flaming cocktail of anxiety and mania.

Oh wait, I was.

As I stared into the mirror, I realized I was overthinking again—a favorite pastime of mine. My thoughts were running wild and doing me no favors.

I carefully selected an outfit for the summer evening—an Italian-inspired floral number courtesy of the boutique off the piazza. I left my hair loose and natural, letting some of its natural waves take flight in this humidity, and opted for minimal makeup. I wasn't sure how to present myself. I knew Italian women could be dramatic and vivacious, but I didn't want to come across as flamboyant in front of Enzo's family. And I wasn't sure I had the knack for vivaciousness.

Then it hit me—why did I even care? Enzo was just someone I met on vacation. In a month, I'd be heading back home, likely never to see Enzo or his family again. Did it matter if I made a stellar first impression?

Pushing aside my chaotic thoughts, I picked up my handbag and headed toward the door.

The summer evening was warm and inviting. The setting sun had painted the sky in its favorite hues of pink and orange. The beauty of the moment did little to quell my nerves, but it was a pleasant distraction, nonetheless.

Enzo was waiting outside the cottage. He looked rather dashing, I had to admit, in his perfectly pressed shirt and trim pants—Italian men sure did wear tight pants. His eyes twinkled in the dying sunlight. His foxy smile melted my fears momentarily.

"Ciao, bella."

I blushed like a little schoolgirl at the easy compliment.

"Ciao."

"All ready?"

I took a deep breath, squared my shoulders, and nodded. "As ready as I'll ever be," I replied, my voice stronger than I felt.

He chuckled. "You look like you're about to commit yourself to a prison sentence, not eat pesto."

I glared. "Just drive."

"Gladly."

With a move I'd practiced over and over in the mirror, I draped a scarf around my hair, shielding it from the potential havoc the wind and helmet could wreak. Enzo revved up his Vespa, and we cruised out of town.

We journeyed along the coastline as the sun sank slowly into the horizon. It was breathtaking, something akin to a scene plucked straight from a movie. I felt a bit like Grace Kelly. Or was it Audrey Hepburn? I was pretty sure one of them rode a Vespa along the Riviera coast.

As we rounded the final bend, the road dipped into a quaint residential neighborhood flanked by mature, lush trees. Enzo guided us to a halt in front of a gorgeous mansion ensconced in a stone wall and iron gate.

"Um, wow?"

Enzo said nothing as he hopped off to open the gate, then rode us through.

The stunning architecture, embraced by lush green vines on either side, held an aged charm that was impossible to ignore. Vibrant flowers decorated the yard, adding splashes of color to the scenery. Despite its apparent age, the building was well-maintained, indicative of the painstaking love invested in its upkeep. Billowy curtains fluttered in the breeze, adding an almost ethereal touch. The moment Enzo cut the engine, the air filled with laughter and music emanating from the house. The tantalizing smells of fresh herbs and garlic flooded my senses. I felt I could halt my journey right here and still deem my Italian dream fulfilled.

"This is your parent's home?" I asked in awe, my eyes climbing to the tiled roof.

He smiled and looked almost sheepish rather than rogue for once—almost. "Si. Si."

"You failed to mention the casual family dinner was at a palace."

"Don't be so dramatic. It's a villa, not a palace."

"What is it exactly that your family does?"

"Uhh. A little of this. Little of that."

"Enzo—who—"

"Stop overthinking. Come."

"Enzo!" Before I could say anything else, a woman's voice echoed from the house. We both looked up to see a woman about our age sprinting toward us. She was dressed in a flowing white dress, her dark hair cascading around her shoulders, her Mediterranean skin perfectly bronzed. In contrast, my pale complexion felt like a blank canvas in need of an artist's love.

"*Ciao, Lucia! Che bella vederti,*" Enzo replied warmly. He leaned in for a quick cheek kiss exchange.

Lucia's eyes landed on me.

"Ciao," she said with uncertainty.

Enzo switched to English. "Lucia, this is Isla. She's a friend of mine from America."

Lucia switched to English, too, and flashed him a skeptical look. "You have friends in America?" Her gaze locked on me—was that suspicion? Her look was a complex mix of confusion, curiosity, and caution.

"I have friends all over this world," Enzo replied nonchalantly.

Lucia smirked, then smiled at me. If her tight expression could be called a smile.

"It's lovely to meet you. Piacere," I said, extending my hand before retracting it as Lucia leaned in for a customary cheek kiss. "Same to you. *Benvenuta* to our home."

After a moment's pause, Enzo added, "Lucia is my cousin."

"Oh? That's wonderful. Do you live here too?" I asked.

She nodded. "Si, I do. For now. I recently moved back to the area and am currently staying with my aunt and uncle until I find my own place."

Turning to Enzo, I inquired, "Is this where you grew up?"

His smile was almost bashful. "Si. This is the ancestral home. My family has owned it for generations. But really, it belongs to all of us. The doors have always been open to aunts, uncles, cousins, and even friends. All are welcome."

The idea of an extended family all living together was so

foreign to me, but I couldn't help but admire it. It contrasted starkly with the isolated living back home, where everyone moved away in pursuit of their fortunes, building new communities and laying roots far from home. Technically, I didn't live that far from my parents, but the traffic and rat race of the Bay Area made forty miles a Herculean journey. Not that I necessarily craved Sunday dinners with my parents, but —I shook off the melancholy thought.

"Well, you'll want to get inside quickly," Lucia chimed in, interrupting my meandering thoughts. "Everyone will be dying to meet your new friend."

"In a minute. Don't rush us," Enzo said, playfully pushing her away.

"Allora. Well, hurry before all the good French sparkling is gone. You know once everyone gets tipsy, your mama starts with the cheap prosecco." She gave me a scrutinizing look before sashaying away.

Enzo flashed me an amused look. I attempted to return the smile, but it felt forced. This encounter wasn't exactly unfolding as smoothly as Enzo had promised.

"I don't think she likes me," I corrected.

He waved away my words. "Don't be silly. Lucia is just a little—fiery. Come on. Let's jump right in. Lucia's right—Mama usually opens the best wine first."

We stepped inside, and my breath caught. Each space was a living, breathing symphony of mirth and camaraderie. The air was thick with laughter, lively conversation, and the intoxicating aroma of Italian cuisine—a heady mix of garlic, tomatoes, and herbs that set my stomach growling in anticipation. A glass of wine was urgently needed.

Enzo promptly guided me toward a side table where an open bottle of French sparkling wine was sweating in a silver bucket with a nice patina. He poured the wine into two slender flutes and handed one to me.

"Take a sip and relax, Isla," he said, his voice conveying understanding. "You're radiating nerves like a kettle about to whistle."

I smiled shyly, trying to hide my anxiety behind my glass. "Can you blame me? This isn't something I was exactly prepared for. I didn't meet Ian's parents for like a year."

He leaned in closer, his voice a whisper, "I am not Ian." His hands brushed my waist in a way that sent the blood rushing to all kinds of places. "Relax, Isla. No one here will bite you. Except maybe me." A playful grin lit up his face as he turned away to greet the arriving family members.

He really needed to stop—stop being so—the only word I could think of was *delicious.*

Drawing in a deep breath, I braced myself to meet the family. Soon we were surrounded by a flurry of Italian chatter. I could only comprehend maybe one word in every thirty, but the joyous reunion of Enzo and his family was unmistakable. After a moment, Enzo pulled away and directed their attention toward me, where I had been waiting awkwardly on the sidelines.

"*Famiglia.* This is Isla, a friend from America," he introduced me, first in Italian and then in English. "She was dying to try Mama's pesto."

The room fell silent for a moment before erupting into welcoming smiles and enthusiastic chatter.

"*Benvenuta*!" A woman approached me, placing her hands gently on my shoulders. "I am Maria, Enzo's aunt. We are so happy to have you!"

"Grazie. Thank you for inviting me. Your home is incredible," I responded.

Maria looked around the room, her eyes sparkling with pride. "Ah, yes. My father renovated it himself. It is truly a beauty. But come, you must be hungry and thirsty."

I held up my glass. "Enzo already took care of the latter."

She flashed a wide grin. "Good boy, Enzo. Show these Americans true Italiano hospitality."

Navigating through the crowd, I was introduced to various individuals, including Enzo's uncle Franco, another cousin named Maria—I really hoped not everyone was going to be a Maria—Lucia again, and her brother Rocco. I made a mental note of each introduction, putting my academic skills to use.

Enzo, ever the gracious host, guided me through the human maze. His hand, warm and reassuring, rested gently at the small of my back—an intimate gesture that seemed to nudge us into something more than a tour guide. As he introduced me to each family member, their traditional Italian greetings made me feel less like an outsider and more like a welcomed guest. Their handshakes were firm, their smiles were warm, and their cheek kisses charming. Despite the whirl of unfamiliar faces and the rapid-fire Italian that I struggled to comprehend, there was a sense of home in this joyful chaos.

Finally, I spotted an older woman coming out of the kitchen, wiping her hands on a tea towel. She was short and trim and wore a breezy black cotton dress with a well-used apron over it. Her jet-black hair was tied up in a top-knot, and despite a few lines encasing her eyes, she had a youthful glow.

"Enzo!" she said with a warm smile when she spotted him.

"Mama. Ciao," Enzo said. I sucked in a breath. The Mama.

She hustled over and planted a big sloppy kiss on his cheek, and pulled him into a tight hug. She pulled away, and they exchanged some Italian, her hand pressing to his cheek affectionately. I got the impression he hadn't been to dinner in a while. After a moment, she noticed me.

"Ah! *Mi dispiace. Sono Alessia.*"

"Piacere. Sono Isla," I said, my Italian sounding clumsy

and gummy compared to their lyrical tones. And apparently, I was instantly ousted.

"Americana?" Mama Alessia flashed Enzo a confused look.

"Si, mama. This is a friend from California. She was dying to try your pesto. Read all about it *Travel & Leisure*." Enzo winked, and Alessia swatted him with her tea towel.

"*Benvenuta*, Isla. We are happy to have you here." Her English was clear but heavily accented and more calculated. She probably spoke it much less often than her son. "I'm so sorry my husband isn't here. He's away this week on business."

"Grazie for having me. I do apologize. My Italian isn't great. Or existent."

She waved away my concerns in that Italian way with a wide smile. "Not a problem. Most of us speak some English. Just glad you're not German! Remember that *boche* Lucia brought home once?"

I hid my smile with my hand. "Not an ounce of German in me."

"Bene." Alessia seemed genuinely relieved.

"Isla's nonna was actually from Mare Sereno. Maybe you knew her?" Enzo said.

Alessia's eyes went wide. "Really? Ah, what a little world. What was her name?"

"Rosa Amante."

"Amante—I don't think I knew a Rosa Amante. Although she was probably much older than me."

"Yes, she would have been. She would be eighty-five now. She actually just passed away."

"I am sorry for your loss." Alessia took my hand, and I tried not to cry.

"Thank you. Her family left when she was young—twelve, I believe. So I'm sure no one remembers her. But she told the most beautiful stories of her childhood here. I had to come see it."

Alessia's eyes beamed. "That is so beautiful. Please, make yourself at home here. You are of the same soil."

I thought I might just melt.

"Ah. Allora. I must get back to the food before your animal uncles get in there. Enzo, make sure our guest has some of the good wine before Franco drinks it all."

* * *

"Are you all right?" Enzo asked as we stepped out onto the terrace for a little air. The villa was stunning but, like most homes here, it lacked the lovely modern convenience of air conditioning.

"I'm doing great. It's a bit overwhelming but amazing," I replied, laughing lightly. I pressed a hand to my flushed cheeks.

"You'll get used to them," he assured me.

"What is it with your mama and Germans?"

He chuckled. "Probably a hangover from the war. Europeans have a lot of hangovers from that thing."

"Oh, that little thing," I teased. "Honestly, this whole thing—it's wonderful. Thank you for inviting me. It feels like a scene straight out of a movie."

"Just don't say *The Godfather*."

I shrugged. "It's too early in the night to tell. You don't have any horses around here, do you?"

He chuckled. "Americans and their movie fantasies."

I shrugged. "It's our way of experiencing adventures."

"Instead of living your own adventure?"

My cheeks flushed, and I looked down, murmuring, "If only it were that easy."

He leaned in closer. "And what do you think you're doing here in Italy, Isla, if not living your own adventure?"

I turned toward him, the moonlight catching the glint in his eyes, amplifying his allure in this picturesque setting. The air between us seemed to hum with anticipation as we inched closer. As gentle as a whisper, he brushed away the errant tendrils of my hair dancing in the balmy breeze. His fingers grazed my cheek, then traced the delicate curve of my collarbone.

"You are so lovely," he murmured, his foreign accent adding an exotic touch to his simple words. I swallowed hard, trying to steady the fluttering in my chest.

"Coming from anyone else, that might sound cheesy," I replied.

"Would you prefer if I said you were hot?"

I giggled like an idiot and lowered my eyes.

Suddenly, a shrill voice pierced the serene moment.

"Enzo! There you are! Your mama is looking for you." Lucia's voice rang out as she approached us.

"Way to kill the mood, cousin," Enzo teased, his tone light. Lucia looked at us, her expression a confusing blend of suspicion and annoyance.

"Stop playing Romeo on the family balcony, will you? You're clearly visible," she chastised, her hand wildly gesturing to the gardens below.

My cheeks heated, and I fumbled nervously with my hair. "We weren't—It wasn't like that," I stammered.

"Sure, sure, it's never like that with Enzo," Lucia retorted, her voice dripping with sarcasm, her hand gestures on overdrive. "Come on then."

Her words left a knot in my stomach. 'Never like that with Enzo' implied what exactly? Was this just part of his routine?

"Let's go in," Enzo suggested, his tone neutral.

As I moved to follow him, Lucia gently tugged at my arm, holding me back. Somehow, in the previous ten seconds, she'd managed to light a cigarette. She took a delicate drag and exhaled in a fluid, almost sensual motion. She was like a tragic

French model with smoky eyes and wild hair. A messy edge contrasted with elegance.

She leaned into me and said in a low whisper. "I get it. You're a pretty tourist looking for a summer romance in Italy, but be careful."

"Excuse me?" I questioned, taken aback.

Lucia glanced around conspiratorially before responding. "Bringing you here seems rather thoughtless, even for Enzo," she admitted, shaking her head. "I don't understand why he'd just throw you into the mix."

"You make it sound as if I've walked into a pit of vipers. Everyone seemed genuinely nice," I defended. Everyone but you, I added silently in my head.

Her lips tightened into a thin line. "Italian families are complicated. They love a good party, and the more, the merrier. But, we are also wary of outsiders. Just try not to take anything too seriously. Enjoy yourself, Isla," she said, her voice carrying a hint of resignation.

With a swift turn, she sauntered off, her billowing dress and dark hair swirling in the wind, reminiscent of a '90s shampoo advertisement. I stood on the steps a little dumbfounded, not entirely sure what had just transpired.

Enzo finally noticed my lagging and came back down. "Are you ok?"

I shook it off and forced a smile. "Yeah. Totally."

Enzo's eyes followed his cousin, and he shook his head with an understanding smirk. "Ignore Lucia's stories and come in. We just uncorked a special bottle from the cellar."

His smile beckoned me in like a lighthouse guiding a ship through a stormy night.

Suppressing my inner turmoil, I mustered a bright smile and hurried to join him.

Chapter Sixteen

We lingered around the appetizer table, nibbling on antipasto. I wanted to dive into everything, but I forced myself to politely select small portions. The fresh rustic bread was warm and fluffy. The olive oil was smooth, with a hint of spice. I plucked some fritto misto from the plate and thought I might pass out from flavor overload.

"Don't fill up. The main course is the real attraction," Enzo said.

I could already feel my stomach testing the fabric of my dress, but my taste buds craved more. Thank god for flowy summer fabrics.

"Bring it on." I grinned.

As if on command, a voice rang out.

"*Tutti! La cena è pronta!*" Alessia emerged from the kitchen, looking triumphant, and announced proudly.

"I assume that means 'dinner is served'?" I asked.

Enzo grinned. "Your Italian is getting better by the moment."

"Some things are universal."

"Come on. Hope you're hungry."

"You seem to say that a lot," I said.

He shrugged. "It's an Italian thing."

I followed the crowd out of the lounge and down the hall. The villa itself was like a visual history book of Enzo's family, the echo of generations filling the space. Black and white snapshots of bygone eras adorned the walls. They shared the space with more recent photos. I tried to take them in as we passed by. There were an awful lot of them on very large boats. Yachts, dare I say? Ok, seriously, who were these people? Antique furniture peppered the rooms, and vivid Italian artwork imbued the space with an irresistible vibrancy.

We stepped into a formal dining room that had a rustic elegance, boasting a long, polished wooden table that stretched out to accommodate the large family. Place settings with gleaming silverware and delicate china were perfectly aligned, and in the center, a variety of open bottles of red wine. The scene had a homey quality to it despite the opulent surroundings.

Enzo's family gathered around the table, their loud and spirited conversation filling the room. I was seated between Enzo and his Aunt Maria, a vivacious woman with silver-streaked hair and sharp eyes.

"*Per favore, siediti,*" Aunt Maria said to me. "Please, sit."

"Grazie," I said with a smile.

With the help of Lucia and another aunt or cousin whose name I couldn't remember, Alessia brought out the pasta course.

"Pesto Genovese," Alessia set down a massive bowl in the center of the table, brimming with bright green leaves and thick noodles I could only describe as *plush*. I think I actually felt my eyes bulge.

"She makes her own pasta, too," Enzo said.

"Stopppp it," I said.

Soon the table was a whirlwind of Italian, with the occasional English phrase thrown my way. I tried to keep up, but the rapid-fire chatter was a blur.

"Isla, Enzo tells me you are a professor of history?" Alessia said.

All eyes turned toward me, and I felt my insides flip flop with nerves. "I am. Yeah, certified nerd over here," I said, blushing slightly.

She chuckled. "Nothing nerdy about that. Or at least it's the right kind of nerdy, I would say. But tell me, you didn't come all the way to Italy just to spend the summer in our sleepy little village, did you? This country has some of the richest historical sites in the West."

"No, not entirely. I spent a week in Milan and Genova before I came out here. Incredible history. I teach some Renaissance courses at my university, and so, of course, that was magical. The sights, museums, castles." I shook my head, realizing I was about to unleash all my nerdy historian chatter.

But instead of looking bored, everyone seemed amused.

"Oh, yes, Milan. Such a sophisticated city. Old and new," Alessia said.

"And the trains actually run on time there," Enzo said, which elicited a genuine chuckle from everyone.

"We are not known for punctuality in this country. I'm sure you've noticed," Alessia added.

"I might've noticed just a bit. Never quite sure if the train will actually arrive, it's true."

Maria waved her hand dismissively. "Because really, where does anyone really have to be? What's so important?"

"Did you get to Florence?" Lucia asked.

"No, unfortunately, I didn't. There's just so much to see in Italy. I haven't been to Rome either. But I guess I'll just have to come back someday."

"Now Florence, that is a place worth seeing!" Franco declared. "Forget the Sforzas. It's all about the Medici."

It might have been his accent, but I think I detected a slight slur in his words. Everybody smiled amusedly, and I had the inkling Uncle Franco might be somewhat of the family clown.

"Something tells me there will be many more Italian vacations in my future." I didn't mean to, but I couldn't help but spare a glance towards Enzo. I also didn't miss Lucia's icy stare.

Aunt Maria turned toward me.

"You know, Isla," she began, a glint of mischief dancing in her eyes. "Enzo here wasn't always this charming gentleman you see now."

I glanced at Enzo, who groaned in mock despair, rolling his eyes in anticipation of what was to come. "Not this again, *Zia*." He turned to me. "Her favorite pastime is embarrassing me in front of newcomers."

"Silencio, Enzo," she scolded lightly, then turned back to me, her smile broadening. She "spoke clearly and slowly. When he was just a boy, no more than six or seven, he fancied himself quite the knight. You see, he'd found this old broomstick and decided it was his mighty sword."

I leaned in and whispered. "Did you think you were the Mustache King?"

Enzo glared at me.

"But that's not the best part," she continued, her voice dropping conspiratorially. "One day, he decided to 'slay the dragon' to save the princess. The 'dragon' was actually his uncle's prized Vespa, and the 'princess' was our neighbor's cat."

My laughter echoed in the dining hall as I pictured the scene—Enzo playing the daring knight, facing a Vespa dragon for a feline princess. I glanced at Enzo, expecting to see him embarrassed. But he wasn't. He was laughing too, the flush on his cheeks more from laughter than from shame.

"And what happened then?" I asked, intrigued and amused by this childhood tale.

"Well," Aunt Maria said, her eyes sparkling with laughter, "Enzo decided to take the 'dragon' down by sticking his 'sword' in the exhaust pipe. The 'dragon' was vanquished, all right, but the poor Vespa... It was out of commission for a month."

Enzo was doing his best to look annoyed, but a smile poked out of his mask.

"I thought you cherished Vespas above all else?" I teased.

"Apparently, it was a turning point in my life," Enzo said with a smirk.

"It wasn't the last time our Enzo would try to rescue a princess then, was it?" she cast a teasing glance in Enzo's direction.

"Zia—"

"He's always been popular with *la signorinas.*"

I felt my stomach drop, the playful tone of the conversation doing nothing to lessen the blow. It wasn't that I was surprised—Enzo was undeniably charming and attractive. I mean attractive. But the open acknowledgment of his romantic history sparked a fresh wave of anxiety.

A wave of laughter swept the table as Maria shared a tale of young Enzo, all of fifteen, trying to woo his first girlfriend with an ill-fated serenade under her window. Apparently, he had chosen the wrong window, waking up the girl's irate father instead.

Despite whatever irritation or embarrassment he felt, Enzo chuckled good-naturedly along with his aunt. His laid-back reaction, however, did nothing to ease my discomfort.

As the laughter subsided, Maria continued, her tone

becoming more serious, "But, of course, Enzo also experienced his fair share of heartbreak."

Enzo stiffened. "Ok, Zia, that's enough."

I turned to look at Enzo, searching his face for some sign, some reassurance. But his expression was unreadable, a mask of light-hearted amusement as he accepted the teasing.

Maria winked at him before turning back to me. "Fine, fine. I've embarrassed him enough for one night." She leaned into me conspiratorially. "But I have plenty more stories where that came from. Would you like to hear about the time he tried to cook pasta for the first time?"

I laughed, but the underlying question remained—was I merely another character in the colorful narrative of Enzo's life, or did I have a chance to be something more? Did I even want that? No, what I wanted was more wine. I subtly reached for the bottle.

Lucia's warning reverberated in my mind, a dark cloud to my festive mood. The undercurrent of unease swelled, growing into a steady drumbeat of caution, and doubts began to take root in me. I did my best to pull them right up. I noticed the knowing glances exchanged between Enzo and some of his cousins, the secretive smiles they shared. They were brief, fleeting moments, but enough to stir a whirlpool of questions in my mind. Was there an unspoken narrative, a hidden history that I was oblivious to?

With the joyous clatter of the family dinner as my soundtrack, I tried to shake off the doubts that plagued me. I focused my attention on putting as much pesto in my mouth as possible because, my god, Enzo had been right about his mama's pesto.

As the detritus of our meal lay scattered on the table—a battleground of crumbs, half-empty glasses of wine, bits of antipasti—the mood shifted. The laughter quieted and gave way to a more profound rhythm of conversation.

Uncle Franco, a man of stature with a booming laugh I'd heard all night, cleared his throat. I turned my attention to him as he began to speak, his voice carrying an undertone of reverent pride.

"Uh oh." Enzo leaned close to me. "Franco's been into the grappa already."

"See, this villa," Franco began, thankfully in English, his calloused hand sweeping across the room in a grand gesture. "It's more than just our home. It's our heritage, our history. Our ancestors built it from the ground up. Every brick, every beam, every corner of this place carries a part of our story. Built from the sweat of the shipping yards."

I leaned in, captivated. The historian in me was thrilled to be offered this firsthand account of Italian family history. Drunk history anyway.

"This villa," he continued, his gaze distant, "has witnessed the birth of every member of this family for the past five generations. It's watched us grow, celebrate, grieve... It's borne witness to our trials and triumphs."

He paused, letting his words sink in. A respectful silence hung in the air, but I could see the tightlipped smiles hiding. Enzo glanced at me, barely containing his mirth.

"The frescoes in the living room," Franco pointed toward the beautifully painted walls, "were painted by Enzo's great-grandfather. He was an artist, blessed with an incredible gift."

I turned my gaze to the walls, taking in the scenes depicted.

"As for this table," Franco patted the old, weathered wood with a palpable smack, "it has been the center of countless family gatherings, bearing the weight of our feasts, our conversations, our lives. If only it could talk, the tales it could tell—"

"And do you have a point, Franco?" Alessia interjected. Everyone giggled. Franco glared at his sister.

"I—I do not." With that, he sat back down theatrically.

An uncontrollable laugh escaped me, muffled by my napkin. Enzo squeezed my thigh under the table, making me jump.

* * *

As the night drew to a close, Enzo guided me to a quiet corner of the garden. Bathed in soft moonlight, Enzo appeared serious. His usually sparkling eyes were clouded with thought.

"I hope you had a good time tonight," he said, his voice barely above a whisper. "I apologize for all the antics."

"It was a colorful night. But it was great," I replied honestly.

He sighed, running a hand through his hair. "Isla, I...I know what Lucia said to you. And I know that you might be doubting things...doubting me."

I was taken aback but remained silent, giving him a chance to continue.

"I can't pretend I don't have a past. Obviously, Zia Maria wouldn't let me even if I tried." We both laughed. "But you're not just some passing entertainment. I hope you know that. I really enjoy spending time with you."

His words were sincere, his gaze steady. A surge of mixed emotions welled up within me, but there was a sense of relief, too. I wasn't sure where this would lead or what I even wanted from this, but it was comforting to know I wasn't just a notch in a bedpost.

"Thank you. But you don't have to justify anything to me. You and I—I mean, we're not even...We're just—"

He interrupted me with a kiss. I startled and stumbled back, but he held me up with one strong arm around my waist. He pressed his mouth into mine, and I opened to him with gusto—my surly garlic breath an afterthought.

"Enzo?" His mother's voice interrupted the moment. "È tempo di dolce!"

"*Merda*," Enzo muttered, and we both burst into laughter. My cheeks flushed, and I was suddenly overwhelmed with embarrassment. What was I doing? Enzo flashed me a grin.

"I think it's time for dessert."

Chapter Seventeen

I awoke to the sound of chirping birds and the warm sun on my face. My body stirred slowly from a deep slumber. Despite the glorious first sensations, I soon felt a headache gnawing at the base of my skull. Too much grappa with dessert had rounded out an already gluttonous evening. But the memories softened the pulsation. I would take a little grogginess to experience last night over and over again. So far, Mare Sereno was precisely what I needed it to be.

I lingered for a moment in my dreamy surroundings, letting the sea breeze tickle my skin.

Finally, my caffeine addiction won out, and I pulled myself up. I fixed an espresso pod and lazily stood by the window, looking out at the bustling day unfolding like a warm embrace.

Eventually, I washed my face, pulled myself together, and made my way down to the little kitchen in the hopes Maria would have something savory and delicious prepared.

Sure enough, she was just setting out the pastries and coffee when I stepped into the breakfast nook. Her face lit up as I came in. She seemed exceptionally bright this morning.

"Buongiorno!" she said.

"Buongiorno. You seem extra chipper this morning," I observed as I helped myself to a small cup of coffee and a croissant.

Maria beamed. "Oh, just a lot to get done for the day. But I always enjoy the festival."

"The festival?" I said rather impolitely, my mouth full of buttery croissant.

She blinked for a moment, then waved it away with a smile. "Oh, well, of course, you wouldn't know about it. Would you? *La Festa delle Luci*. The Festival of Lights. It's our favorite summer festival here in Mare Sereno."

I swallowed my food this time before speaking, washing it down with a sip of strong coffee.

"What's it all about?"

Maria smiled, and her face took on a nostalgic look as though remembering many festivals past.

"La *Festa delle Luci* is a traditional event celebrated every year to mark the end of summer and the beginning of the harvest season." She piled empty dishes—Ava and Lucas', I assumed—onto a tray as she spoke. "It has its roots in ancient pagan rituals later incorporated into local Christian traditions, as so many were around here. It honors our patron saint, Santa Lucia, the patroness of light and sight, who is believed to protect the town and bring good fortune."

I smiled. I loved how everyone around here had a tale to tell.

"The history dates back to the early days of the town, when the local fishermen would light lanterns on their boats as a tribute to Santa Lucia, seeking her blessings for a bountiful catch and protection from the dangers of the sea. Over time, the event evolved into a vibrant community celebration not only for the fishermen but also the farmers and townspeople who would come together to celebrate the end of a successful season and the beginning of the harvest."

"That sounds magical," I said, taking another bite of pastry.

"Oh, it is. The town is transformed into a wonderland. Twinkling lights, lanterns, and colorful decorations adorn the streets, houses, and businesses." Her hands made wild gestures as she described it all. "We will have lively music, dancing, food, games, and local art. People of all ages from all along Liguria participate."

"Do people still light the lanterns?"

"Oh, si. That is the culmination. Some people spend weeks making theirs ahead of time. Others make them at the little booths during the event. At the end of the night, everyone carries them through town to the sea."

"That all sounds incredible," I said, already dreaming of including it in my courses.

"You will come, si?" Maria asked.

"Oh, si. I wouldn't miss it."

"Bene. Well, I must get to work. I'm baking some cannoli for the fundraiser."

Mare Sereno, usually bathed in the warm hues of the sunset against the cerulean sea, was now illuminated by a different kind of light. As I stepped into the main square, my breath hitched at the sight. Hundreds, possibly thousands, of glowing lanterns floated in the evening sky, turning the night into a breathtaking spectacle of shimmering lights.

"I'm going to drop these off at the booth," Maria said, gesturing towards the wagon full of cannoli she'd been working on all day. "I'll take those." She reached for the bag of supplies I was carrying.

"Are you sure you don't need any help?" I asked.

She waved a dismissive hand. "No, you go enjoy yourself. Have some good wine, eat some delicious food, dance. Just don't forget to come buy some cannoli later."

I smiled. "I'll buy at least two."

Maria grinned and trundled her goods off to the fundraising booth.

Closing my eyes, I absorbed the surrounding sounds. Guitars strummed softly in the background, merging with cheerful chatter and laughter. I strolled through the transformed piazza, eyeing stalls selling an array of local delicacies and vibrant handmade crafts.

Children rushed past, their faces glowing with excitement, their small hands clutching lanterns and gelato, ready to join the dance in the night sky. A small band commanded attention with folky tunes from a makeshift stage as happy couples of all ages moved to the rhythm. A group of elderly ladies sat at a booth, folding colorful paper into intricate designs with well-practiced hands. One looked up and waved. I returned the gesture.

At a wine stall, I procured a small glass of fruity red. As I turned around, I spotted him across the cobblestone piazza. I don't know why I was surprised, but his presence still caught me off guard. He spotted me, too, and flashed a slow, subtle smile, then gave a slight wave. We stood there across from each other, the tension between us palpable as unsaid words hung in the air. Finally, I laughed, feeling absurd for behaving like a nervous teenager at her first dance. Gathering my composure, I walked over to him.

"You look beautiful," Enzo said, his eyes appreciating my summer dress and the extra attention I'd given to my appearance. "And taller."

With a playful move, I slid my dress aside to reveal my tall wedges. "I had some help. I don't think I can dash across the cobblestones in stilettos like a true Italian woman, but perhaps these will suffice."

"That's all a myth, anyway."

I tilted my head. "Is it?"

He scrunched his face and shrugged. "Ok, maybe it's true. But I always thought they had a death wish running around in those spikes."

"You clean up fairly nicely as well," I said, noting his stylish European summer attire. He looked like he belonged on the cover of a Riviera magazine.

He rolled his shoulders back in a nonchalant shrug. "We Italians are known for our stylish dressing, aren't we?"

"You do have a reputation to uphold. It's true."

He glanced around the bustling piazza. "So, what do you think of our little festival?"

Inhaling deeply, my lungs filled with the scents of sea salt and citrus. "It's beautiful. Honestly, it's everything I wanted it to be."

"You keep saying things like that."

"Because you keep fulfilling my fantasies." I winked, and I'm pretty sure his eyes widened. "I had visions in my mind about what this place would be like. But visions rarely match reality. We build things up in our minds, especially when our only reference point is glossy Instagram photos or, in my case, memories relayed through a nostalgic lens. But this place," I paused, taking in the scene. "Actually lives up to its reputation. My grandmother used to tell me stories about it, and I always assumed she was embellishing. But she was accurate. Her memories were true."

"I am happy to hear that. We sometimes have a distorted view of what this place might be like, too. It's home to us, and it offers everything you could want. But we don't know how other people see it. There are some things we probably exaggerate and some things we take for granted. That's the way of life when it's your home, isn't it?"

I nodded. "I get it. I'm from a place people travel from all over the world to see, and even though I grew up there, there are things I've never done."

"Such as?"

I pondered for a moment. "Like visiting Alcatraz."

His brow furrowed. "Alcatraz?"

"It's a famous prison."

His face twisted, and I laughed.

"I know. It's a bit morbid. But it has a profound history in the area. And it's on an island. Historically, inmates tried to escape, but they had to swim across the freezing cold San Francisco Bay to reach land."

"Did anyone ever succeed?" He asked.

"No one knows for sure. There have been about a dozen escape attempts, but most were recaptured, shot, or drowned in the bay during their attempt. However, there are a couple of inmates who got off the island and were never seen again."

Enzo appeared thoughtful. "Wasn't that in a movie?"

I laughed. "Yes, an old Clint Eastwood movie from the 70s."

"Ah yes, now I remember. It is rather morbid, though, touring such a dark place."

"Oh yeah? And how many people were tortured to death in your castles or led to slaughter at the Coliseum?"

He waved his hand dismissively. "But yours sounds like an amusement park attraction."

"I guess you're not far off. People charter boats to go and tour it. You can even stay the night there for a haunted house experience."

The look of shock on Enzo's face was hilarious. "I will never understand you Americans."

"Don't look at me like that. Like I said, I've never actually been there. So when people ask me, 'what do you think of Alcatraz?' I have to admit, well, I've never actually been there. And there are other things like that too. You grow up in a place, and you just assume things will always be there, so you don't bother. I don't know."

He laughed. "Sure, sure. There are certainly museums in Italy I've never visited, which people travel from all over the world to see. I don't think we have to love something just because it's local. We're allowed to have opinions on the matter. We're allowed to spend our time as we see fit."

"Hear, hear. I like that approach. Only spending our time doing things we want to do." I took a sip of my wine, then realized how absurd that sounded. The idea that we could only spend time doing things we wanted was definitely not a part of my home country's work ethos.

"Well then, come on, you must meet some more of my friends," Enzo said, taking my hand. I hesitated as my nerves fluttered.

"What's the problem?" Enzo asked.

"Nothing. I guess I'm just a little nervous about meeting new people."

"Why? You've met so many already. Why stop now?"

I shrugged. "I don't know. It just seems..." I struggled to articulate why I was nervous. Everyone I'd met had been friendly and open—well, almost everyone. What was it about Enzo's inner circle that made me edgy?

I shook my head. "Nothing. Just ignore me. I'm just having one of those moments."

"Don't worry, I've got your back." Enzo linked his arm through mine and guided me through the bustling piazza.

As we walked, the sound of Italian music intermingled with modern pop. Children ran and laughed, launching sparklers into the air. Blissful couples strolled with gelato in hand while elderly individuals perched on benches, their faces creased with wide smiles. Crowds clustered in corners, their laughter ringing out as they raised wine glasses aloft. Revelry pervaded every corner of the piazza, wrapping us in a warm summer embrace. I had never felt such elation—it was almost unsettling. Where was the familiar shadow of uncertainty that usually resided deep within me?

"What's amusing?" Enzo inquired.

I shook my head, grinning. "Nothing. Everything's perfect."

"As it should be," he returned. "Ah, there they are. Let me introduce you to some of my closest friends. Don't fret. They're going to adore you."

"Like I worry about what other people think," I replied, my smile wry.

Enzo chuckled. "You're more transparent than you give yourself credit for."

"Enzo!" a woman called out, spotting him. She was waving her hand eagerly.

"Come along then," Enzo encouraged.

We ambled towards a small gathering clustered around a tall pub table, upon which light snacks were spread. Wine glasses rested in each person's hand, their attire—flowing summer dresses, finely tailored shorts, and loafers—exuding a casual yet purposeful elegance.

"Ciao, Enzo," the woman who'd called out greeted us, leaning in to plant a kiss on Enzo's cheek. "*Non ero sicuro se eri in città.*"

"Ciao, Elena. *Possiamo parlare in inglese*?" Enzo asked, glancing toward me.

Elena looked at him curiously, then seemed to notice me. "Ah, si. Yes."

Turning to me, Enzo introduced, "This is Isla. She's a friend of mine from America."

Their expressions warmed instantly. "Ah, benvenuta! Welcome!" Elena exclaimed, mirroring the cheek kiss Enzo had given her. She pulled away, her eyes sparkling with an unexpected enthusiasm. "I am Elena. Welcome, welcome."

I smiled at her vibrant greeting. "Thank you. This is a wonderful festival."

Her grin widened. "It's the biggest event our little town hosts. People come from everywhere each year. I was just telling Enzo we were glad he made it."

A man leaned in to offer his own cheek kiss. "Piacere, Isla. I am Fabio."

I shared a glance with Enzo, silently questioning if his name was genuinely Fabio, but his confused expression suggested Fabio Lanzoni didn't hold the same cultural significance here. I turned back to Fabio. "Likewise."

"Mi dispiace, my English is not good," he admitted.

I offered a comforting smile. "I'm sure it's better than my Italian, which I'm afraid is virtually non-existent."

Elena waved dismissively. "You don't want to talk to Fabio, anyway. I am far more interesting."

"And I am Gio," chimed in a third member of the group, kissing my cheek. "And how do you know our charming Enzo?"

Enzo shot me a roguish grin. "We met recently."

"He tried to run me over on his Vespa," I said.

"So she hired me to be her tour guide." He winked.

Eyebrows rose around the table.

"A new business venture?" Gio asked.

I interjected, hoping to defuse the growing awkwardness. "Not exactly. He offered to show me the area. I suppose we clicked."

"And you're here by yourself?" Elena inquired.

"Indeed. Solo traveling for the summer. I feel I owe you a huge thank-you for taking me under your wing."

"Enzo, he love a stray," Fabio quipped, fanning the flames of my latent doubts.

"Disregard them, Isla. They know nothing," Enzo countered.

"Only everything about him since infancy," Gio riposted, prompting easy laughter and helping to melt away my lingering tension.

"I think we're out of wine," Elena observed.

"An unforgivable crime," Gio declared. "Stay here. I'll go in search. I don't trust anyone else to select the right bottle."

"He's a character," Enzo noted.

"I gathered," I replied.

"How long are you staying?" Elena asked.

"For the summer. Another four weeks left."

Elena clapped gleefully. "What an amazing holiday. I'm jealous."

Laughing, I retorted, "Jealous? You live in this paradise every day."

She waved a hand dismissively. "Even paradise can grow tedious. Limoncino can only be savored so many times. I envy your ability to leave and try something different for an entire summer. It's been years since I've done that."

"Watch your tongue about our limoncino!" Gio returned with a freshly uncorked bottle of Chianti.

"This is my first time trying something like this. It's not a common thing to do where I'm from. We don't get a lot of vacation, and gap years aren't popular," I confessed.

"Yes, I've heard you Americans are quite married to your work," Gio remarked.

"That's not too far from the truth," I agreed, laughing. "But I'm fortunate. I get summers off from my job. I work at a university." I felt a surge of nervous energy, and words began to pour out.

Elena's eyebrows shot up. "A university? How marvelous. What do you teach?"

I sighed, feeling the weight of my chosen profession. "History."

"Why do you say it so...sourly?" Elena asked.

How could I explain?

I felt an inadequacy in my career. Scrolling through social media, I saw college friends revolutionizing industries with their groundbreaking apps. Stories of entrepreneurs and innovators making a name for themselves by age thirty caused me to question my own path.

My profession felt rooted in the past, quite literally. While I loved history and its myriad stories, I wondered if I was making a significant impact. I saw my friends shaping the future while I analyzed what had already occurred.

Despite my love for teaching and imparting knowledge, a nagging feeling whispered that I should be doing something more "forward-looking" with my life. These insecurities grew as I wrestled with reconciling my passion for history with my desire to make a meaningful impact in a rapidly evolving world. I worried my expertise was becoming obsolete and feared that my students might view me as a relic rather than a valuable source of insight and inspiration.

"I don't know, it just doesn't feel like an interesting profession," I admitted, shaking off my introspection.

"What's more fascinating than history?" Gio contested.

"I suppose what I mean is, it doesn't feel very useful. I feel as though everyone I know is creating an app or becoming an influencer. They're doing something grand and entrepreneurial. Meanwhile, I'm entrenched in the past. Literally."

A hushed silence followed my confession.

"But the past created us," Gio argued. "Innovation is wonderful but look around. Look at what has endured for thousands of years. Those are the things that matter."

"Si, our country is one vast museum," Elena interjected, prompting chuckles.

Her defense of my profession brought a smile to my face. I supposed it made sense. A country with millennia of history beneath our feet would value the past.

"Thank you. I agree. Sometimes, though, in a highly modern society, it feels as though the past holds us back. We're pressured to constantly look ahead, to push forward."

Enzo raised his hand. "Progress has its time and place. But sometimes, I can't help but think that the drive for progress can prevent us from fully enjoying life."

"Salute," Elena concurred, raising her wineglass. "Cheers to the past."

My smile widened as we clinked our glasses and drank. At that moment, the wine tasted like the best I'd ever had.

"I love the way Italians embrace their traditions. Your family the other night—that was like something out of a book."

"Ahh, you saw the royal palace, eh?" Gio said.

Enzo flashed him a glare.

I laughed. "It was definitely a grand home."

"Did you meet the Shipping King himself?" Gio asked.

I furrowed my brow. "Who?"

"No, he wasn't there," Enzo said. "Just ignore Gio."

Suddenly, the crowd fell silent, and the streetlights dimmed.

"Shh! The lighting is about to begin," Elena announced.

Enzo looked down at me. "You're in for a treat."

Chapter Eighteen

Soon, the entire piazza and its surroundings were bathed in shimmering light. The atmosphere was reminiscent of a rock concert, albeit set in ancient times. The night sky was aglow, and magic seemed to twirl around us. A gentle breeze wafted in from the sea, but a comforting warmth enveloped me. Perhaps it was the mesmerizing scene, Enzo's comforting presence, or the effects of the wine. Either way, I felt as if I was floating alongside the lanterns.

"This is incredible," I murmured. Enzo leaned in, indicating he had heard me.

"I've seen it my entire life, and it never loses its magic. There's something truly enchanting about it."

"Who's the Shipping King?" I asked.

Enzo shook his head with an annoyed quasi-laugh. "Aye, Gio. Big mouth."

"Is it your dad?"

"Si. Papa is in the shipping business."

"You mentioned that, but—I take it he's successful?"

Enzo sighed. "Si. He runs a large company out of the Genova port. And yes, he's been very successful."

"Ahh, so you're rich," I teased.

He smirked. "My papa is, perhaps. But he's not me."

"Why didn't you go to work for him?"

"I did for a time. But it just wasn't my dream. It wasn't work I enjoyed. And maybe that makes me ungrateful but—"

"No, it doesn't. It just makes you your own person."

"I love my papa. And while it wasn't their first choice, he and Mama were supportive of me wanting to build my own thing. But the truth is, he still bothers me to come back. Offers me all kinds of perks."

"So if Vespas AND tour guide don't work out, you have a *backup* backup."

He chuckled. "Nice to know I have so many options."

Unable to resist, I edged closer. I half-expected him to withdraw. His friends were here. This was his world, his life. And here I was, potentially causing a spectacle. However, he didn't pull away. Instead, he reciprocated, draping his arm around my waist. I stiffened momentarily, then relaxed into his embrace. For the first time in what felt like forever, I felt free to simply exist—to be myself, to be present, to be part of this world.

Looking up at him towering over me, his eyes shifted to meet mine. As he angled his body toward me, our gazes locked under the moonlight, highlighted by the glow of the lanterns. A spark ignited in his eye. I felt aflame, as though I were levitating. He leaned in, his lips inching towards mine.

"Enzo!"

The moment shattered.

"Fabio, how nice of you to interrupt," Enzo said dryly.

Fabio flashed us a knowing grin. "Oops. Sorry, sorry. Lucia is here, and she is looking for you," he said in his broken English.

Enzo rolled his eyes. "Of course she was. Okay, we will be right there."

He flashed me an apologetic look, and I brushed it off. I couldn't decide if I was disappointed or grateful for the interruption. But either way, I wasn't exactly thrilled to face down Enzo's icy cousin again.

We walked back to the little table where Lucia had indeed joined the group.

"Lucia," Enzo said.

"Ciao, Enzo." They exchanged kisses. "Ah. Isla. Ciao."

"Ciao, Lucia. It's nice to see you again."

Lucia offered me a smile, but it felt forced and weak.

"Did you come alone, cugina? Is Rocco here?" Enzo asked.

Lucia hesitated for just a moment too long, then shook her head.

"No," she said, dragging the word out. Her eyes rolled to the side, and Enzo followed her gaze. A woman was walking toward us. Enzo's entire demeanor shifted at her introduction, his face paling and his body stiffening.

"*Merda*," Elena muttered.

Great, now what?

"Lucia," he said under his breath in a scolding tone. "*Perché?*"

"Aye, Enzo. You don't own the festival. What do they say in America?" She eyed me. "Free country?"

Enzo rolled his eyes, then turned toward the approaching woman.

She was striking in appearance, with long, dark hair flowing in thick waves over her shoulders, a fitted black dress hugging very shapely curves. She turned toward us with dark eyes that seemed to hold a secret that only she knew. The way she held herself was both captivating and intimidating. But it wasn't just her beauty—everything about her presence was big. She radiated energy, defining the sultry Italian night. I imagined her drinking red wine and dancing late into the evening, with a trail of suitors following after, desperate for the simple scent of her. I swallowed a sticky lump in my throat. How exciting to have yet one more bronzed goddess in our mix. Oh, and look. She was wearing heels.

"Valentina," Enzo said, his voice noticeably strained.

"Enzo. *E 'bello vederti.*" Valentina leaned in for a cheek kiss.

Enzo replied in English, "It's good to see you, too. Although I didn't expect to see you here tonight."

Valentina flashed a tight-lipped smile. "*Perché parli inglese*?"

Enzo flashed me a look, and Valentina finally registered my presence. Her dark eyes were like hooks, piercing right into my soul.

"Ah," she, too, switched to English. "It is the Festival of Lights, Enzo. Everyone in town is here. And who is this? Don't be rude."

Her gaze lingered on me, sizing me up with a mixture of curiosity and disdain. I tried to offer a friendly smile, but it faltered under the weight of her scrutiny. And I thought Lucia was intimidating.

"Valentina, this is Isla. She's a...friend. Visiting from the States," Enzo said, his voice unusually nervous. "Isla, this is Valentina."

Valentina leaned in to offer a cheek kiss. "Piacere, Isla. You are a long way from home."

My heart raced as I returned the kiss, sensing an underlying hostility in Valentina's tone. I tried to ignore it, telling myself that perhaps she was just being protective of Enzo. His group of friends seemed to be especially tight-knit.

But even after such a brief interaction, I knew there was a story here.

"Where are you from, *amica*?" Valentina continued.

"Oh, America," I replied, nervously offering already established information.

Valentina smirked. "Yes, Enzo said as much. Where in America? I have been there."

"Oh? I'm from California. San Francisco?" The words came out in a squeak. God, what was wrong with me? I didn't get intimidated by other women. Not even Mediterranean sea goddesses.

She nodded. "Lovely place. I did a gap year in the United States after secondary school before university. I was lucky enough to stay in many places, but I had an extended stay in New York and Los Angeles." I noted that, while still accented, her English was exceptional.

"Oh, how wonderful. I would love to know all about your experience," I said, trying to shatter the awkward moment. Now I had the good fortune of picturing her rubbing elbows with the beautiful people of our two most glamorous cities.

"Will you be joining us?" Enzo said a little nervously. I flashed him a look, but who was I to tell him whom he was allowed to invite to join a party I, too, was invited to? I might've been imagining it, though, but Fabio, Elena, and Gio also looked a little put off by Enzo's invitation. Maybe Valentina wasn't very popular in this crowd.

"Oh, I don't want to interrupt. I didn't realize you would be...well, occupied." Her eyes landed on me.

"Nonsense," Elena said in a pacifying tone. "The more, the merrier, Vala."

I was getting the sense that Elena was the peacekeeper of the group.

Valentina smiled and slipped into a position in the middle. Gio raised the bottle of wine to her, and Valentina nodded. He filled a glass.

"Salute to new friends then," Valentina said, her eyes

landing on me. I shifted uncomfortably but forced my spine to stay erect. I wasn't going to be intimidated.

Enzo's expression stayed sour, and he flashed Lucia occasional annoyed glances. Okay, there was definitely a story here. A big neon sign was flashing, EX-GIRLFRIEND.

"Where are you from, Valentina?" I asked. I hid my nervousness behind my wine glass.

"Oh, from here. Mare Sereno," Valentina said.

"Valentina is an old family friend," Enzo explained. "We really sort of grew up together, didn't we?"

"Yes, old friends indeed," Valentina replied.

The words were innocent enough, but it didn't take a psychologist to sense the history between them. Well, that was just dandy.

"When did you get back from Milan?" Enzo asked.

Valentina smiled. "Oh, just a few days ago. I wanted out of the city for the summer, si? So stuffy."

"She might be moving back!" Lucia said with a happy squeal.

Enzo's expression darkened. "I thought you hated it here."

Valentina pursed her lips. "Hate is a strong word, Enzo. Having different priorities is not hate."

"*Hai detto che era un puntino noioso della mappa. E solo i non ispirati rimarrebbero qui,*" Enzo spat out in clearly irritated rapid-fire Italian.

"Harsh," Gio said in English, shaking his head. He leaned toward me. "She said this is a boring map dot, and we're all uninspired."

Ouch. I wanted to crawl under the table to flee this awkwardness.

Valentina rolled her eyes and threw up her hands. "Aye! Enzo, *Sei così drammatico!*"

My head was now spinning, and clearly, the tension was about to bubble over. I pressed my mouth to my glass and drained it. Elena, clearly sensing my discomfort, quickly refilled my glass.

I flashed her an appreciative look.

"Okay, let's move on to another subject, si?" Elena said.

Enzo and Valentina stared each other down for a moment before both their expressions lightened.

Valentina swiveled her attention back to me. "So, what brings you to the Riviera?"

I took another sip of wine. "Oh, just wanted to get away on a nice extended vacation."

"I did not think you got vacations in the United States," she said with a wink.

"Vala, be nice," Enzo scolded.

She flicked her hand. "Relax. I am just teasing."

I laughed nervously. "You're not far off. It's definitely not a top priority for most American companies. I'm lucky enough that I work at a university. So I have summers off."

She raised an eyebrow. "University? Are you a teacher?"

"Yes. Well, a professor. History." I took another sip of my wine. Wow, it was going down fast tonight.

"Brainy then. Not Enzo's usual type." She flashed a knowing smile that set my teeth on edge.

"Oh?" I said nervously.

She smiled. "I suppose I might be an expert in that area."

"You're insulting yourself, Vala," Gio said.

Well, that confirmed it.

"That's enough," Enzo said.

I caught the smirk on Lucia's face, which she quickly hid behind her wine glass.

"Can we talk about something else?" Enzo said.

A group of street musicians started playing nearby, their lively tunes filling the piazza.

"No better way to change the subject than to dance," Elena said, evidently acting as the group's peacekeeper.

"Best idea ever," Gio said.

"Bene. Enzo, shall we dance? For old time's sake?" Valentina asked, her eyes sparkling mischievously.

Enzo gave me an uncertain look, but I brushed it aside with a feigned wide smile. I wasn't going to play the jealous date.

"Go ahead! I want to make sure you can actually dance before I embarrass myself with you anyway," I urged.

Enzo gave me a grateful look before he, with a resigned sigh, led Valentina to the impromptu dance floor. I noticed Lucia hanging back, her gaze fixed on Enzo and Valentina.

Elena extended a hand to Fabio. However, he refused, waving his hands in front of his face. "No. I won't be dancing."

Despite the lively and upbeat music, I felt a stark contrast in my emotions. I looked at Enzo, wanting to share this moment with him, but his attention was focused on Valentina. She twirled in his arms, her laughter echoing in the night. Suddenly, I felt like an outsider.

"Don't let it bother you," Elena said, leaning in close to me.

I took a sip from my wine glass and forced a thin smile. "Oh, it's no big deal. Enzo and I aren't—well, you know. We're just friendly acquaintances. We only just met." I felt a pang of embarrassment at my nervous rambling.

Elena gave me a look that bordered on pity, and it was all I could do to suppress my urge to flee.

"Don't underestimate the power of a friendly acquaintance. Things can move quickly over a glass of wine and a hot Italian summer," she advised, raising her glass in a toast.

I felt a spark of defensiveness. "I don't think I'm quite so reckless or naïve as that, thank you."

She smirked. "And what if you were? Would there be any harm?"

I tilted my head, considering. "You tell me."

Elena laughed lightly. "I've struck a nerve. I didn't mean to."

I shook my head, feeling embarrassed by my defensiveness. "No, it's fine. No harm done."

Elena pressed her lips into a thin, unconvinced smile. "Look, Enzo and Vala have a long history."

"I gathered as much. She's not exactly discreet," I admitted.

"She never is. But it's history. In the past."

My gaze landed on them, still dancing. I felt like an intruder, unable to shake off the undeniable spark between them that seemed to exist far beyond my understanding. It was intoxicating and daunting at the same time.

"Doesn't look that way," I muttered, almost under my breath.

"Valentina is—well, she's petty. Always has been. She saw you and smelled a threat she couldn't resist. It's just how she is. That's why she and Enzo are not together anymore."

"Not together anymore," I repeated.

Elena smirked. "Don't let it ruin your fun."

Just then, Gio sidled up beside me. "He thinks he can dance, but he's wrong. Let me show you."

He winked and extended his arm. I laughed and gratefully accepted his offer.

The music was upbeat, and Gio was quick on his feet. He twirled me around in a version of a swing dance. Luckily, he was adept enough to move me around without much effort on my part. Dancing wasn't exactly in my repertoire of award-winning talents.

We twirled around, laughing. Enzo caught my gaze, and for a moment, our eyes locked. His gaze held a silent apology, but I simply flashed him a flirty smile and leaned into Gio. I didn't want to play games, but I was done sitting on the sidelines.

As the lights started to fade, so did everyone's energy. We'd all had our share of wine and our share of dancing. I was bone-tired.

* * *

"So, do you care to enlighten me on the situation with Valentina?" I asked Enzo as we began the slow walk back toward my cottage.

He worked his jaw and sipped his take-away wine. "It's nothing. Just old family stuff."

"Something tells me she's not exactly family," I said, giving him a wry look. "Elena told me you have a history. But even if she hadn't, it was fairly obvious."

He sighed. "Yeah, sorry. Vala likes to make a scene. We dated for a while. But it was a long time ago. Water under the bridge, as you say, yes?"

"Yes. That's the expression. But it doesn't seem like it's under the bridge. It seems very much right on top of it."

Enzo chuckled lightly. "Come on, now. You don't strike me as the jealous type."

I laughed. "I'm not—I'm not jealous."

He pinched my side. "Sure you're not. You Americans. Don't know how to share."

I flashed him an annoyed look. I didn't like being made a fool of, especially not in a foreign country surrounded by strangers.

"I just think it would be polite to warn me about any future awkward situations, okay? I don't like feeling caught off guard like that."

He looked genuinely apologetic. "I am sorry. I truly did

not know she would be here. The last I heard, Valentina was in Milan. I didn't realize she had come back."

"Was it serious?"

He sighed. "That's a loaded question."

"I don't think so."

"Serious? We cared about each other very much. We have known each other all our lives. But we were on different paths. She wanted to move to Milan, pursue a faster pace. I don't care for the city. I like the museums, the culture, sure. But I need to come home to the sea," he explained, shrugging as if his poetic description answered everything.

"It's hard to picture you two together."

"Why's that?"

I finished my wine and tossed the cup into a passing recycling bin. "She's just—well, she seems kind of mean."

He laughed. "Yeah. She's not the nicest person in Italy. That's part of why we didn't work out."

I wanted to probe further, to know every detail, as was my habit, but I knew I needed to drop it. It wasn't really my business, and he was right. I had no right to be jealous of the ex-girlfriend of someone I barely knew.

I smiled warmly. "I'm sorry. I was getting worked up over nothing. I'm just a little nervous."

"Hey, relax, okay? There's nothing to be nervous or worked up about. Just drink wine and enjoy your life, okay?"

I smiled. "Okay."

Easier said than done.

Chapter Nineteen

My head was still swimming with the magic of the previous night. Of Enzo's touch. The lights and laughter. I was doing everything I could not to think about Valentina.

Filling my days with new friends was invigorating but also draining. Taking advantage of another sparkling sun-soaked day, I thought I'd hop on the little commuter train and check out a tiny museum at a town up the coast my little off-the-grid guidebook had mentioned.

I settled into a little window seat and let my mind take it all in—the rustic charm of the train carriages, the rhythmic lull of the locomotive's pulse, and the picturesque views of the Italian Riviera as far as the eye could see. Rolling green hills crowned with charming cottages that looked as though they'd been borrowed from a fairy tale. Vineyards basking in the golden sunlight. The serene sea, whose twinkling surface stippled with light, seemed to dance all the way to the horizon.

The museum was housed at the back of a small church, Santo Stefano. I paid the three Euro entry and stepped from the heat of the day into the cool damp of the old building. I wandered through the silent museum, my footsteps echoing in the hush of the intimate galleries.

The main exhibit was a nautical history, beautifully arranged, brimming with weathered nautical maps, model ships that ranged from large galleons to smaller fishing boats, and a variety of maritime artifacts that each had a story to tell. I was drawn to an ancient, elaborately detailed map, its edges frayed and faded with time. The old paper was marked with the routes of historic voyages, sea monsters playfully drawn in the uncharted waters, and the coastline of the Riviera, not too different from today's. I traced the lines with my eyes, my mind whirring with tales of adventure and exploration.

Beside it, a glass case housed a stunningly detailed model ship, its masts towering and sails intricately stitched. I peered closer, marveling at the care and attention to detail in the craftsmanship. The ship seemed to contain an echo of the past, a glimpse into the grandeur and grit of maritime life in the days of yore. I could almost hear the creaking of the wooden planks, the rustle of the sails, and the song of the sea whispering tales of voyages.

The exhibit also held a variety of other fascinating artifacts —an old captain's log, its pages yellowed with age, the ink faded, but the words were still legible; a compass that had guided unknown adventures; an antique spyglass; even a set of well-worn deckhand tools. Each item was a piece of the puzzle, a part of the vast tapestry of maritime history that had shaped the life and culture of the Italian Riviera.

There was an uncanny sense of familiarity about the exhibit, a resonance that made me pause. Perhaps it was the undercurrent of the sea that ran through Enzo's life, the unspoken threads of his family's past that now seemed somehow connected to these relics of maritime history.

After leaving the hushed corridors of the museum, I found myself instinctively wandering down a cobbled pathway toward the harbor. The picturesque scene unfolded effortlessly before me—boats gently bobbing on the water, pastel-colored houses clinging to the hillsides, all bathed in the warm glow of the late afternoon sun. The Riviera appeared as though it was posing for a picture postcard, its enchanting beauty practically glowing.

I found an inviting stone bench overlooking the harbor, warm from the sun, and the view from there was absolutely spectacular. I couldn't help but feel like I had stumbled upon a private, breathtaking painting of the world reserved only for the lucky few who sought it out.

Unzipping my bag, I pulled out my planner for the upcoming semester. The peace of the harbor, the inspiration from the museum—it all felt like the perfect backdrop for brainstorming the structure of my courses.

My eyes roamed over the peaceful tableau as I scribbled thoughts. There was so much more to this small slice of Italy than I had ever known. I watched as fishermen brought in their afternoon catch and tourists meandered along the promenade. I thought about how to integrate local history and culture into the curriculum, touching on legends and lore.

With the quiet hum of the harbor in the background and the warmth of the setting sun on my skin, I felt a sense of profound peace and connection.

I checked the time and realized I had to catch the next train to make it back to Mare Sereno. Apparently a glutton for extroverting overload, I'd agreed to attend a dinner party with Gianna. I felt a little over-socialized, especially after the non-stop activities of the last few days, but I was also trying to really make the most of this summer. I wanted to push myself out of my shell, so I wouldn't revert to the introverted book-worm who could lock herself away and ignore the world for days on end.

I packed up my day bag and strolled back through the

town toward the station. As I left the little town behind, I had a new feeling that this place wasn't merely a beautiful landscape—it was my classroom, my inspiration. A mystical place lingering between past and present.

***

"This house is incredible," I said, my eyes wide with wonder as I looked around the ornate yet eclectic villa. I'd expected everyone here to live in tiny little apartments above family *pescherias*. I was seriously starting to feel a twinge of villa envy.

Gianna smiled. "Caterina has a very unique style. She's an artist, you know? Very successful, too. And, of course, it lends her a certain something." Gianna waved her hand at the mix of sculptures and paintings, both modern and antique. It was a beautiful juxtaposition, everything vibrant and watercolor-like.

The entryway was a work of art in itself, an architectural marvel that combined rustic charm with modern elegance. The floor was a medley of polished stones, each one a different shade intricately laid out to form a beautiful mosaic pattern. The walls were adorned with sconces casting a warm, inviting glow, highlighting the artistry on display.

The ceilings were a marvel of their own, decked with ornate stucco work and interspersed with exposed wooden beams reminiscent of the villa's historical roots. Occasionally, skylights punctuated the ceiling, allowing beams of moonlight to filter in and dance on the vibrant tapestries and dazzling artwork.

"I've never seen anything quite like it."

"I'm sure she will tell you all about it, but she has worked all over the world. She has collected many pieces and has been inspired by the things she has encountered. You're going to love her." Gianna leaned in conspiratorially. "And I can always count on her to buy my rare imports, so I love her too."

I laughed. "I already do," I said, almost under my breath. I caught sight of myself in an ornate mirror in the villa's foyer. The sleeveless summer wrap dress in a bold cherry red that Gianna had loaned me now seemed the perfect choice. I'd curled my hair into soft waves and put on a little more makeup than usual for a beach day. I knew this crowd would be bold based on Gianna's description, and I wanted to feel the part, at least a little.

"Gianna!" A woman came rushing over in a sleek black dress that was both chic and functional. She wore low black pumps with a stylish chunky heel, and her hair was tied back in a twist at the nape of her neck. She gave me the distinct impression of an event planner.

"Sofia, ciao," Gianna leaned into the woman. "You look positively busy."

"*Sì, sì. Sempre pazzo. Chi è questo*?" She turned to me.

"Oh, this is Isla. A friend from America."

"Bene! Piacere. I am Sofia, Caterina's assistant. Which mainly means ensuring you always have a drink, no?" She beamed at me with big blue eyes.

"Piacere, Sofia," I said. "I look forward to that drink."

Sofia laughed and beckoned us forward. "Come. The party is already underway. You will be most welcome, yes."

The hallways of Caterina's villa were akin to a labyrinthine gallery, a testament to her eclectic taste and world travels. Each turn unveiled a new panorama of art and culture.

"She could charge admission here," I said.

Gianna smirked. "I think that would offend the guests who delight in her coveted dinner invitations. But, yes, she probably could."

As we ventured deeper into the villa, I was struck by the richness of the tapestries that lined the walls. They were a kaleidoscope of colors and textures, each one telling a story of a different time and place. Some bore intricate designs from Persia, their patterns weaving intricate tales of mythical beasts and heroic feats. Others were vibrant depictions of folk tales from South America, their lively hues and bold strokes exuding an untamed energy. Walking through the hallways of Caterina's villa was like journeying through a museum of world art, each piece a window into a different culture, a different era.

Modern masterpieces—or what I assumed were masterpieces as I was no expert—were interspersed among the age-old treasures, their abstract forms, and bold colors providing a stark contrast. The chaotic beauty of it all was mesmerizing. And perhaps a testament to Caterina's appreciation for the unpredictable and The Avant-Garde. I thought of Luna and how she might actually drop dead from wonderment here.

We finally stepped into the main room, and it was already alive with revelry. About a dozen people were gathered, all clutching drinks and small plates of appetizers. Everyone was engaged in thoughtful, friendly conversation. The energy in the room was palpable. Some smooth gypsy jazz played in the background, and I thought the words were English.

"I don't speak much Italian," I said under my breath to Gianna.

She squeezed my shoulder gently. "It's not a problem. As you can already tell, everyone here speaks English fluently, for the most part. Francesca is a little wary of speaking English, but just ignore her." I watched Gianna's eyes land on an elegant woman who had the look of an aging starlet. Jet black hair wound up in a bouffant, a slinky blue dress that fell to the floor, and jewels dripping from around her slender neck. Subtle wrinkles encased her eyes and mouth, but she was still beautiful. She could've been anywhere between forty and seventy.

"Former actress," Gianna said in a little whisper. "She still thinks she's on the stage half the time."

I had to smile.

A group huddled by the fireplace, deep in conversation in a blur of fast-paced Italian. They were the epitome of chic, their sophisticated elegance radiating from their designer outfits to the way they held themselves and their drinks. I felt slightly dizzy from the beauty of it all.

"Come, let me introduce you, and let's get ourselves a refreshment," Gianna said.

We made our way toward the drinks table, where there were some ready-made cocktails as well as wine, and we helped ourselves. I took a long sip of wine, trying not to drain the entire glass in one go in an attempt to quell my nerves. I'd never been accused of being a social butterfly back home, and that didn't seem to change now that I was halfway across the world.

"Gianna!" A woman in a long, flowing dress waved at us. Gianna waved back.

"Caterina. *Felice di vederti*. Thank you so much for having us. This is the friend I was telling you about, Isla. She's from America. Isla, this is Caterina, our gracious hostess."

"How wonderful," Caterina said, leaning in for a cheek kiss with Gianna and then me. "Benvenuta to our little town and to my humble home."

"Humble is the last word I would use to describe this home, I'm afraid," I said. "It's exquisite."

Caterina blushed and waved a hand dismissively. "You are too kind. American flattery will get you far here," she said with a grin.

"I'm just very grateful for the invitation."

"Of course. We are a group that welcomes those from all over the world. We love nothing more than to hear the stories of different adventures. You must tell us everything. What brought you here, what you were doing, and what you think?"

"Let her relax," Gianna said. "At least let her get moderately tipsy before you start piling on the questions."

"Of course. The bar is plentiful, and please help yourself. Come, let me introduce you to everyone else," Caterina said.

I followed her as she waltzed into the room like a czarina about to hold court.

"Isla, this is Marco. Marco, Isla, Gianna's friend," Caterina said. We exchanged cheek kisses.

"And this is Piero and his lovely wife, Maria."

"Lovely to meet you," I said. Great, another Maria.

"Don't worry, I won't quiz you later," Gianna whispered.

A thought struck me then about introductions here. Back home, introductions were almost immediately followed by occupations. This is Maria, and she's an accountant, but not here. It seemed that here, people existed separately from their occupation. It was a strange concept for me. My career seemed to define me.

"And this is Francesca. Don't mind her sour expression," Caterina said. Francesca flashed her an annoyed look that I couldn't tell was real or just theatrical.

"Piacere," I said. Francesca leaned in for a kiss but with less enthusiasm than the other guests.

"Ciao," Francesca said.

"Francesca doesn't like to speak English," Caterina said. "She finds it beneath her."

Francesca glared at Caterina and then fired off something in Italian that made everybody laugh.

"No, Francesca just doesn't like to do things that she's not perfect at," Marco said. "She doesn't realize that no matter what she says, it sounds like the music of a harp."

"And as you might have guessed, Marco is a poet," Piero added.

"Ok, and last but possibly least, Signor Aldo. He's one of the oldest and most respected winemakers in the region."

Signor Aldo was a man of perhaps seventy, with a thick mop of salt and pepper hair and a muscular frame despite his age. He smiled warmly. "You have come on a good night, Isla. I have brought something special tonight for dinner."

"I can't wait," I said.

I grinned at this cast of eclectic characters. They'd embraced their quirkiness, making it cool and modern. Maybe I would actually feel right at home here.

"And that charming cad over there is my son, Leo," Caterina said, nodding to a trim young man in fitted summer linen with a shock of thick, dark hair. He clutched a low ball of amber liquid and leaned into the fireplace. He stood tall and handsome, his eyes meeting mine across the room. A slow smile spread across his face, and he raised his glass in a silent toast. I felt a mix of emotions–flattery, nervousness, and an undeniable intrigue. I took a deep breath and smiled back, ready to dive into the whirlwind that was the Italian dinner party.

"Come, let us get this party going," Caterina said. "Sofia, turn up the music. Let's open a bottle of the good sparkles. None of this local Prosecco. Let's have some real Champagne!"

I caught a glimpse of Francesca's raised eyebrow, and I wondered if she was just opposed to anything that wasn't purely Italian.

I heard a beautiful pop, and soon we were all clutching long, delicate flutes filled with beautiful golden effervescence.

I was on my second glass of champagne when Caterina's son slid in beside me as I awkwardly stared at a huge sculpture of a grotesque face.

"Teste di moro, 16th century," he said.

I flashed him a look. "Oh?" Up close, I noticed he was much younger than me—possibly even a decade.

He stared at the twisted head carving. "Traditional form of pottery from Sicily and a common Sicilian souvenir, but this is the real deal. Mama loves this thing, but I find it a little disturbing."

I tilted my head and studied the colorful Medusa. "It is a little creepy. Looks a little like a planter."

"Often they are used that way."

"Let me guess, there's a legend there," I said.

Leo chuckled. "You are starting to know our customs well. Si, there is a legend. You see these stylized human faces of a man and a woman? The man's face is usually depicted as a Moor, while the woman's face is typically Sicilian. The legend traces back to, I think, maybe the 11th century, during the Arab rule."

Okay, he had me hooked like an unsuspecting lake trout.

"There are multiple versions of the tale, but a popular one is that once upon a time in Palermo's district called Kalsa, which was a Moorish neighborhood at the time, there lived a beautiful young Sicilian woman who loved to spend her time taking care of the plants and flowers on her balcony. One day, a young Moorish merchant who was passing by saw her and immediately fell in love with her. The feeling was mutual, and they started a passionate love affair."

"How scandalous," I said.

"Si, si. However, the woman discovered that the Moor had a wife and children waiting for him in his homeland. Upon learning this, she was overcome with rage and jealousy. She decided to take a drastic step to ensure that the man would stay with her forever. So, one night while he was deeply asleep," he leaned in close. "She cut off his head."

"Yikes. Talk about a woman scorned."

Leo smiled like a fox. "In her continued devotion to her

plants, she used the man's head as a pot in which she planted basil. The plant flourished, fed by the nutrients within the head, growing lush and vibrant, arousing the envy of all who passed by. This sight became so admired that people started crafting ceramic pots in the shape of the Moor's head. Thus, the tradition of the Sicilian ceramic heads was born."

"That is...quite gross."

He shrugged. "History is brutal."

"Don't I know it?" I said with a laugh. "You're quite knowledgeable. Are you a teacher?"

He smiled. "No, just learned a lot when your mother is an artist. Besides, I just like history."

My insides warmed. "Me too."

"We haven't been officially introduced, although I saw you make a charming entrance. I am Leo," he said, extending a hand.

"No cheek kiss?" I said playfully.

He laughed. "I am culturally sensitive."

I laughed and shook his hand. "Piacere, Leo. I'm Isla."

"And what brings you to Mare Sereno, Isla?"

"To study Sicilian heads, obviously. I was looking for a way to grow better basil plants."

He grinned.

"Aye, Leonardo, stop flirting with my guests," Caterina came hustling up and slipped her arm through her son's. "Come on. I need help. The dinner is about to be served."

Leo took my hand and kissed it theatrically. "A pleasure."

As dinner commenced, I once again found myself surrounded by a cacophony of Italian chatter, but it felt much less awkward here with this band of artists and vagabonds than it did under the intense scrutiny of Enzo's family. The evening wore on, and I found myself entranced by the cadence of the party. It was a symphony of flavors, laughter, conversation, and the occasional blunder that only added to the charm of the night. (I mean, who *really* knows the difference between Parmigiano-reggiano and pecorino-romano? That was not in the guidebook as need-to-know, thank you very much.)

Fueled by the flowing wine, I felt a surge of confidence and decided to join in a traditional Italian toast, even though my American accent butchered the lyrical words. To my surprise, it was met with chuckles and applause, and the guests raised their glasses in a salute of my efforts.

"What do you think of the wine?" Piero asked, leaning across the table.

"It's all so good. I don't think I've had a bad glass while in Italy, but this is particularly exceptional." I sipped and, emboldened, went on. "I've been learning a ton about Italian wine. I even went to a class at Gianna's."

Gianna grinned. "She was the A student."

"Gianna knows her wine!" Signor Aldo chimed in, making Gianna blush.

"Coming from you, that is quite the compliment, Signor," Gianna said.

"California produces some pretty great Italian wines these days, but definitely not like this," I said.

The room fell silent, and all eyes turned toward me, then slowly shifted to the end of the table where Signor Aldo sat. His brows furrowed, and he gave me a long, hard look. "California?" he echoed, his voice a low rumble. "Italian wines?"

I felt my cheeks heat up as I nodded. Word vomit started to bubble. "Yes, there's Napa, Sonoma... they have some really good wineries that—."

Signor Aldo snorted, shaking his head.

"Italian wines," he said, emphasizing each word, "are Italian because they are made in Italy. Our soil, our sun, our climate... these things cannot be replicated. Just because you have some seeds doesn't make it Italian."

I'm pretty sure my face paled as the embarrassment literally threatened to kill me.

"Aldo, shh!" Gianna scorned. "Don't be such an old crank. I happen to carry a nice little section of wines from California in my shop."

She flashed me a look, and I wanted to kiss her with gratitude.

An animated debate followed, with the guests passionately discussing the merits and drawbacks of Italian and Californian wines. Mortified, I sat silently as the conversation swirled around me.

Gianna struggled to contain her laughter. She leaned in and whispered, "Welcome to Italy, where every dinner includes a debate on wine." With a wink, she raised her glass, her eyes sparkling with amusement.

"The next thing you know, you'll be ordering a cappuccino after dinner," Gianna joked with a grin.

I gave her a wary, sidelong glance. "Should I not?"

Gianna smirked. "It messes with your digestion!"

I shrugged. "But they are a delicious way to end the meal."

Caterina burst into laughter beside us. "Americans."

I flashed a playful glare. "We believe one should do what one pleases."

Caterina raised a glass with a grin. "To your freedoms, then."

I smiled and raised mine as well. "Long may we live free of the tyranny of the milk overlords and wine traditionalists."

The entire table burst into laughter at my comment.

"Bring her back anytime," Marco said with a laugh. "She's fine company."

I silently exhaled with relief.

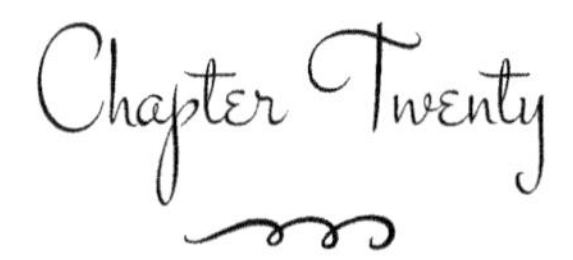

Chapter Twenty

Staring back at my reflection in the mirror, I recognized a certain tiredness that hung under my eyes, remnants of last night's feast, and the generous pourings of wine. But there was something else there, something that took me by surprise—a vibrant glow, a vitality that I hadn't noticed in a long time. Maybe it was the Italian sun, the crisp sea breeze, or perhaps, just maybe, it was the joy of being myself.

Thinking back on the previous evening, I realized I'd allowed myself to be flawed, awkward, and vulnerable. And nothing catastrophic had happened. Even my accidental insults of wine and cheese confusions hadn't been catastrophic. In fact, it had been fun—a lot of fun. I'd allowed myself to live, to breathe. And maybe I was reaching, but it kinda sorta felt like they all liked me. Mission: Italian Dinner Party—a success!

I had been taught all my life to seek stability, to avoid the tumultuous nature of fleeting passions, and to steer clear of the pain and loss that came with shattered illusions. Yet my tireless pursuit of stability had led me straight into the arms of grief and disillusionment. Was stability itself not an illusion?

Enzo came to my mind. So what was the big deal about letting myself enjoy a summer romance? Just a fling, no love, no commitment. I had been conditioned my whole life not to look for those things. I needed stability, not fleeting passions and careless endeavors. Not a carefree rendezvous that would surely only lead to heartbreak and loss once the illusions were shattered.

I was doing it again—driving myself crazy, backing myself into yet another corner. I over-thought everything—it was one of my greatest talents. If there were a reality show for over-thinking, I would take it to the finals every time. I didn't know what was broken inside of me that I couldn't just allow myself to live.

So what did I do? One thing I knew was I would stop fighting this thing between Enzo and me. I'd allow him to take me into this magical fold of adventure and wild times. I would allow myself just to live for once, just to sit back, taste the wine, enjoy the smell of the sea, and feel the wind. Enzo, Gianna—they were right. This was the essence of life, or at least it could be. Sometimes, life really was just about the wine.

And the wine... it really was so good. I chuckled at the thought of returning home with a mouthful of stained teeth, a souvenir from my wild Italian summer. A fleeting thought of Ian and his borderline obsession with dental hygiene brought a small, sardonic smile to my lips. But the smile disappeared as quickly as it had come. I was no longer Ian's fiancée, no longer a part of his picture-perfect life. He was a closed chapter in my story, and I refused to let him steal any more of my thoughts, my time. Ian was in the past.

But this moment, this decision—it wasn't about Enzo either. This was about Isla—me, finally taking the reins of my life, finally doing something I wanted to do. And right then, what I wanted was to sit by the sea with a glass of wine and soak in the breathtaking view. So, that's precisely what I was going to do.

My phone pinged with the sound of an incoming email. I lifted the screen, and the email preview made my stomach turn over. It was from Ian. I hesitated and nearly set the phone back down. I couldn't imagine there was anything he had to say that I needed to read right now. I started to set it down, then snatched it back up again. I repeated the process twice more, then finally forced myself to open the Gmail app.

Isla,

I hope this email finds you well. I know we said we'd handle all the house matters when you got back, but something's come up. I've been thinking, and I believe it would be best for both of us if I bought out your share of the condo. This would allow you to have a clean break, and it would be more convenient for me as well.

The truth is, I'd like to stay there. And I can't imagine you would—given the memories.

Let me know what you think.

Best,
Ian

. . .

My heart pounded as a whirlwind of emotions surged within me. There was a pang of hurt—the house had been our shared dream, a symbol of our future together. And Ian wanted to stay there? That could only mean one thing—Miranda was moving in. I knew it in my gut.

And then there was the indignation. The audacity of Ian to make such a proposal while I was thousands of miles away —it felt like a slap in the face.

But there was also a strange sense of relief. Selling my share of the house would indeed give me a clean break, a chance to leave behind the painful memories and start anew. He made a lot more money than I did, so he'd naturally put more into it. But I had still contributed a small amount of savings to the down payment and contributed to the monthly mortgage. With the strong appreciation over the last year since we bought it—I could be looking at a large chunk of cash I hadn't expected.

I leaned back in my chair, staring out the window at the coastline. I felt a wave of uncertainty, my mind a chaotic mix of my past with Ian and my unknown future.

For a moment, I allowed myself to feel the hurt, the anger, and the relief. But then I took a deep breath and began to draft a response to Ian. This was one more step I needed to take to move forward, and I was determined to handle it with grace and dignity.

Chapter Twenty-One

I scrolled through the pages of the guidebook on my phone's Kindle App—my obscure specialist book about Riviera historical sites. I'm pretty sure I'm the only person who bought the poor guy's book. But this was the spot. Glancing up from the screen, I took in the humble yet grand church standing proudly before me. Meticulously preserved, its intricate craftsmanship showcased a strange mix of modesty and grandeur. Dominating the façade was a stunning stained-glass window depicting a delicate rose, one of the most coveted pieces of glasswork in Italy, or so I'd read. Who would have thought it would be here in this tiny map dot? A wave of warmth washed over me as I thought of my grandmother standing in this very spot, ready to attend the weekly service. Although I wasn't particularly religious, I found myself whispering a small prayer of gratitude for her indirect guidance to this beautiful place.

"She's beautiful, isn't she?"

I spun around and nearly laughed at the sight of Leo sauntering toward me, radiating youthful confidence. He wore very short, pale blue chino shorts and a short-sleeved shirt that tried to pass as a t-shirt but was clearly so much more.

"Oh, hello. Yes, it's incredible. I'd read about it, and my grandmother used to tell me stories. But seeing it firsthand is different."

Leo nodded, standing beside me. "She's our town's pride and joy. It's one of the oldest churches in Italy. Construction began in 1215 AD and was mostly completed by 1263 AD," he informed me, gesturing to my phone. "But I'm sure you've read that already. History professor, after all."

Returning his smile, I pocketed my phone. "Guilty. But I like the way you tell it. What else can you tell me about it? Anything I wouldn't find in the guidebook?"

His smile broadened, clearly delighted by my interest. "I do know a little legend. I know you're fond of them."

"Can't get enough. I'm all ears."

Leo looked back at the window. His voice was laced with dramatic flair as he began his tale. "Allora, according to legend, the window was created by a master glassmaker named Alessandro Pisano. Alessandro was famous not only for his artistic talents but also for his unrequited love for a beautiful woman named Rosa."

"There's definitely a theme to these local legends."

"Unrequited love affects the best of us. Rosa, who had taken the veil and devoted her life to the church, was beloved by the people of Mare Sereno for her kindness and selflessness. Alessandro, in his deep love and admiration for Rosa, decided to create the most beautiful stained-glass window as a tribute to her beauty and spirituality. He spent months sourcing the finest glass and pigments from across Italy, with the window to be his crowning masterpiece. Rosa was deeply moved by the tribute but reminded Alessandro of her spiritual commitment. Heartbroken but accepting of her decision, Alessandro made a vow—as long as the rose window remained in the cathedral, his love for Rosa would illuminate the town of Mare Sereno like the sunlight through the stained glass. From that day on, the stained-glass window became a symbol of enduring love and dedication in the town. It's said that when the sunlight hits the window just right, you can see Alessandro's silhouette in the glass, forever watching over Rosa and the town he loved."

Though the story may have been a pure fabrication, Leo's enthusiasm sparked a sense of whimsy within me. "How much of that is true?" I asked.

Leo shrugged, a playful grin on his face. "Who knows? But it makes for a nice tale."

"My nonna was named Rosa. She would have appreciated the tale."

"We are all captives of our legends. There is magic in our little slice of the world," Leo said.

"I don't doubt it. Thanks for sharing."

"And what's next on your agenda?" Leo inquired.

"Oh, I don't know. Just more exploring, I guess. Trying to find inspiration."

"Inspiration for what?"

I blushed even more. "I teach a class on Renaissance and medieval history. I'm looking for ideas for the course next semester."

Leo tilted his head, a smile playing on his lips. "Why does that make you embarrassed?"

Looking away awkwardly, I replied, "I'm not embarrassed."

"Then why do you blush?"

Turning back to meet his eyes, I said sarcastically, "Isn't teaching dated history a little uncool?"

Leo chuckled. "Who am I to say what's cool? Have you met my mother? Seen my home? We are oddballs, all of us."

Unable to resist, I joined in his laughter. "I appreciate that."

Leo's grin broadened. "Come, have a coffee with me. The day is hot, and we have more legends to discuss."

I considered his offer. Initially, I was going to decline—I didn't need another Italian man trailing behind me—but then I remembered Leo was a decade younger than me. His intentions were likely more friendly than romantic.

"Sure, why not?" I agreed.

With a flourish, Leo pointed out a charming café on the corner. For such a small town, there must be at least a dozen little cafes, enotecas, and the like within walking distance of the piazza.

We settled in, enjoying the view of the cathedral against the backdrop of the rolling hills. A light breeze wafted in, soothing the sun-kissed skin on my arms, which were turning a honey-gold under the Mediterranean sun—a stark contrast to my usually pale complexion, thanks to the perpetual fog in San Francisco.

"Did you grow up here, then?" I asked as the server brought around two espressos with biscotti.

"Si. Mama was from Florence, but she came out here to paint one summer and never went home."

"Florence—I've never been, but I know I have to."

"That's a crime," Leo shook his head. "For a lover of history, it doesn't get much better. And the art is, of course, world-class. As a Florentine, art is in our blood."

"Was it isolating being here?"

He shrugged. "Well, admittedly, I went to boarding school, first in Milan, then France. Then I studied in London. But when I was done with all that, I knew I wanted to come back. There is something about this place. They say it's the sirens in the sea."

"No wonder your English is so good."

He smiled. "Grazie."

"What do you do for work now?"

"I work for mama on the business side. It's a good gig, as they say. I help get her work into galleries, fulfill orders." He shrugged.

"Sounds like a wonderful life." The words were completely genuine. It sounded like a dream.

As we chatted, our china cups softly clinking and the hum of conversation from surrounding tables blending into a comforting soundtrack, I noticed a familiar face among the passersby—Enzo. Our eyes met, and surprise flickered across his face, swiftly replaced by an inscrutable expression as he took in the sight of Leo. Furrowing his brow, he approached our table.

"Isla, Ciao," Enzo greeted, his eyes landing on Leo with a scrutinizing look.

"Ciao, Enzo," I responded, keeping my voice friendly.

"What are you doing?" Enzo asked bluntly.

"Oh. This is Leo, Caterina's son. Do you know Gianna's friend Caterina? The artist."

"Not really, no," Enzo said with a note of incredulity.

"Leo, this is my friend Enzo. Leo and I were just discussing some local history."

"History?" Enzo echoed.

"Yes, we ran into each other outside the cathedral. I was admiring the famous Rose window," I said.

Leo, ever the gentleman it seemed, stood and extended his hand toward Enzo.

"Piacere, Enzo."

Enzo merely glanced at the extended hand before turning his intense gaze back to me.

"Allora. Isla, can I talk to you for a moment?" Enzo's tone caught me off guard.

I glanced at Leo, who also looked taken aback by Enzo's rudeness. What was I missing here? But then Leo nodded in understanding, and I got up and followed Enzo a few steps away from the table.

"What's going on?" I asked, struggling to decipher his expression.

"Who is he, exactly?" Enzo's voice was low, his gaze darting back to Leo.

"I told you. He's Caterina's son. I met them at a dinner party last night Gianna took me to. Which, by the way, was so fun. I have so many things to tell you. Mainly how I made a complete ass of my—"

"I don't like him," Enzo blurted out, running a hand through his hair.

I laughed, then realized Enzo seemed serious. "What? Why?"

"I just... I don't trust him," he said, failing to mask his frustration. "He looks shady."

Laughing incredulously, I responded, "Enzo, you're being ridiculous. You don't even know him. Besides, he's like half our age."

"Doesn't mean he's not hitting on you. You have to be wary of these guys."

"Oh, please. You know, even if he was, I don't just run around hooking up with every Italian I meet."

Enzo opened his mouth as if to argue, then closed it, letting out a sigh. Jealousy flashed in his eyes, an unexpected twist that made my heart pound.

"Guys like him prey on tourists."

I tilted my head, feeling a surge of anger. "Oh, and isn't that what you've been doing? Wooing some poor unsuspecting tourist?"

"Isla, that's not—"

"I'll see you later, Enzo," I cut him off. I returned to Leo, who had been waiting patiently with a mix of amusement and confusion in his expression.

"Isla—"

I held up a hand. "No. If you're going to act like a child, go home and take a nap."

My heart was pounding as I plopped back down.

"I am...sorry," I said, unsure of what else to say. Leo seemed more amused than upset.

"Beautiful American tourist? It's not surprising the locals will fight over you."

Nervously, I laughed. "It's not like that."

Leo waved his hand dismissively. "Don't worry, Isla. Take it as a compliment. This Enzo fellow will be over it by tomorrow."

I spared a glance behind me and watched Enzo's Vespa fade into the distance. I couldn't help but think, He might be, but I might not be.

Chapter Twenty-Two

I stepped into Gianna's shop, sweaty and damp from the unexpected Italian summer rain. Gianna looked up from behind the counter, where she was sorting through some papers, and laughed slightly at my disheveled appearance.

"My goodness. What's wrong with you, apart from being soaked?" she asked.

Sighing, I sauntered over to the counter, wiping water from my forehead. "Having terrible taste in men is what's wrong."

Smirking instead of frowning, Gianna pushed her papers aside. "This sounds like it warrants the good stuff." She reached behind the counter and pulled out a rustic bottle of red wine, waving it in front of me. I nodded eagerly, and she poured us two glasses. Handing me one, she then slid onto a barstool beside me.

"Allora. Tell me everything."

Sighing, I took a sip. "It's just—he's so infuriating."

Chuckling, Gianna asked, "Enzo, I assume?"

"Are all Italian men that hot-headed and reckless?"

She bobbed her head as if considering, then nodded. "I'm afraid so. There's fire in our blood. We can't help it."

"Well, it's infuriating," I retorted, taking an extra-large gulp of the wine.

"What did he do this time?"

"He just acted like a teenager. I was admiring the rose window at Santa Cruz Cathedral," I explained, pausing as Gianna nodded. "And then Leo showed up."

"Caterina's son?"

"Yes. We talked a bit at the party about history and art. He's a history nerd like me. We started chatting about the window, and then we decided to have a coffee. Enzo happened to pass by and overreacted."

"Did Enzo find you in a compromising situation?" Gianna inquired, wiggling her eyebrows playfully.

I laughed. "No! We were just sitting and talking. It was the most innocent thing in the world."

She nodded, understandingly sipping her wine. "I see. Enzo is a good guy, really. But he does have a reputation for being, how did you say it, a hot head?"

"Well, it's juvenile."

She chuckled lightly. "It is. But come on. You're going to tell me that men in America don't act the same way? With all their American football and NASCAR racing? That's a lot of testosterone."

Laughing, I admitted, "Yes, I know. But we sometimes delude ourselves into thinking that European men are more sophisticated and civilized."

"I'm afraid evolution hasn't caught up to any of the male species across the globe."

I raised my glass with a sigh. "Well, at least we have good wine."

She raised her glass. "I think what you need is a break from Enzo. In fact, a break from all men."

"I think you might be spot on."

"I have an idea. There's a talented Spanish guitarist playing at Ristorante Marina tonight. Dress up and come with me. We'll drink a little too much wine, dance, and flirt with the bartender. It'll be a fun girls' night out."

"I think 'flirting with the bartender,' so to speak, is the cause of this problem."

She waved her hand dismissively. "There is no problem. Ignore him. He's just being a man-baby. You don't owe him anything."

I laughed at her apt description.

"Besides," Gianna went on, "he doesn't own you. Don't be quick to relinquish your freedom to a man you barely know. Even one as sexy as Enzo."

I chuckled, but her words gave me pause. He *was* sexy. Dangerously so. But was I giving up my freedom too quickly? Was I too accommodating to the men in my life rather than living life on my terms? I didn't intend to hurt anybody, but I was allowed to sit and have a beverage of choice with anyone I wanted. After all, I barely knew Enzo. We were just... I wasn't sure what we were. A summer fling? We'd shared some fun times and a few kisses, but I owed him nothing. Plus, he clearly had a vibrant social life that didn't involve me. Looking Gianna directly in the eye, I nodded and raised my glass. "Let's do a night out then."

Gianna clapped her hands. "Bravo! This will be so much fun. Do you have something black and slinky to wear?"

"Not really. I hadn't planned on dressing up while I was here."

"No problem. We'll go shopping. I know Mare Sereno seems like a sleepy fishing town, but the women here love to shop. We'll find something beautiful for you. Something simple, yet elegant and fun."

I felt a warmth inside me. "That sounds like a wonderful plan."

* * *

A couple of hours later, we stepped into a quaint clothing boutique on the north end of town. I loved the accessibility of everything here. A thirty-minute walk could take you end-to-end. The boutique smelled of incense, sea salt, and something warm and comforting, like tea. The shop attendant lit up when she saw us and hurried over.

"Gianna, Ciao!" They exchanged a cheek kiss and then a light embrace. The shop girl pulled away and looked at me.

"Ciao, Mia. This is Isla. She's a friend from America."

"I didn't know you had friends in America, Gianna."

"Just one friend. We met a few weeks ago. She's staying in Mare Sereno for the summer."

Mia beamed. "I'm delighted to have you in my little shop. Thank you for coming in. What can I help you with?"

"I need a dress, apparently," I said.

Mia chuckled. "Well, you've come to the right place. Any particular kind of dress?"

"Gianna says it needs to be slinky."

Mia chuckled again. "Of course she does. *Allora*. Perhaps something black? Are you going on a date?"

"Yes, with me." Gianna slipped her hand through mine. "Girls' night out. We're going to see Rafael at Marina's. You should join us."

"Oh! I do love his guitar. Ok, something you can dance in, si? A little tight but flowy at the bottom?"

"That sounds perfect. You seem to be the expert," I said.

Mia nodded approvingly and began scanning the shop. Then she took me by the hand and led me to a little sitting area. "Here, rest a bit. Would you like some Prosecco?"

Surprised, I glanced at Gianna. "I didn't realize I was in the Red Room."

Both women chuckled. "You cannot properly shop for clothes without Prosecco!" Gianna proclaimed.

"Well, then, I only want to do things properly."

Moments later, I had a glass of crisp, fruity Prosecco in my hand, and Gianna and Mia were showcasing a display of beautiful summer dresses. It felt a little like an Italian version of Pretty Woman. We finally settled on a black A-line number with a fitted bodice that accentuated my curves and made me feel like an old-time movie star. Looking in the mirror, I felt glamorous.

"It's perfect," I declared. "Absolutely perfect."

"Si," Gianna echoed. "Add a little red lipstick, and Enzo won't know what hit him. That is, if we were going to let him see it," she added with a wry smile.

Chapter Twenty-Three

Ristorante Marina was transformed from the night I had gone there by myself. We went to a back room apart from the main restaurant that had a small stage and pub tables. In the early evening hour, golden light spilled from its windows, casting a welcoming glow on the surrounding stones. Inside, exposed brick walls were adorned with framed paintings of Italy's landscapes, while each wooden table was set with delicate lace placemats and flickering candles.

A man whom I assumed was the famed Rafael stood on the small, elevated platform fiddling with a guitar. He sported a white shirt, black vest, and matching trousers, a mixture of traditional Spanish and casual elegance.

"He's nice to look at," I said as Gianna, Mia, and I slipped into a table at the back. The place was already packed and inching toward standing room only.

"Gianna agrees," Mia teased. "She never misses a Rafael night."

Gianna swatted Mia. "*Stai zitto*!"

Mia giggled.

Gianna, it would seem, had a little crush.

We ordered a round of Aperol Spritz, and with it, the server brought out a complimentary selection of olives, cheeses, sliced bread, and olive oil. I was never getting on a scale again, and I thought I was going to be just fine with that.

The melodic strum of a guitar brought the room's chatter to a hush.

Gianna's eyes went wide as Rafael struck the first few chords. As Rafael played, his dark hair fell into his eyes, which were closed in deep concentration. His fingers danced expertly over the strings of his polished guitar, each note resonating with palpable emotion. As he plucked and strummed, the intimate room vibrated with the melody, and the entire room was soon a captive audience.

The restaurant staff moved silently, almost invisibly, among the tables, refilling glasses of wine and collecting plates. They were careful not to disrupt the enchanting atmosphere, their movements as fluid and harmonious as Rafael's melody.

Gianna leaned in and whispered to me, her eyes bright, "Rafael doesn't just play his music—he lives it. Each strum, each chord, it's a piece of his soul."

I nodded, finding myself drawn to the melody as it wove around us. Every chord was raw, passionate, and strangely intimate. The rhythm was mesmerizing—a lullaby and a cry for freedom all rolled into one.

Rafael, his eyes still closed, seemed to be channeling every ounce of his emotions into his fingers, shaping the melody as a sculptor would a masterpiece. Each note danced in the air before merging into the night.

A lump formed in my throat as the chords of his guitar washed over me, stirring a well of emotions I hadn't anticipated. It was as if the music reached inside me, touching parts of my soul I didn't even know existed. It was haunting and beautiful, a salve and pain.

Tears welled in my eyes, unshed but threatening to spill

over. Gianna, noticing my state, reached out and gently squeezed my hand. But she didn't say anything—there were no words to say. The music was speaking for us, transcending language and culture.

As the last strum faded into silence, the emotions it stirred lingered, leaving a quiet ache in its wake. I felt changed somehow, touched by the magic of Rafael's music. His song wasn't just a melody but a powerful, resonating story that left its listeners forever marked.

"Isla, are you okay? You seem a little... overwhelmed," she asked, concern lacing her voice.

I paused, taking a deep breath. I took a heavy sip of my wine and forced a smile. "Sorry, that was—powerful."

"Si. Rafael's music is more than music. It's a beautiful, brutal experience."

I laughed through choked-back tears. "I'm definitely having the feels."

"Do you want to talk about it?" Gianna asked.

"No." I forced a calming breath. "I don't know, Gianna. I thought this trip would help me heal and find myself again, but now there's Enzo and he's complicating everything and I'm not sure if I'm ready for it."

Gianna's hand on my arm was warm, reassuring. "It's okay to feel vulnerable, Isla. Relationships can be scary, especially when you're far away from home. And when you've gone through so much. But you deserve happiness, and if Enzo is a part of that, maybe you should give it a chance."

I took another sip of wine, my voice barely a whisper. "I just miss my old life sometimes. Or I guess I miss the predictability of it all. Knowing where I was going and what I was working toward. Now—" I shook my head. "I have no idea what I'm doing. Adding Enzo into the mix—plus his family and ex-girlfriend—everything feels so complicated."

Gianna reached over to hold my hand, her grip firm and

comforting. "Change can be terrifying, but it can also be beautiful. You're on this journey for a reason, and you're stronger than you give yourself credit for."

I felt the tears finally escape, trailing down my cheeks. "What if it doesn't work out? What if I end up even more lost than I am now?"

Gianna squeezed my hand, her voice steady and full of conviction. "You'll never know unless you try, Isla. Sometimes, we need to take risks to find our happiness. Trust your instincts. And remember that you're never truly alone."

Wiping my tears, I nodded. "Thank you, Gianna. I'm so grateful I met you."

Her smile was warm as she replied, "I'm here for you, Isla. Now, let's enjoy the rest of our night and this amazing music."

As the evening wore on, the wine kept flowing. Each glass seemed to take the edge off my worries, and soon I found myself laughing more freely, my words becoming less coherent. Gianna, ever the responsible one, watched me with a mix of amusement and concern.

"Maybe you should slow down a bit, Isla," she suggested after I'd knocked over a glass of wine in a bout of laughter, the red liquid pooling on white table linen.

"I'm perfectly fine," I insisted, despite the fact that I was having trouble picking up the fallen glass. Gianna raised an eyebrow at me, a smirk tugging at her lips. "Well, maybe not perfectly," I admitted, joining her in laughter.

"Maybe it's time to call it a night," Mia added. Even in my jumbled state, I deciphered her amused smirk.

"Fine, fine," I muttered.

Gianna helped me out of the restaurant, my arm draped over her shoulder for support. The cobblestone alley seemed to sway under my feet, and the laughter that bubbled up from my chest was uncontrollable.

"I'm a fantastic dancer," I slurred as I attempted a wobbly pirouette, nearly sending both of us sprawling onto the cobblestones.

"I'm sure you are," Gianna chuckled, steering me away from a water fountain I was heading toward with an alarming lack of coordination. "But perhaps we should save the dancing for when we all have a clearer head."

The walk back to my cottage was a blur of laughter, impromptu dance moves, and heartfelt confessions.

When we finally reached my cottage, Gianna and Mia helped me up the steps and into the living room. I flopped onto the couch, giggling at my own clumsiness.

"All right, crazy girl," Gianna said, her voice gentle but firm. "I think it's time for you to get some sleep."

"But I'm not tired," I protested, even as a yawn stretched my mouth wide.

Gianna merely raised an eyebrow at me, her expression saying more than words ever could. Eventually, I relented, allowing her to guide me to my bedroom. She helped me change into a comfortable shirt and into bed, tucking the bed covers around me.

"Thank you, Gi-gi," I murmured as my eyelids began to droop. "For everything."

Gianna squeezed my hand but said nothing.

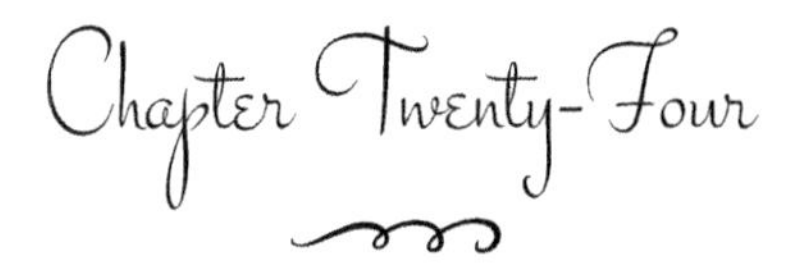

Chapter Twenty-Four

Enzo was annoyed with himself for behaving like a caveman. He honestly didn't even know what had come over him. When he saw Isla there with an attractive guy—a noticeably younger attractive guy—something in him just snapped. He shook his head and downed his cappuccino.

"What's with you this morning?" Lucia asked, glancing at him over her croissant.

Enzo met her gaze but didn't respond.

"Enzo?"

"Nothing. I just had a little...misunderstanding with Isla yesterday. It's weighing on me."

Lucia subtly rolled her eyes.

"What's that look about?" Enzo asked.

Lucia sighed and set down her cup. She pulled out her cigarette case and lit one up. "I just think you're getting worked up over a girl who doesn't matter."

He regarded his cousin curiously. "Doesn't matter? That's a bit harsh."

She exhaled dramatically, delicate plumes of smoke curling around her coffee cup. "You know what I mean."

"No, I don't think I do. Explain."

"She'll be gone at the end of the summer, in like three more weeks. And you'll never see her again. So, it's not worth worrying about. Don't waste your energy."

Lucia wasn't necessarily wrong, but her dismissive words didn't change the fact that Isla mattered—to him.

"Besides," Lucia continued, "she's dull."

"Dull?"

Lucia nodded. "Look, I can see she's pretty. And I understand that's your usual type—"

"She's also very smart. And engaged. And fun."

"If you say so. But she's wound up like a bomb. You don't want to play with that."

"You need to be nicer," Enzo replied.

"I'm a grown woman, Enzo. I don't have to do anything," Lucia retorted, dragging her cigarette.

"I know you've never forgiven me for breaking up with Valentina, but this is—"

"That's not true!" Lucia interjected. But Enzo saw the truth in her eyes. Lucia and Valentina had been good friends. Still were, in fact.

"Yes, that whole situation was difficult for me at first. I love you both. I didn't want to see you break up. But I'm not mad at you for it. You have to do what you have to do."

Enzo nodded. "I'm glad you can see it that way. Valentina and I were just not right for each other, you know?"

"I know. You don't have to explain it again." Lucia waved her hand dismissively.

"I feel like I do. Despite what you say, you won't let anyone else get near me. It's been years. It's time to let it go."

She sighed and snubbed out her smoke. "Can you blame me for being protective of my favorite cousin?"

Enzo smirked. "Yes, I can. When it gets in the way of my love life. You're intimidating. No one wants to get near you."

Lucia pretended to be offended, but Enzo saw the spark of satisfaction in her eyes. Lucia reveled in being intimidating. That was something that had bonded her and Valentina together. They were both women who enjoyed being the queen bee. Warm kindness wasn't exactly their strong suit. At first, he had found that attractive about Valentina. It was a fierceness that he couldn't get enough of, and if he was honest, it was quite the turn-on. But after a while, it just started to wear on him. She was always putting on a front. She could never just relax. She was so afraid of being taken advantage of that she had to act like the ice queen all the time. It was hard to have any real connection when she was constantly taking his sense of humor the wrong way. Pretty soon, Enzo just got sick of it. He wanted someone who could laugh with abandon, someone who could just exist, be vulnerable and silly. Valentina was never silly.

"So, are you getting serious about this girl, then?" Lucia asked, casually sipping the last of her cappuccino. Though she spoke nonchalantly, Enzo could sense her sincere concern beneath her tone.

"She's not this girl. Her name is Isla. And no, I'm not getting serious about anyone or anything. You know me. But I would like the chance to just hang out with a girl without you giving her the third degree."

Lucia sighed and raised her hands. "Fine, I surrender. I will be nicer."

Enzo smirked and picked up the menu. "Good, now what are we having for lunch?"

Chapter Twenty-Five

The morning after my night out, my head felt as though it was stuffed with cotton wool. Nursing a double shot of espresso, I heard a knock at my cottage door. Squinting against the bright sunlight streaming through the windows, I glanced at my clock: 9 a.m. Maria, hopefully with something savory and strong?

I pulled myself up and shuffled over to the door. Instead of a cheesy croissant with my name on it, however, there stood Enzo on my doorstep.

He looked a bit sheepish, his hands tucked into the pockets of his slim shorts.

"Buongiorno," he greeted, flashing me a tentative smile.

"Buongiorno," I replied, rubbing my temples. "You're looking awfully cheerful for this hour."

He chuckled, scratching the back of his neck. "I've always been a morning person. You look—forgive me—a little less cheerful."

I yawned. "Yeah, well."

His eyes softened, taking in my disheveled appearance. "Rough night?"

"You could say that," I admitted, suddenly remembering his outburst over Leo. I rubbed my eyes, too hungover and tired to deal with this right now. But here he was. And despite my irritation, he looked even more delicious than Maria's fresh croissant.

"So, what brings you here so bright and early? Did you bring a peace offering in the form of pastry?"

"Sadly, I have no pastry."

"I'm docking points for lack of forethought."

"That is fair." He hesitated, appearing uncharacteristically unsure. "But I did want to apologize."

I crossed my arms, leaning against the door frame. "For your lack of croissant?"

"I had no right to get jealous over Leo. He's a friendly acquaintance, nothing more."

"Anything else you'd like to add?" Despite my desire to crawl back into bed and sleep off my late night, I was secretly enjoying watching him squirm a little.

He winced, running a hand through his hair. "I can be a bit... volatile."

"A bit?" I repeated, raising an eyebrow.

"Okay, a lot," he admitted, giving me a shamefaced smile. "But I'm working on it."

I studied him for a moment before sighing. "So you won't just jump to conclusions next time? You'll give me the benefit of the doubt?"

His brow furrowed at the turn of phrase.

I clarified. "I mean, you'll give me some trust. Not automatically assume I'm out to do wrong."

He smiled thinly and nodded. "Ah, si. I'm sorry, Isla. I should have already done so."

I folded my arms and nodded curtly. "And you'll remember that I'm a grown woman to whom you have no claim, and you don't get to tell me what to do or who to talk to?"

He paused for a moment, and he looked a cross between shamed and amused.

"Si. You are your own woman."

"All right. Apology accepted. Just... try to keep your Italian temper in check next time."

He looked relieved, his shoulders visibly relaxing. "I promise."

I shook my head, a small smile playing on my lips. "You're lucky you're charming and that I'm a sucker for swarthy men."

He pressed a hand to his heart and flashed me a grin, his brown eyes sparkling with mischief. "Is that a compliment, Isla?"

"Take it as you will," I replied, leaning back against the door frame. "Now, if you'll excuse me, I have a hangover to nurse."

He chuckled, stepping back. "I happen to know just the thing for terrible hangovers."

"Please don't say limoncino. I think I might throw up."

He grinned. "Wouldn't dream of it. Pick you up in one hour?"

"For what?"

He just grinned. "One hour."

I groaned. "Fine. I'm too tired to argue."

"And pack your swimsuit."

Before I could protest, he turned and walked away, leaving me with a throbbing headache and a small smile on my face. Despite his hotheadedness, Enzo had a way of making things right. And as much as I hate to admit it, his charm was a salve to my wounds.

The sea glittered like a welcome mat, and the beach was lined with an expanse of golden bodies eager to soak up everything the Riviera had to offer.

"This scene is straight out of a postcard. Or some glamorous 50s movie," I said, my eyes scanning the shimmering panorama. There was nothing like this gilded tableau to make me feel ever so drab.

"There she goes with the movies again," Enzo teased. I ignored him. "I have the sinking suspicion you haven't allowed yourself a simple beach day since you've been here."

I flashed him a look. "And what would make you say that?"

"I think you're the type who believes a holiday isn't meant to be relaxing."

I responded with a mock glare.

The corners of Enzo's mouth twitched upwards as he caught my mock glare. "Oh, come on, Isla. Don't tell me you're not the type to fill up your travel itinerary with every museum, every historical site, every art gallery in town?"

I fought back a laugh but finally conceded with a sharp nod. "Okay, you might be onto something there. But in my defense, history is kind of my thing."

"Sure, sure. That's what the cities are for. But the Riviera —" Enzo splayed his hands out toward the sea. He set down our beach bag on the sandy shore. "You're going to experience the Italian beach culture. The art of doing nothing and enjoying everything."

"*Il dolce far niente*?"

"Exactly."

With an exaggerated sigh, I flopped down on the beach towel he had spread out. "I suppose I can handle one day of relaxation." I squinted up at him, shielding my eyes from the sun. "But only because you insist."

Enzo chuckled, reaching for the sunscreen. "It's a tough job, but someone's got to make sure you relax. And regazza? If you can't relax in paradise, there maybe be no salvation for you."

The next thing I knew, Enzo slipped off his tee shirt, revealing a form fit for da Vinci. I sucked in a breath as I tried not to ogle the corded muscles and bronzed skin. I don't know why I was surprised. Clearly, Enzo filled out his clothes quite well. But there was something about him that hinted at someone who spent long days in the sun, working naturally, as the body was intended to do. I supposed he was outdoorsy and active. He spent his days on the water, restoring machines, riding his Vespa.

Before I could stop myself from staring, Enzo caught my lingering gaze. I quickly averted my eyes as my cheeks—and other places—flushed with heat.

"Is somebody staring at me?" Enzo said with a smirk.

"No. I just thought there was a giant spider about to bite your neck."

"Ahh I see. And did you stare it away?"

I flashed him a mock-annoyed glare. "Don't be so arrogant. I'm a historian. I can't help but stare at pieces of art."

Enzo chuckled. "Would you like me to put sunscreen on you?"

I nodded and started to remove my beach dress. But I hesitated, suddenly flooded with embarrassment. I wasn't usually shy about my body. I was fit enough. I attended my workout classes regularly. I ate well. But I was suddenly mindful of the slight padding I'd put on due to a month of pasta and good wine. I hadn't really given it a second thought until now, but now suddenly, I was stripping down to next to nothing in front of all these bronzed deities. My slinky black revenge bikini suddenly felt like nothing but dental floss. I inhaled and ripped off the Band-Aid.

"I'm not the only piece of art in the room," Enzo said, his eyes darkening. My insides warmed beneath his lidded gaze.

"About that sunscreen, then?"

Enzo grinned and reached for the bottle. He gently applied it to my bare back, the chill of it sending tiny pricks down my spine. It might've been my imagination, but it seemed his hands lingered a little longer than necessary. I imagined those strong hands gave incredible massages.

"They are here!" The voice snapped Enzo and me out of our moment. We both turned to see Gio running toward us.

"I managed to get her out of a textbook for a day," Enzo said, flashing me a teasing grin.

"Well, he finally made me an offer that sounded interesting," I said.

Gio smirked. "Good, good. You can't leave the Riviera without spending a day on a boat."

I raised my eyebrows. "A boat? That little tid-bit was left out." My stomach and head protested to the idea of being out on choppy water. I've never had much for sea legs, despite growing up on the coast. And definitely not with a hangover.

"Don't worry. It's completely relaxing. Fabio will drive, we will all drink. We'll just cruise around the bay. You'll get some sun. Pretend like you are Grace Kelly," Gio said.

"Finally, I get to be Grace Kelly," I said.

"You're thinking of Monaco, Gio," Enzo said.

Gio spread his hands out. "Same difference."

I laughed.

"Where is everyone?" Enzo asked.

"Fabio is getting the boat ready. Elena has gone to fetch more refreshments. And Lucia should be here any moment."

My stomach tightened slightly at the thought of Lucia.

Enzo seemed to sense my hesitation and gently touched my arm. "Don't worry. I've talked to her."

I swiveled my head to him. "Talked to her?"

Enzo shrugged. "I told her she needed to be nicer."

"Is she not nice?" My voice squeaked a little.

Suddenly, my anxiety flared to life. It was now confirmed that Lucia didn't like me. The fact that Enzo felt the need to have a conversation with her... that sort of sealed the deal, didn't it?

"You look worried," Enzo said.

"No," I said, an octave higher than necessary. "I just don't want anyone making a big deal about something that doesn't need to be a big deal," I said, the words coming out garbled.

Enzo smiled lightly. "Have you been drinking already?" I glared. "Don't worry about Lucia. Don't worry about anything. Just worry about having a fun day out on the water with me."

I saluted him. "Yeah, ok. You've got it."

"Who needs a cold drink?" We turned to see Elena coming down the beach, dragging a cooler.

"I definitely do," I said.

* * *

Gio was right—the day was relaxing. The sea was smooth, and Fabio cruised around the bay with a gentle cadence. The salty sea air did wonders for my aching head, and soon, I forgot all about my throbbing hangover. I forgot about Lucia's judgment. I forgot about my insecurities. I was in the moment more than I had been in a long while.

Then Gio opened his mouth.

"I think it's time for a swim," Gio said.

I groaned from my lounge chair. "And ruin this moment? No, thank you. I'm perfectly content where I am."

"Come on," Enzo urged. "A quick swim will make you feel better."

"Pass," I declared, pulling my hat down over my face. "Leave me alone."

There was a long pause, and I suddenly felt the mischief brewing. I did not have time to scream or protest before Enzo and Gio picked me up and threw me into the water.

I shrieked, but the initial shock of the cold was quickly replaced by soothing relief. The saltwater seemed to wash away the remnants of my cloudy head, and I found myself laughing and splashing around with everyone.

"See? What did I tell you?" Enzo said with a self-satisfied grin.

I splashed him and glared. "You are not forgiven."

Enzo splashed me back. "We'll see."

Despite my initial reluctance, the day unfolded into one of the most enjoyable ones I'd had since arriving in Mare Sereno. Enzo was right—there was a charm to the Italian beach culture, the way people seemed to genuinely enjoy the simple pleasure of a leisurely day with the sea and sun. And there was something about the sting of the tepid salt water that washed away all traces of late nights.

Maybe a day of doing nothing was exactly what I needed. It was a reminder that sometimes, it's okay to step away from the hustle and bustle, to simply enjoy the moment. This was the way people were meant to live—in close-knit communities, in tune with nature. It was a way I had forgotten to live—a way I'd never even had a chance to live.

"So," Enzo began as we climbed from our small pocket of the Mediterranean Sea—I'm sorry, was I really just swimming in the MEDITERRANEAN SEA?—"Has the art of relaxation won you over?"

I flashed a reluctant smile. "I hate to admit it, but I think you might be right. This… it's nice."

Enzo's eyes twinkled with delight. "Nice? I know your vocabulary is better than that, professor."

"It's quite divine," I said in a terrible British accent.

He nodded curtly. "Much better."

"Enzo! *Vieni*?" Fabio was calling him from down the beach.

Enzo leaned back on his elbows and sighed.

"What's that about?" I queried, laughing.

"They want me to play beach volleyball."

"Oh, the horror!"

Enzo rolled his head toward me. "I'm better than everyone."

I nodded. "And humble. Good, good."

He rolled over on his elbow. "They know it. They do this every time. They challenge me three to one. If I win, they buy drinks. Vice versa."

I laughed. "Three to one hardly seems fair." He shrugged nonchalantly. I raised my brow. "Ah. You're that good, are you?"

"It's really not fair. To them."

I fell back against the sand and laughed. I cupped my hand and shouted toward the gang. "Beat him, and I'll buy!"

Enzo shot daggers right through me. "I hate you."

"I know. It's charming."

He fell back, letting his head fall into the sand. "I mean it. I will never forgive you."

I leaned in close to his ear. "And here I thought you were a good Catholic boy."

Chapter Twenty-Seven

Elena, Gio, and Fabio were in a battle of wills against Enzo. He wasn't kidding—this was a gladiator sport at his expense. But in their defense, my God—this man needed to be defeated. I wasn't entirely sure whom I should be cheering for. I fished around in the cooler for the rosé, mindlessly refilling my glass, my eyes glued to the spectacle.

"Ridiculous, isn't it?"

I spun around to see Lucia standing next to me.

"It's pretty funny," I said.

"Every time we come here, it's the same shit." She pulled a pack of cigarettes from her cross-body bag and lit one.

"I guess it would get old after a while," I said.

She exhaled a plume of smoke, and while, as a rule, I detested smoking, she did make it look terribly chic.

"Enzo tires of many things quickly, but for some reason, this years-long volleyball feud persists. The Habsburg–Valois Wars of sport."

"Nice reference," I said.

She shot me a look but didn't comment.

I don't know what emboldened me—okay, it was probably the wine—but I suddenly had the courage to say what I'd been thinking for the past few weeks.

"Lucia—"

She looked at me with an expression that said, *Whatever you're about to say better be worth my time.* I swallowed my familiar cement block.

"There is something I've wanted to speak to you—"

"Speak?" she all but interrupted, her brows knitted.

I cleared my throat.

"Talk. Talk to you about." Get it together, Isla. You have a freaking Ph.D.

The words came out slowly. "I sense you may not particularly like me."

She stared at me like she was studying my chemical makeup. Finally, she exhaled smoke and shrugged.

"I don't even know you, Americana. Don't be so self-conscious about whether people like you or not."

"I'm not being self-conscious," I clarified. "I think we both understand what I'm talking about."

She looked me over with a discerning gimlet eye.

"What does it matter?" she said.

"We just don't have to be enemies," I said.

"Who says we are enemies? That's a very strong term. Especially in Italy."

I tried to smile. "I just think we could get on better than we do."

She folded her arms, cigarette dangling between two long red nails. "Does my opinion really matter to you?"

I shrugged. "I haven't decided whose opinion matters to me yet. But, generally, I prefer it when people like me. Or at least when they don't dislike me for no good reason."

"Do you often give people a good reason not to like you?"

I chuckled at her sharp question. "Not intentionally. Look, I like Enzo. Quite a lot. And I would like you and I to be on friendly terms. It seems like everyone else likes me. Or at least doesn't have a problem with me."

She smirked. "This lot—the four bandits, mama calls them." She dragged again. "Isla, we are not enemies, you and me. You mistake me. I think you're fine. I just think you're wrong for Enzo."

"Why?"

She took a drag. "I have my reasons."

"Okay, fine. Why is it any of your business whom Enzo spends his time with?" I asked.

"Because Enzo is my dearest cousin," she said with a small laugh as if it should be perfectly obvious.

"He's a grown man, Lucia. You're not his mother, and he's not a little boy."

She waved her cigarette in my direction, and I coughed on the smoke.

"You don't know anything about Enzo. Enzo is complicated. You're just going to get yourself hurt."

I stood a little straighter. "You don't know anything about me, either. Why don't you let me be the judge of that?"

To my surprise, she managed a half-hearted smile. She drew another puff from her cigarette, then extinguished it in the sand. She picked up the butt and slipped it into her bag.

"*Aspetto, ragazza*. You seem like a nice girl. Maybe in another life, we could all be friends. I haven't told Enzo anything against you or suggested he shouldn't enjoy his time with you. I merely warned him about his family's likely reaction. I understand things are done differently where you come from. But here, family and tradition are important. His mama doesn't want him to elope with an American girl. She wants—needs—him to marry a good Italian Catholic girl."

I almost choked on my wine at her presumptuous words. "Marriage? Who's getting ahead of themselves now?"

She shrugged. "Welcome to Italy. Why can't you understand this?"

"I don't know, because it's 2023."

She shook her head with a laugh. "You Americans. You think you're so enlightened. I get it. You come from a very diverse place. We don't. Look around you. You have our blood, and you still stick out like a sore thumb."

I huffed incredulously. "I think everyone is getting ahead of themselves here. I'm on vacation, not husband shopping."

She shrugged. "Okay, good. So why don't you cut your losses now? You can't possibly be thinking of staying in Italy."

I opened my mouth to protest, but her words hit a sore spot within me. They threatened my resolve. My self-confidence.

"I never said I was thinking of staying in Italy," I said, trying to hide my insecurity.

"No, maybe not. But you are thinking it. You have romantic dreams about it. I know you do. Every American does."

"Nice stereotype."

She shrugged. "Doesn't make it less true."

"So what if it were true? Is that so bad? Is it so bad to have romantic dreams? I would think you'd be flattered that I consider this place as a potential future," I said. I remembered the rosé in my hand and sipped with purpose.

She made a little quipping sound. "It's your heart, I guess. But our family is never going to accept it."

My eyes trailed across the beach to the furious game in progress. Maybe not, I thought. But I think his friends will. No, no. I was losing myself.

"He doesn't strike me as the settling down type, anyway. So who cares?" I said.

Lucia snickered. "You're not wrong. But Zia Alessia worries it could be a girl like you who might change that."

I thought of sweet Alessia and wondered if she really did worry about me. Maybe her kind, pesto-fueled hospitality was just that—hospitality.

"My nonna was from here. I'm not so much of an outsider as you think," I added.

"You're free to make your arguments, Americana. But don't expect to win," Lucia said.

I felt a mix of annoyance and flattery at her insinuation. The notion that they considered me capable of taming a wild spirit like Enzo was intriguing. But I quickly brushed it off. Everyone was jumping to conclusions, including me.

"Look, I understand and respect everything you're saying. But this is nothing more than a summer friendship. Okay? I'll be heading home next week, and Enzo will be a fond memory. I'd prefer to keep it that way, free from drama. I'm certainly not seeking any."

Lucia studied me for a moment, then sighed. Her expression softened. "*Mi dispiace* if there was any 'drama,' as you call it. No one wants you to have a bad time in Italy or to leave Mare Sereno with negative impressions. That includes the locals."

"You sound like a travel brochure," I joked.

She chuckled at that. "Okay, we've had our serious talk, si? Let's just have our wine and calm down. I can already feel my buzz wearing off."

I smiled, raising my empty glass in agreement.

"Tell me the truth. Do they let you win? Do you have a fragile ego?" I teased Enzo as he returned from his sweeping victory on the volleyball court. I was propped up on my elbows in the sand, my glass of white wine—a crisp Pinot Grigio with notes of apple (I'm learning)—nearing its end. We had sneaked off to a small private cove well-hidden by a rocky overhang.

"You clearly know nothing of Italian pride. Fragile ego or not, their pride would never allow such a thing," he retorted.

Smiling, I drained my glass.

"More?" Enzo reached for the bottle.

"Probably not just yet. I am in the perfect phase. The phase of haze," I giggled.

"More than perfect, I think," he replied.

"Nope. Just perfect. I am light as a feather. Happy. My God, Enzo, I am *happy*." The realization came over me like a bucket of ice water, waking all my senses.

He grinned. "About time."

Sneaking closer, he slyly topped off my wine. I spared him a suspicious look before indulging.

Sighing, I said, "My Nonna would have loved it here. She

probably did love it here. I bet she sunbathed on this very beach." A small smile played on my lips at the thought.

Feeling his gaze on me, I turned to see a soft, nostalgic look on his face. "You really loved her."

My smile waned. "I did. Do you think anyone in Mare Sereno would remember her?"

"It's possible. They would be very old, though, wouldn't they?"

I sighed. "Yes, I suppose."

My heart ached with longing for her. I felt a sudden urge to talk about her, to share her story, and before I knew it, I was pouring my heart out.

"She practically raised me," I admitted. Enzo sat silently, his eyes encouraging me to continue.

"When I was just a little girl, it dawned on me that my parents weren't quite like other parents. They didn't come to school functions or take me to the park. They were too engrossed in their own lives—their work. Both doctors."

"A very noble profession. But demanding, sì?" he interjected.

"Sì. Particularly where we're from. I'm not sure how much you know about our healthcare system, but it's very much pay-to-play. Doctors can make a lot of money, and while some are among the world's best, they work relentlessly. My parents were both surgeons. They met in medical school and spent more time at the hospital than at home. When they weren't working, they were networking. To them, I was an afterthought, a responsibility delegated to a nanny. Sorry, I didn't mean to bore you with a sob story."

Enzo gently touched my shoulder. "You're not boring me. I like knowing about your past. I'm sorry it was like that for you. I am sure they loved you. Some people—they just have a hard time showing it."

Feeling flushed, I lowered my gaze and sipped my newly

refilled wine. "It's ok. I mean, I'm not hung up on my parent's every flaw. At a certain point, you just move on, I guess. But Nonna Rosa was the one person who was always there for me. She was warm, loving, and playful. She always made time for a craft or to play with me. Like, really play. Down on the floor, with my dolls." Smiling at the memory, I felt the sting of tears in my eyes. Sniffing them back, I continued. "She was everything to me for so long. She was fiercely proud of her Italian roots. She told me many beautiful stories about this place."

"Did you stay with her often?"

I nodded. "I did. After a while, she convinced my parents that nannies weren't necessary. She took over when they couldn't—which was often. She tucked me in every night, cared for me when I was sick, and taught me to make pasta from scratch." I shot Enzo a glance. "Sadly, her culinary skills didn't really stick."

Enzo laughed.

"Anyway, she was my anchor in the storm. When she died —I just—lost it. I wasn't only mourning my grandmother. I was mourning the only real parent I'd ever known. Mourning my best friend."

Tears were now falling freely, blurring my vision, and I no longer bothered to stop them. They needed to fall. I needed to let her memory soak into this beach, this sand. Her essence needed to find its way home.

Wiping my eyes, I said, "I'm sorry. I'm a mess."

Enzo brushed a tear from my cheek. "Don't be sorry. Feel what you must feel. Grief like that takes a long time to heal."

Swallowing hard, I admitted, almost inaudibly, "After her death, I... I fell into a deep depression. It was a very difficult time. A dark time."

"Isla... You don't have to—"

"I need to finish," I interrupted, my throat tightening. "I pushed everyone away, including Ian. That was the beginning of the end for us. I was so angry with him for leaving me, but the truth is, it was partly my fault. My depression, my inconsolable sadness, drove him away. I mean, why would anyone want to be with someone like that?"

Enzo seemed to ponder my words, his expression thoughtful. Then he reached out, gently took my hand, and pulled me closer. "Isla. Ian was a fool. *Fottuto idiota*! If he couldn't stand by you in your darkest times, he didn't deserve you in the light."

His words were kind, but they didn't dispel my fear.

"You don't understand. I was gone. I could barely function. I can't risk going back there again," I said.

"And you're scared that if you let yourself be vulnerable again, you expose yourself to that," Enzo finished for me, his voice tender.

My next words came out in a choked whisper. "Ian told me that after he saw how badly I could fall apart, he didn't think I was strong enough for him. He worried about what would happen to me when life inevitably threw more at me. He even wondered what would happen if we had a child. He questioned whether I would be one of those women who 'drowned her own babies.'"

His expression turned to one of horror. "He did not say that."

I shook with anger as I recalled the dreadful conversation. "He did. He said it scared him to think about a future with someone like me. It was during that time he met Miranda." It was hard for me to even say her name. "She was consulting at his company, and I guess she's not the type to drown babies." I sighed.

A string of Italian words, likely profanities, slipped from Enzo. "That's pure cowardice." He turned to me, his gaze filled with resolve. "I'm not an expert. But I do know when you love someone, you stand by them, no matter what."

I shook my head. "That's a lovely sentiment, but I don't think it's reality. People break all the time. Marriage is just a contract, after all. Just because you sign on the dotted line doesn't mean you're bound together forever."

Enzo was quiet for a moment, then said, "Take the whole concept of marriage out of it. Forget about legalities and contracts. Consider the commitment between two people who love each other."

I gave a half-hearted laugh. "That's very romantic too, but that's not real life either, Enzo. People fall in and out of love all the time. Love is fleeting. I think it's a bit ridiculous to think there's one person you're destined to be with for the rest of your life. Eternity, depending on your beliefs. People change. They grow, and often they grow apart."

"Maybe. But don't you think there might be some people who have a connection so strong, a bond that can withstand anything? Don't you think people can choose that? I'm not saying it's magic or something beyond our control. I'm saying that when you love someone, you choose to stand by them. Life is hard. I know you think I just spend my days drinking in the sun, but I understand the difficulties of the world, too. The key to getting through it with a smile is to surround yourself with people who will be there for you when things go wrong. Jobs and fortunes are lost. People get sick. Kingdoms crumble. People die."

I managed a small smile at his sentiment. I wasn't sure I fully agreed with him, but his perspective was more optimistic than mine had been recently. I needed more of that positivity in my life. I needed someone who could see the sunshine and not just the rain clouds looming on the horizon.

"I'm sorry. I've ruined the mood," I said.

"Not at all. Life is too short to only talk about the frivolous things. We could sit here discussing the merits of cheese, or we can be real. I choose real."

"Thank you. I am rather sick of discussing cheese."

"Did you at least have fun today?" Enzo asked.

"I did. Honestly, Enzo. Thank you. This has been an incredible summer. I don't know what I would've done without you."

Enzo chuckled. "I think you would've done just fine without me. I think it is I who have to thank you. You added an unexpected flair to my summer."

Suddenly, the words I had been holding back spilled out. "I wish I didn't have to go," I said. I regretted them almost immediately because I didn't want to think about the inevitable goodbyes or the potential of staying.

"But it's not over yet," he said. I was relieved he didn't try to argue or convince me to stay or suggest some other wildly romantic notion. I didn't want to ruin this moment. I just wanted to be in it.

"No, it's not over yet," I said, looking up at him. "We still have memories left to make."

He leaned in closer, and I did not move away. I didn't stiffen or protest. I allowed his hands to touch my neck, my shoulders. His lips to touch mine. And soon, we were locked in a deep kiss—the kind of kiss that fuses two people together. His mouth opened, urging mine to do the same. My whole body erupted into tiny flames as he leaned into me, pressing his mouth harder to mine. All I wanted was to melt into him.

"I have wanted to do that," he confessed, in between our lips and breath.

"Me too," I admitted.

His hands moved from my shoulder to my waist, and he pulled me close. His nose traced the line of my neck, a hurried desire palpable between us.

"I'd like to do more," he said.

My stomach turned over with nerves and anticipation. What was I afraid of? I was a grown woman living life on my own terms. I could do this. I needed to do this. I wanted to do this more than I could ever remember wanting to do anything.

"As do I. I want to do more. Right now," I said.

I could feel his desire as he leaned back on the beach blanket. Our bodies pressed into each other, moving in a tangle of grasping hands and passionate kisses. He reached into his pocket and pulled out the protection we needed.

I nearly laughed. "It's like a well-scripted movie," I whispered.

He nuzzled my neck. "Maybe an American one."

I sent Enzo a message and waited. I saw the small bubbles start and then disappear. I stared at the screen. I shouldn't have done it. Not the super-sexy, romantic, sleeping-together-in-an-Italian-beach-cove part—I definitely should have done that. But I shouldn't have opened up emotionally like that, laid myself bare. It was too much. It didn't matter that we shared something, that we had a connection—I had word-vomited all my dark demons all over a beautiful Italian beach. Was it any wonder he was politely ignoring me today?

I threw back my espresso and debated having another. I was already too jittery but also, somehow, exhausted. Everything was starting to pile up on me. I shook my head.

My phone pinged, and I nearly jumped. I almost dropped it trying to pick it up and swipe open the lock screen. A WhatsApp message lit up my screen.

"Ciao! Sorry, busy morning. I actually need to go up to Genova for a couple of days. I have some business to take care of. Let's connect when I get back, si?"

I blinked. I didn't know what to make of it. I mean, it was a reasonable excuse. He had a life. Did I really expect that he was just waiting around for my texts night and day? It might be the leisurely days of a long Italian summer, but he still had a life and a job. I wasn't his entire world.

I set my phone down and forced myself to breathe. It had nothing to do with me, really. He was just going about his life, which was something I needed to do, too. My days here were coming to an end, and I really needed to start thinking about what I was going to do next.

For one, where was I even going to live when I got back?

Ian wanted to stay in the condo. And fair enough—I was the one who had abruptly left and told him to do whatever he wanted with the place. True, I said those words out of some very justified anger, but I still said them. And he'd had the past eight weeks to do just that. With Miranda. My face scrunched up as her name came to my mind, and I tried to push it far away. Miranda wasn't the enemy here. Sure, she'd exercised some very poor judgment in getting together with someone already spoken for, but ultimately, this was on Ian. Ian was the liar. Well, have at him, Miranda.

What I needed to do was what I always did best—focus on my work. I had a seminar to plan. I popped open my laptop and pulled up my Google Doc.

The Medieval Mediterranean. It was coming together in my mind. The castles and battles and whimsy. Maybe I could even introduce the Mustache King, I thought wryly. The idea tickled my lips.

It was such a bizarre slice of time in history. And when one thought of those dark years of religious wars and persecution and grim living, they didn't associate it with this glittering gem of a place. It was an interesting juxtaposition.

I gathered my laptop and notes, threw my hair into a messy knot, and slipped on my sandals. I was going to seize this day and stop worrying about what Enzo thought. I had to live my life and stop living it on the whims of fussy men. If he wanted to pull away, that was his problem.

The day was as beautiful as ever, with lapping waves and a gentle breeze. The heat was reaching a crescendo as August settled in, but the sea air kept it manageable. I slipped into the little cafe with the ocean views and found a shady table on the terrace. I pulled out my computer and went to work plotting out the course.

I heard a woman's voice above my own thoughts. It was somehow familiar, even though the words were in Italian. I glanced up. Valentina was walking by, chatting on her phone. As she was finishing her conversation with a curt "Ciao," she spotted me. Our eyes locked awkwardly for a moment then she offered me a ghost of a smile. She was stunning as ever in an understated but sophisticated black shirt dress that skimmed her knees, paired with buttery soft leather sandals. Her dark hair cascaded down her back, and she carried a small leather tote. She was effortlessly put together despite the sweltering heat of the day. I hated her for it just a little.

"Isla, Ciao."

"Ciao, Valentina." I smiled as best I could.

"What are you up to?" She said, the words lazy and punctuated as though she'd forgotten how to speak English.

"Oh, um, work. I'm planning my courses for next semester. They kick off a lot sooner than I'd like to remember."

She paused awkwardly, then gestured toward the seat opposite.

"May I sit for a moment?" she asked.

I resisted the urge to climb under the table and pretend not to hear her.

"Sure. Please."

She nodded and slipped into the chair like it was a delicate dance move.

"It is so hot today. August in Italy—they don't tell you how it turns into a cesspool. Even on the coast."

I laughed nervously. "It is a little unbearable. The sea breeze helps, though."

"It's why I came back here for the summer. Milan right now is the very definition of unbearable. Take the heat and throw in a million people, too many cars, and hordes of tourists. And no air conditioning anywhere. At least that's something you Americans do right."

I tried to ignore the jab in the underhanded compliment. "We do love our comforts."

A server came by, and Valentina ordered an espresso in rapid-fire Italian that was so lyrical it made my eyes water.

She refocused her dark gaze on me. She looked pensive, as though trying to work out a math problem in her head.

"Was there something on your mind?" I asked. I sipped my water bottle.

"Now that you bring it up, si. Enzo. He's on my mind."

"Ok then. I'm not sure why I expected this not to be an awkward encounter."

She smiled thinly. "He's a good man, and I know he's taken with you. But I also know he can be impulsive, and I'm worried he's rushing into things."

For a moment, panic rushed through my brain. Did she know about yesterday in the beach cove? I took a moment to compose my thoughts. Even if she did, who cares?

"I appreciate your very friendly concern, but I think Enzo's a big boy."

Her expression went a shade darker. "It's presumptuous to think you know him like I do."

Her words struck a chord in me. She wasn't wrong. At the end of the day, what did I really know about Enzo? He was charming and carefree and seemed to genuinely care about the world and people, but I'd known him for only six weeks. It wasn't that hard to keep up a pleasant front for six weeks.

"Are you saying this because you're genuinely concerned for Enzo's delicate sensibilities or because you still have feelings for him?" I said.

Her gaze wavered for a moment, her dark eyes flickering to the side. But she instantly regained her stony mask. "I will always care for Enzo. We have a long history. But I also genuinely believe he's making a mistake."

"A mistake? What mistake is that?"

"Come on. Don't be thick-headed. If you're a professor, then you are smart."

"Shows how much you know. Academics are notoriously thick-headed."

She snickered. "Then let me be clearer. Enzo has a big heart full of passion. He falls easily. And you are leaving in what, a week? Life in Italy is not all scenic Vespa rides and romantic sunsets. It's a real place with real people and real challenges."

My shoulders tensed. "I know that." But did I? Wasn't it so easy to believe that this place and everyone in it was a long, permanent holiday? Before Valentina could lecture me more, I continued.

"Yes, I've enjoyed a nice long Riviera vacation. I have drunk more wine and eaten more pasta than I ever thought possible. But I do realize it's a vacation. I know everyone has a life to get back to, including Enzo. I'm leaving soon, as you pointed out, and I will take with me many happy memories, but that's all. Enzo isn't some fragile flower that needs your protection, Valentina. He knows I'm leaving—he has from the start. And frankly," I felt my frustration and my confidence rising. "Frankly, whatever Enzo and I have going on is so not your business. It's the farthest thing from your business. And I think—I think you really need to find something else to worry about."

If she was affected by my speech, she didn't show it. "Good. I'm glad you see it that way," she said fairly. "You aren't his first summer fling. You won't be his last."

The words were thrown out like the delicate flick of a razor blade. One so sharp, the sting of the slice doesn't hit you until you see the blood.

"But you'll still be here, won't you?" I said calmly. She didn't dignify the comment. At first, I hadn't seen the appeal of Enzo to someone like Valentina. Sure, he was gorgeous. But she seemed so much more driven than he was. Wasn't she more suited to some financier in Milan? But maybe she saw his potential as the shipping heir and not just a Vespa playboy.

I stood abruptly, my chair scraping back and making the patron next to me jump. He flashed me an annoyed glare.

I snatched up my computer and handbag. "I'm glad we've had this talk. Good day, Valentina. Don't melt in this heat."

I turned on my heel and all but ran away.

I didn't exhale until I was around the corner. Then I burst into a fit of laughter tinged with tears.

Chapter Thirty

Three days passed before I heard anything from Enzo. Despite being entitled to our own lives, our summer hadn't followed this pattern. We hadn't gone more than a day since he tried to kill me with his Vespa that first day. This silence only solidified the truth that gnawed at my insides—Enzo was pulling away. I didn't blame him. I was leaving, and the last time I saw him, I'd unloaded all of my inner turmoil, my darkest demons laid bare.

In that time, I tried to embody everything I'd learned about il dolce far niente. I read two books while lounging on the beach, shared good wine with Gianna, and enjoyed an evening aperitivo by myself, staring out at the lapping sea. And it was all wonderful. I didn't need Enzo to enjoy this little paradise. I only needed myself. But his absence felt like a pulsating void.

When my phone finally pinged, I had to do a double take upon seeing a message from him. My finger hesitated over the screen, fearing what he had to say. What if he was about to announce he'd met someone in Genova and was never coming back? Or that he and Valentina were running away to Milan?

Maybe he was going to say he'd enjoyed our time together, but the sun had set... I shook off all the worst-case scenario thoughts and picked up the phone. Text messages can't hurt you, Isla, I reassured myself. Taking a breath, I opened the message.

"Hey! Finally back in town. I didn't miss you, did I? When do you leave?"

I reread the message. He didn't know when I was leaving? That stung a bit. But I chided myself—did I expect him to mark it on his calendar in bright red letters? Shaking off the feeling, I typed a message back.

"Still here! Don't leave for a few more days."

"Excellent. Then we have time for one more rendezvous."

I set the phone down, unsure of how to respond. Was his tone different, or was I just imagining things? I picked my phone up again.

"Yeah, sounds good! You have my number."

After sending the message, I decided to take a long shower. I had a few days left in Italy, and I wasn't going to spend them worrying about what others thought of me. I intended to enjoy some more pasta, drink more wine, see a few final sights, and go for a long swim. Maybe I'd swim every day until I left.

I was heading to the beach. Enzo was right—I hadn't spent enough time simply relaxing while on vacation. I had conditioned myself to always be on the go, see every museum, and make the most of every moment. Lounging around was for home, wasn't it? Not when you were in one of the most beautiful, historic places in the world. But maybe I'd been wrong. If you can't relax on the Italian Riviera, where can you? I put on my swimsuit and a cover-up dress, collected my beach things, and dropped my Kindle into my bag. I might even read fiction today. Show everyone just how well I could relax.

I took my time walking down the twisty cobblestones,

savoring the sensations of this place. My impending departure made every sound, sight, and scent seem more vivid. When I rounded the corner, and the beach came into view, I stopped in my tracks. Enzo was sitting at a little café table, deeply engaged in conversation with Valentina.

My stomach did a flip-flop. I hadn't seen him in days, and his text that morning had been vague. Was Valentina the first person he wanted to see upon coming back? Panic started to dance within me. I turned to leave but hesitated a moment too long. Enzo spotted me. His initial smile faded as he realized how this might look. He got up immediately and started toward me. Panicking, I turned around and began moving in the opposite direction.

"Isla, aspetta! Wait!" Enzo called.

Ignoring the urge to keep walking, I stopped and awkwardly faced the opposite direction. Forcing a smile onto my face, I turned back to him.

"Enzo, hello." My words sounded formal and awkward, reflecting my nervousness. He stared at me for a moment.

"Where are you going?" He asked.

I glanced at the horizon. "Um, the beach. Yes, going to have a beach day."

"Are you—are you okay?"

"Of course. Why would you ask?"

He rubbed the back of his neck. "You saw me just now and ran off."

I chewed my bottom lip and tried unsuccessfully not to look at Valentina.

"Yeah, sorry. I just saw that you were busy. So, I didn't want to bother you."

He spared a glance back at Valentina. "I came down to run some errands and ran into Vala at the market. We popped in for a coffee to catch up."

"Uh, huh." My voice went up two octaves. "Okay, well, I won't keep you. Nice to see you."

I turned to leave, but Enzo grabbed my hand and pulled me back around. I closed my eyes and breathed.

"What's going on? Why are you acting like this?"

"Like what?"

"Like, I don't know. *Come si dice*? Cagey? Is that the word?"

"I'm not being cagey. I just—look, Enzo. I get why you've been keeping your distance."

"What do you mean?"

"I know things between us have escalated beyond what either of us set out to do," I said.

"Is that how you see it?"

I shrugged. "I didn't come here looking for romance. I came to get away and clear my head. Figure out what I was going to do next. And it's been so fun with you, but—"

"So, you regret the other night?"

"No! No, that's not what I'm saying at all. It was wonderful. All of it. But let's face it. It's almost over. I'm leaving in a few days, and maybe it's better if we just let this fizzle out. I know you're pulling away and—"

"I'm pulling away? What are you talking about? You are the one literally running away from me in the streets."

I sighed, forcing my voice to stay calm. "I haven't seen or talked to you in days. I just figured—"

He laughed incredulously. "Because I was away on business. I wasn't ignoring you. I was just busy. Isla, I love spending time with you. But I do have a job and a life that I need to attend to every so often. I've blown off a lot of work these past few weeks to spend time with you."

"I'm sorry, I didn't mean to stress you out or—"

"You aren't. I wanted to. But sometimes, I have things I can't ignore. I had a client in Genova that is a little demanding, so I needed to personally work on his project. And, well, I thought maybe you needed a little space. I didn't want to crowd you."

"Oh," I said, feeling the disappointment swell. So it had been intentional. "Right, of course. And I just want you to know that I'm not expecting anything more than this. We've had a fun summer. And the other night was beautiful. And I'll take those memories home and always think of you fondly."

"Fondly?" He half laughed.

I blushed. "I know. Stupid word. I use stupidly formal words when I get nervous."

He stepped closer. "I noticed. It's part of your charm."

Catching a glimpse of Valentina subtly turning to look at us, I thought about her position. What was the point of letting this go on anymore when we were both going to get hurt?

"I should go. I really do want to spend some time on the beach."

"Si, okay. How about dinner tonight?"

"Enzo, I don't know."

"What is the problem? I don't understand?"

I shook my head. "I don't want to get into this on a street corner." Flashes of being dumped in the Neiman Marcus linen section flooded my mind. I'd had enough public confrontations for one lifetime, grazie. "Can we—we can talk later?"

He nodded slowly. "Sure."

"I'll—I'll message you later once my head is a little clearer." Or once I'd had enough wine to give me some courage, I thought. "Yes, let's do dinner. That would be great."

I didn't say anything else as I walked away.

Chapter Thirty-One

We sat at a small bistro, the soft music and crashing waves creating the perfect ambiance. A good bottle of wine and some pasta sat between us. A girl's got to eat, after all. Might as well eat with Enzo. It should've been nothing short of romantic, but tension crackled in the air like a live wire.

"So now that you have a belly full of wine and pasta, do you want to talk to me?" Enzo asked.

I nervously fiddled with a piece of bread. "I'm sorry. I know I was acting really weird this afternoon. I'm just trying to process a lot of things."

"Like what?"

I sighed. How did I explain any of this without sounding insane? "I'm leaving in a few days."

Enzo half-laughed. "Yes, I know. You keep reminding me. As much as I'd like to forget it, I don't think that's possible."

"Let's just both be honest, okay? I don't want anyone to get hurt here."

"Who's getting hurt? I'm not a child, Isla. You don't have to worry about my delicate heart so much."

I met his eyes. "But what about mine?"

He blinked, seemingly never having considered the possibility. "I'm not going to hurt you. Why would you think that?"

"You wouldn't intentionally, I know. But that doesn't mean I'm not going to get hurt, anyway. I'm coming off a pretty rough phase of life. And I just don't think I can go through it again."

I sipped my wine as a distraction.

"I don't understand. Where is this coming from?"

I couldn't bring myself to bring up Valentina or even Lucia. I didn't want to sound like a crazy, jealous idiot. "I'm just—I'm a lot more fragile than I've let on. Ian—he's still really fresh in my mind."

"Forget Ian. He is no longer in your life, Isla."

I shrugged. "I wish that were the case, but it's not entirely true. We own a house together and—"

"Sell it."

His words were so casual, they annoyed me. I hadn't wanted to think about—let alone talk about—the fact that Ian wanted to buy me out and stay there, but now I couldn't hold it back. The words erupted out of me.

"He wants to buy me out. Of our condo. He wants to live in the house we bought and decorated together with his new girlfriend. And that betrayal—I don't know, there is just something about that particular thing that is worse than anything. Worse than meeting someone new or breaking the engagement. He wants to live in MY HOUSE with HER."

All of a sudden, tears came pouring out, ruining my perfect cat-eye liner. Damn it.

Enzo was silent for a moment before he finally spoke. "So what?"

I glared at him. "So what? How can you be so callous?"

Enzo sighed. "I'm not being callous. Just listen. Why don't you let him? Sell your share to him and stay here. In Italy."

His words hung in the air, the implication heavy. I looked at him, my mind whirling.

"Don't be ridiculous," I said, reaching for my wine and draining it.

"Why is that ridiculous? What's stopping you?"

I huffed, indignant. "You make it sound so easy. Just leave my entire life, pack a bag, and move to a foreign country. Start over. Come on, Enzo. This is real life, not one of your little stories."

He ignored my jab.

"And why not?" Enzo retorted, his frustration evident. "Ian is the past now."

"It's not about Ian!" I snapped, eyes burning. "It's about me! I am not like you, Enzo. I can't just let go of my past and embrace the unknown. I need... I need stability. I need certainty."

"And you think you'll find that back in America? With your ex-fiancé living in your house with his new girlfriend?" Enzo's words were laced with bitterness. "Is that the stability you're looking for, Isla?"

I flinched at his tone. "That's cruel. And believe it or not, Ian was not the defining factor of my life. I have a job. I have friends."

He nodded, lips tightly pressed together. Finally, he continued. "You came here to find yourself, didn't you? But all you've done is run away from anything that challenges you."

I shook my head. "That is so unfair." The words were barely a whisper.

"Unfair because I'm honest?"

The frustration was now morphing into anger. Who was he to judge my life? My decisions.

"You are saying things you don't even understand. I'm

here on a ninety-day tourist visa. I couldn't stay even if I wanted to."

He stared at me, processing. He raked a hand through his dark hair. "Yeah. I guess I hadn't thought about it."

I shook my head. "You don't think about a lot of things, Enzo." I sighed. "I—I should go before this escalates any more."

"Is this goodbye?"

I blinked back the threat of more tears. "I don't know. Maybe. I just need to be alone right now."

Before I could make things worse, I hurried out of the restaurant.

The end came so fast. Too fast. The final days were a blur or trying to soak up every last morsel of Mare Sereno, trying not to think about Enzo, and trying not to stress about my life back home.

"I can't believe you're leaving," Gianna said, her eyes misty with unshed tears. She plucked the cork from a new bottle of what she claimed was a very special vintage. With a flourish, she filled up two crystal glasses, the scarlet liquid shimmering in the sunlight.

I sighed deeply. "I know. I'm absolutely shattered about it. But I always knew it was coming. When I got here, eight weeks seemed like such a long time. It's amazing how quickly it goes."

Gianna nodded, her dark curls bouncing gently. "I know. Nothing like summer on the Riviera to pass the time."

"Or lose time," I said with a smile. "Thank you for everything. You've been an amazing friend to me all summer. I'll never forget you."

She smiled thinly, her eyes still glossy with emotion.

"Don't sound so mournful, Isla. You will come back someday."

"So certain?"

She shrugged. "She is a siren, Mare Sereno. Once you hear her song, you can never forget her."

I laughed lightly. "I think you're right about that. And hopefully, you'll make it out to San Francisco someday. I don't know what my life will be like. I don't even know where I'm going to live," I said with an uncertain laugh. "But wherever I end up, there will always be a space for you."

Gianna's eyes sparkled. "I have always wanted to go there. And now I have a good excuse."

We sat there for a moment, lingering in good wine and the warm day. The sun cast a golden hue on the terrace, and the scent of blooming flowers filled the air.

Finally, Gianna turned to me, her expression tender. "Are you going to miss him?"

I did not turn to face her, nor did I answer right away. I didn't know how to answer exactly. Or maybe I just didn't want to answer.

"Yes, of course. But," I shook my head. "Just like my stay here. It always had an expiration date."

Gianna tilted her head, a hint of sadness in her eyes. "Are you sure?"

"Yes," I said, hearing the wobble in my voice. But what could I say? There was no changing the way things were. "It is what it is. And I'll always have fond memories."

"Well, Mare Sereno and everyone in it is better to have known you."

"You're just saying that," I said. Gianna laughed.

"I would never lie. You've been a spark of joy for everyone. Do me a favor?"

"All right."

"Don't lose that spark when you go home. Remember this version of yourself always."

I swallowed my lump and squeezed her hand.

* * *

When I heard the knock at the door, I startled. I stared at my open suitcase. The room was in shambles—my life strewn about the floor.

It had to be Maria preparing for my checkout. I was going to miss her morning pastries and warm smile. Catching a glimpse of myself in the side mirror, I noted I had mastered the art of chaotic chic that morning. Instinctively, I tucked some rogue tendrils of hair back into its sloppy top-knot and approached the door.

But when I opened it, the last person I expected to see was there.

We stood there for a moment, silence enveloping us, neither of us knowing what to say.

"Maybe I'm not the person you want to see right now," Enzo said by way of greeting. I leaned into the door. I needed something to steady myself.

"No, not at all. I mean, yes, I am glad to see you. But I didn't expect it." I shook my head. "Do you want to come in?"

Enzo eyed the disheveled room and stared back at me with a small smile.

"I'm packing. Sorry for the mess. Let me clear some space."

"It's ok. Don't worry about it. I won't stay long and bother you. I know you have to get moving. I just couldn't leave things the way we did the other night."

I sighed. "I know. I'm sorry." I pressed the heel of my palm to my forehead. "I shouldn't have stormed out like that. I'm just processing a lot. And not always doing it gracefully."

I waited for a moment as Enzo seemed to be collecting himself. "I owe you an apology, too."

I laughed slightly, that being the last thing I had expected. "For what? You have nothing to apologize for."

"But I do. I didn't recognize the state you were in. I wasn't taking it seriously. I was being selfish, expecting you to just do what I would do in your shoes. To somehow dismiss all the things you have to work out in your life, your career, your home, and just live some sort of carefree existence. I know that's not how the world works, and I shouldn't have made you feel bad for needing to take life seriously."

I'm sure my expression fell as I felt a heavy weight drain from my body. I stumbled back slightly. I didn't know how much I needed those words until they slipped from his lips. How much I needed the validation that everything I had been feeling wasn't crazy but, in fact, normal, understandable. Maybe even healthy.

"Thank you. I don't think you know how much I needed to hear that."

He offered a tight-lipped smile, and for a moment, we just stood there, staring at each other awkwardly. Finally, he turned back to the disaster that was my cottage.

"When do you leave?"

I sighed. "Tomorrow. I'm catching a taxi to the train, then to the airport in Genova."

He nodded, not knowing what to say. I didn't know what to say either. What a summer it had been. I was leaving here a different person, that was for sure.

"Enzo, I hope you know. I am going to miss you. I've really enjoyed our time together. But I we always knew it had a shelf life, and I think maybe I pushed you away, just a little. In anticipation, you know? I couldn't bear getting hurt again, so I didn't want to get too close."

He smiled regretfully. "I know. And I understand. There's

no blame here. We had a glorious summer. You taught me many things, Isla."

I smiled. "Same. I'll never look at limoncello—limoncino, excuse me—the same way again. Or pesto. Or fritto misto. I'm pretty sure my entire worldview on the culinary experience has been turned on its axis."

He chuckled. Then he offered me a dramatic bow. "Then we here have done our job."

"I am really glad I met you, Enzo," I said.

He smiled somewhat nostalgically. "Perhaps in another life, we would have found a different path, yes?"

I smiled. I liked the idea of that. "Sounds like a romantic sentiment. I guess we are star-crossed lovers. Not meant to be in this world."

"Yes, something like that. We come from different worlds," he said dramatically. We shared a mournful smile, and finally, Enzo sighed and nodded definitively.

"Safe travels, Isla. I'm glad to have known you. I think you've made our little town a better place."

I walked him to the door. He turned to me, then leaned in and placed a gentle, final kiss on my lips.

He whispered, "We'll always have limoncino."

And then he was gone.

Chapter Thirty-Three

"Enzo, you're being so dramatic," Lucia admonished, her dark eyes gleaming with unsaid words. The sun-bleached terrace was warmed by the afternoon sun, the clinking of cutlery echoing from the nearby restaurant. She pulled a silver lighter from her purse, and the tip of her cigarette lit up, glowing fiercely against the Mediterranean backdrop.

"You never liked her, anyway," Enzo retorted, his voice low but firm. He cradled a bottle of beer in his hands, the condensation leaving a damp imprint on his fingers. The sun kissed his weathered face, casting a shadow over his eyes, but it provided little comfort. He stared at the sea, its azure expanse offering no solace to his troubled thoughts.

Lucia took a long, leisurely drag from her cigarette, releasing the smoke into the balmy air. Her gaze never left him, studying the lines etched on his face as she sipped her espresso.

"It's not that I didn't like her. She was nice. She was pretty, smart. She just wasn't right for you," Lucia stated, her tone matter-of-fact.

Snubbing out her spent cigarette in an ashtray, she drained the last drops of her coffee. She called for the server and gestured toward Enzo's bottle. "I'll take one of those beers, please." She turned back to face Enzo, her eyes serious. "Isla was too tightly wound, too careful. You need someone more... spontaneous."

"As if Valentina was spontaneous," Enzo said bitterly.

"Don't put words in my mouth. I didn't say anything about Vala. Clearly, that didn't work out either."

"Isla's been through a lot lately," Enzo defended, his gaze distant, looking at something Lucia couldn't see. "You have no idea the weight she's carrying."

Lucia shrugged lightly, not unkindly. "Life can be hard. But her burdens and the sadness—they don't change the fact that she wasn't right for you. You need someone lighter. Someone without all that baggage."

Enzo's laugh was dry, a mere shadow of his usual vibrant humor. "Look around you, Lucia. Who among us doesn't carry baggage? Do you think any of us make it to adulthood without a little baggage?"

"Perhaps," Lucia conceded, a note of amusement dancing in her eyes. "But don't you think Americans seem to carry more baggage than most?"

Enzo sighed, the sound almost swallowed by the sea breeze. Isla came from a faster-paced world with more stress, that was for sure. He drank the last of his beer, the crisp carbonation doing little to dull the ache in his heart. He ordered another, his gaze still fixed on the endless blue sea.

"Take it easy, Enzo. It's barely lunchtime," Lucia.

"Why don't you mind your own business for once, Lucia? If I want to drown my sorrows, I will."

Lucia leaned back with a smirk. "Fine, fine. I'm just not used to seeing you so worked up over a girl."

And she wasn't wrong. Enzo didn't usually get this agitated. It was true he was a bit of a romantic at heart, but he was used to things ending and accepting it, not being left in emotional shambles. He wasn't one to wallow.

"Give me a break. It's only been a couple of days. Let me grieve," Enzo said.

"And what exactly are you grieving, Enzo? A summer fling? A woman you barely knew? Come on. You're getting a little too sentimental in your old age."

Despite the sting of her words, Enzo had to admit that she had a point. He'd barely known Isla, but they had shared something, hadn't they? A connection that was trying to bloom but was cut short before it could fully blossom. He sighed. He was looking for something where there was nothing.

"You're right," he conceded, wanting to change the subject more than anything. "I think I just need a good, long ride up the coast. Stop at Giovanni's, have some fritto misto, and spend a little time with myself."

Lucia tapped her beer glass with her long, red nail. "There, that's the Enzo I know. Enough of this moping. Perhaps you guys can be pen pals," she teased, a glint of her old mischief in her eyes. Enzo managed a small smile. "Now, are you coming to Sunday dinner or not?"

He sighed. Perhaps Lucia was right, and it was time to reacquaint himself with normal life.

Chapter Thirty-Four

I looked around the room, feeling like a stranger in my own home. What was this place? What was this room now devoid of both things and feelings? A room we once shared, thinking we were building a future together. I shook my head. It all seemed so strange, like someone else's life. Someone else's memories. It was as if I was now watching it in slow motion on an old film.

I tossed the remainder of my things into the suitcase and assessed the room. Was there anything else I wanted to take with me?

Ian and I hadn't had all that much when we'd moved in together. I'd spent the majority of my life up till then as a student, crammed into small apartments as the debt mounted. I relied on roommates for furniture. My iPad for a TV. A small desk that doubled as a dining room table. I was usually too busy to do much cooking beyond a quick bean burrito, so my kitchen was pretty bare, too.

The things we'd collected together—the furniture we were starting to accrue, the kitchenware, and dishes—it all felt like fragments of someone else's life now. Did I even want it?

I stared at my collection of personal effects—a few boxes of mementos and clothes, a couple of pieces of art, some throw pillows. I couldn't decide if it was freeing or depressing. I was going to go with freeing so I didn't get even more depressed.

I heard the shuffle of doors downstairs. I stiffened. Oh God, Ian wasn't supposed to be here. Didn't he say he was out of town for the weekend?

I scrambled up, pulling my sweaty hair back and straightening my t-shirt. I spared myself a glance in the mirror. Exhausted from jet lag and overwhelmed by everything, this was not the impression I wanted to make upon our reunion.

But what could I do? And honestly, what did it even matter anymore? I gave myself a weak smile and zipped up my suitcase.

I stepped out onto the small landing and lugged my suitcase down the stairs. I stopped short when I saw something I didn't expect. Miranda was standing beside Ian. Or at least, I assumed it was Miranda. Miranda, the new me. The person who now occupied these walls that I had so painstakingly painted and decorated, the hardware that I had picked out, the drapes I had hand-ordered. Who was this interloper in my space? But I suppose the question was, did I even care anymore? Did I care if she took something I no longer wanted?

"Ian," I said, not knowing what else to say.

For a moment, both Ian and Miranda just stared up at me, a little deadpan.

"Isla. You're back."

"I am."

Ian did a subtle side-to-side shuffle. "I didn't know you'd be here."

"I emailed you about it. Did you get the dates mixed up?"

"I guess so. I didn't realize... How was Italy?"

His words came out staccato and forced. The awkwardness danced around us all, thick with tension.

I swallowed a lump in my throat and forced a smile. "It was great. Just what I needed. But you know, good to be back. Getting things in order." Back to reality, I thought. Back to a life I no longer knew or understood.

Ian's eyes flicked toward the redhead at his side. She was plainer than I expected. Not that she was ugly by any stretch, and I wasn't trying to be mean-spirited—she just wasn't the shining, ravishing harlot I'd envisioned had stolen my fiancé from me. She was just sort of average, with too much makeup and wiry limbs.

"This is... Miranda?" It came out like a question, his voice upticking. I saw the discomfort flash in Miranda's eyes as well.

"Hi," I said. I didn't have it in me to be cruel or catty, but I didn't think either of them deserved any more grace than I felt like offering. They were both to blame for this. I'm not one to blame the other woman as the sole Jezebel who breaks up a home. But then again, she knew what she was doing.

"It's, uh, nice to meet you," Miranda said. Her voice was light, airy. Sort of babyish. But, of course, it was. When I thought about it, she was Ian's type. He liked them quiet, sort of subservient. It balanced out his dominating personality. Had I been like her once? Willing to let him pull me along down whatever path he chose?

"Well, I just came to pack some things. I have the movers scheduled for Monday," I said.

"Movers?" Ian said.

I laughed, wondering if he was delusional or just plain stupid. "Yeah, the movers. To move my things. Out of this house, which I no longer occupy." I spread my hands out, indicating the surroundings. "The house that you now share with your paramour there."

"Oh, right," Ian said nervously. "I just didn't realize you'd be taking any furniture."

I blinked. "I'm sorry, did you think I was just going to give you all of my things in addition to my house?" The words were directed at Ian, but my eyes were trained on Miranda. That is what she thought, wasn't it? She thought she was just going to step into a ready-made life. Did he expect I was going to give the ring back as well? That he would just slip it on her bony little finger, and they would just pretend that it never happened, like switching out an actor in a soap opera after an unexpected firing or death? I wasn't giving them that satisfaction.

"It's just that it all goes with the house. I mean, the whole thing was sort of custom-ordered," Ian said.

I chewed on his words for a moment. You know what? Ian was right. It did belong to this house, this life. And I was done with all of it.

"You want the furniture? Ok. You can have it all. You can have every last spoon. I'll send an itemization to the lawyer to add to the buyout price."

Ian looked completely taken aback—his mouth drooped like a codfish as if to say something, but no words emerged.

I turned my attention away from them, picked up my suitcase, and walked down the staircase with as much dignity as I could muster, given the situation. I walked past them toward the front door. I could smell her overpowering perfume, the artificial scent somehow even more inelegant after my time drowning in the succulent natural scents of Italy.

"I wish you all the happiness," I said, turning toward Miranda. "And I wish you the best of luck."

I turned and shut the door.

Chapter Thirty-Five

Enzo strolled along the piazza, his head cloudy from both a little too much wine last night and a dark cloud that had settled over his world in the past week. This was unlike him. He had honestly never let matters of the heart get to him quite like this. He wasn't heartless—he was just good at loving, living, and letting go. Isla's departure had left a gaping hole in him that he had not anticipated.

He was lost in thought when he found himself in front of Gianna's wine shop. A small smile tickled his lips as he remembered wine tasting with a newly arrived Isla. Was that only at the beginning of summer? It felt like a lifetime ago already.

With a deep breath, he opened the door and stepped in. Gianna had the air conditioning on, creating a pleasant oasis from the sticky August day outside.

"Bongiorno," Gianna said cheerfully, not looking up from her desk. "*Un momento per favore.*"

Then she glanced up and saw Enzo. Her face lit up, but her smile had an undertone of sympathy, and Enzo wasn't sure he liked it.

"Ciao, Gianna. *Come stai?*"

"Oh, I'm fine. Melting in this heat, finally had to turn on the air conditioning. Not excited about the energy bill later. But I have to protect the wine."

He smiled lightly at the attempt at casual conversation. "We do what we must to survive in August."

"Indeed. Can I help you with anything? Were you looking for something specific?"

Enzo sighed and glanced around. "No, I'm not even sure why I stepped in. I was just walking by and thought I'd say hello. Secretly hoping you had air conditioning."

Gianna chuckled. "Why don't you sit? I will open a little chilled Prosecco?"

"I wouldn't say no," Enzo said, thinking of the pounding in his head. It was basically lunchtime. That didn't make him a complete lush, did it?

He settled into a high-top pub table near the window. He glanced out at the bustling day, but the vibrant colors of the Riviera seemed muted today. Gianna hustled over a moment later with an opened bottle and two glasses. She filled them up and slid one to Enzo, then slid into the seat opposite.

"Salute," she raised her glass.

"Salute." They both sipped and then settled into an awkward silence.

"So, do you want to tell me why you're really here?" Gianna asked.

"Air conditioning and Prosecco, obviously. This is nice," he said, eyeing the wine.

"It is. But I know you didn't come in here to taste my average table Prosecco before noon."

"You know, I miss her more than I thought I would," Enzo finally admitted.

Gianna smiled understandingly. "I know. I do too. She was a vibrant light that shook up this little sleepy town. And I know you cared for her. And she cared for you, too."

Enzo sighed. "I did. I hadn't meant for it to go how it did. It was the last thing I was looking for right now. But life likes to mess with you like that, doesn't it?"

"I've never known you to be so sentimental," Gianna said with a little laugh.

Enzo chuckled. "That makes two of us. I guess I'm just a little bluer than I thought."

Gianna exhaled. "I know. That's how it goes sometimes with a summer romance. She had a life to get back to on the other side of the world."

"And I always knew that, you know? I always knew it was temporary. You can't expect anything more from an American traveler. They can't just stay in Europe because they feel like it."

"Not without a good reason." Gianna winked.

"She didn't think she fit in here," Enzo said, finding the idea preposterous. She seemed to fit in just like a glove.

"Well, you know how it can be around here. It's a small town, not always welcoming to outsiders. Especially someone so different. And, well, there are people who want to see you with a local girl." She winked.

Enzo rolled his eyes playfully. "You sound like my mama."

Gianna shrugged. "Alessia is a wise woman. I am just a simple wine shop owner. I merely report back on the gossip."

Enzo tilted his head. "And what kind of gossip was there surrounding me and Isla? Something I should know?"

Gianna strummed her fingers on the table. "You did not hear this from me. Isla didn't want you to know because she didn't want to start any drama. But Valentina said something to her that upset her."

Enzo stiffened, and a small seed of anger sprouted inside of him. "What did she say?"

Gianna shrugged. "Oh, you know, classic Valentina. Just that you and Isla weren't meant to be together. That she didn't belong here. Something like that." Gianna shook her head.

Enzo's eyes widened, and he gestured in the air. "Aye, Vala! Why would she do that?"

"I think Vala is still holding onto the idea of you two being together. She saw Isla as a threat and wanted to scare her off. And it worked, at least a little. It wasn't the only factor, obviously, but I think it helped cement Isla's decision to go back and cut ties."

"I had no idea," Enzo said, annoyed and frustrated. "Isla never said anything to me."

"She wouldn't, would she? She didn't want to cause drama."

"I'm going to confront Valentina. When is she going to get it through her head that we are done? Things like this don't exactly endear her to me."

Gianna smiled. "Don't get too upset. It was a bitter thing to do, but it didn't really change Isla's choices. At the end of the day, she had a life to get back to. A life that wasn't here. She couldn't just stay because she likes the pesto."

Enzo slowly shook his head. "And here I have lived my life believing in the ultimate power of pesto."

Gianna chuckled. "People come and go in our lives at just the right time, I think. We all needed a little Isla in our lives. And she needed us. And so that's life."

Enzo nodded. Gianna was right. He smiled thinly and finished the last of the prosecco. He stood.

"Thanks, Gianna. I needed that."

"Any time. We're open for wine and therapy six days a week."

Chapter Thirty-Six

"Wow, that's quite a story," Luna said as we slurped down half of our cappuccinos. The aroma of freshly brewed coffee enveloped us, mingling with the smell of gluten-free pastries from the glass display case near the counter. The coffee shop, a blend of industrial chic and homely comfort, was an eclectic mix of exposed brick walls, mismatched vintage chairs, and coffee-stained wooden tables. Expensive espresso machines hissed and spat in the background, competing with the murmur of conversation and the occasional clatter of dishes from the small kitchen. An indie song played softly on the stereo, lending a melodious undertone to the chorus of city life.

The taste of the coffee lingered on my tongue with a bitter aftertaste. This had always been my favorite coffee shop in the city, but now, the cappuccino just didn't feel right. Even if I was permitted to drink it after the clock struck noon, it just wasn't Italian enough.

It had been nearly two weeks since I'd been back in San Francisco, and I still hadn't found my groove. It didn't help that I now called an Airbnb condo on Van Ness home sweet home.

"I know. I'm sure I'm being entirely dramatic. It just felt so, I don't know, significant? It was just something, you know?" I shook my head, knowing I wasn't really making any sense. The sounds of the city seeped in through the open door of the coffee shop. Outside, the symphony of San Francisco went on—the distant echo of cable cars clanging, the rush of cars, the sporadic buzz of bike bells, the chattering pedestrians on the sidewalk.

Every so often, a gust of wind would swoop in, carrying with it the scent of the sea and the distant foghorn from the bay. The city felt alive, vibrant, and in that moment, both painfully close and impossibly far.

Luna reached across the table and touched my hand. I met her blue eyes, big, bright, and honest. "I do understand. I know it's hard to put something like that into words, but I get it. I've been there before."

I smiled. "Oh yeah? Long-lost summer fling?"

Luna laughed girlishly. "Something like that. Something similar happened when I was abroad. I mean, I was a lot younger, basically a kid. But, you know, I often wonder what might've happened if I had been brave enough to pursue it."

"What happened?"

"Well, it wasn't all that spectacular, really. Just a summer abroad during my graduate program in Spain. And I met this guy, and, you know, we fell pretty hard. But in the end, I had to go back to my life, and he had a life there. It just wasn't meant to be. But I often wonder." Luna smiled nostalgically.

I nodded. "We all have lives. And Enzo and I, well, our lives just don't go together."

Luna studied me. "But why not? I mean, I know you have a job and a life here. But are you really so in love with everything about it that you wouldn't be willing to do something different?"

I chewed my lip and then busied myself with finishing the rest of my cappuccino. I sucked it down until nothing but foam remained. I licked the milky air.

"I don't know, Luna. I want to say that I am that adventurous person who could just drop everything and fly across the world for a chance at love. But that's not real life. That's a romance novel."

"Who says? I mean, really, you've said yourself you've spent your whole life doing the right thing, doing the thing you're supposed to do. And look where it got you. I mean, no offense, but Ian turned out to be a total ass. And your job, well, you've expressed your dissatisfaction with the whole bureaucracy and politics of your department. Maybe you should take a break."

I furrowed my brow. "A break? What do you mean?"

"You can put in for a sabbatical, you know. I think even up to a full year."

I had never even considered a sabbatical. Wasn't that what summer breaks were for?

"Is that a thing people do?"

She shrugged. "Yeah, all the time. Well, I mean, maybe not all the time. But professors take semesters off, and they do different things. They research. They teach at universities in other places. They just get their head right. I can't say your dean would say yes, but it certainly wouldn't be a weird request. One of the art professors spent a whole year teaching in Southern France and then came back."

I chewed my lip again. I thought through the implications. "Huh. I'd never really thought about it. But they've already assigned the classes for the semester. Which starts in literal days."

She shrugged. "Yeah, maybe this semester wouldn't work

out, but you never know until you ask. You're good friends with your dean, right?"

"Friendly enough."

"I'm sure she would understand. Maybe she has a romantic streak. Even if you didn't want to go back to Italy and see this thing through with Enzo, you could still go have an adventure. I mean, don't take this the wrong way, but the Isla that came back from Italy was a much needed upgrade."

Luna's eyes were so hopeful. Could I actually do that? Was I really brave enough to take an entire semester off from the job I knew and the life I knew to embark on some crazy journey? A handful of weeks over the summer was one thing, but another six months? Where would I go? Where would I live? Did I have the money?

I would once Ian bought me out...

"But aren't there, like, visas to consider and all that? I mean, can you just go somewhere for six months?" I said. I nervously chewed on my thumbnail.

"All I know is people do it all the time, so it can't be that difficult. Look, Isla, I can't tell you what to do. I'm just saying that life is pretty short. And I don't know, sometimes I think the universe gives us signs, and it's on us to listen."

I took a deep breath, trying to imagine what my life would look like if I took the leap. It was terrifying, but at the same time, exhilarating. Could I really let go of my carefully planned life and embrace the unknown?

As I pondered the possibilities, a newfound sense of determination began to grow within me. Maybe Luna was right. Maybe it was time to take a chance and see where life could lead me. There would always be a job to return to, but opportunities like this didn't come around every day. Maybe it was time to embrace a chance.

"Ok. I'll think about it. Maybe I'll float the idea by my

dean. Test the reaction." I sighed. "I can't believe I'm saying this, but maybe it is time for a change."

Luna's face lit up, her eyes sparkling with excitement. She reached across the table to squeeze my hand. "Whatever you decide, just remember that you have friends who love and support you. Life's too short to live with regrets."

I wanted so desperately to believe Luna was right.

"By the way, you're still coming to my art show tomorrow night, right?" Luna said as we exited the coffee shop onto Market St.

"I wouldn't miss it. You're going places, Luna. I know it."

She chuckled. "What, you don't think *starving artist* is a good look for me?"

"It's excellent marketing, but let me tell you about the divine glory of eating pesto."

Chapter Thirty-Seven

I approached the gallery, feeling a certain amount of malaise. I was looking forward to seeing Luna's work and, of course, would never miss it. However, a gray cloud seemed to hang over the things I once enjoyed fervently.

I did my hair and makeup, then slipped into a flowing summer dress reminiscent of my time in Italy, despite the perpetually icy winter weather of San Francisco. I pulled a cardigan around me for good measure.

Stepping into the stunning gallery on the Marina with views of the Bay, I gratefully accepted a glass of champagne and a canapé from a roaming server. I tried to taste and savor it, but everything felt dull as if my senses were in slumber.

Scanning the room, I spotted Luna holding court amid a circle of admirers. She wore a black jumpsuit with a bright blue belt that accentuated her enviable hourglass. Her black hair was tied up in a messy knot that looked both artful and intentional. I smiled, enjoying the way she lit up a room. Her passion for her work was intoxicating. She made some money selling whimsical children's art and had taught some electives at the university, but her real love lay in capturing people and experiences on canvas. Her last painting of the crumbling Tenderloin district had moved me to tears. She enjoyed teaching but would love nothing more than to traverse the globe, capturing humanity's tender moments.

I strolled the small corridors, admiring the vibrant watercolors and landscapes by other local women artists, some renowned, some novices.

Then, a painting caught my eye. I squinted at it from across the room. It called to me like a beacon. I walked over and stood in front of it. My jaw nearly dropped. I recognized that outlook, the curve of that shoreline, and the little restaurant atop the cliff. Someone had captured the light and the vibrant colors perfectly. It was Mare Sereno. No, it couldn't be. Mare Sereno was just an obscure little town on the other side of the world. I shook my head, denying my own thoughts. I was imagining things. Many coastal villages looked like this one.

But that restaurant on the cliff was uncannily similar. A chill crept up my spine.

"Exquisite, isn't it?" A woman of about sixty in wide-leg, high-waisted linen trousers and a cropped sweater that showed off her willowy frame approached. She sported a collection of dangling gold necklaces and thick eyeliner. I thought I recognized her from the website and assumed she was the gallery owner.

"It is. Absolutely stunning," I said.

"The way she captured the light. The essence," she said, waving her hand dramatically.

I nodded, feeling tears prick at the back of my eyes. "Do you—" I hesitated, feeling foolish, "—know where it's supposed to be?"

"Yes, actually. It's a little coastal town on the Italian Riviera. The artist spent the summer there, and it captured her heart."

I swallowed. "Do you know the name of the town?"

She furrowed her brow and squinted down at the bottom of the painting. "Yes, it's right here. 'Portrait of Mare Sereno.'"

I nearly dropped to the floor. It couldn't be.

"Are you okay?" she asked.

I shook my head slowly and then laughed. "Yes, I'm fine. I actually know the place."

Her eyes lit up. "You do? Oh, how funny. What a small world. It's a tiny little place, from my understanding."

I nodded. "It is. Just a little sliver along the Ligurian Sea. My grandmother was from there."

Her face lit up with delight. "Oh, how marvelous! What a wonderfully small world indeed. The painting is for sale if it strikes your fancy."

The idea excited me. A piece of my summer to hang on my wall forever. But the price tag made me shake my head. "Oh, thank you. I'll keep it in mind."

She smiled understandingly. "Well, I believe the artist is here, actually. If I see her, I'll send her over. I'm sure you two will have a lot to talk about."

"Thanks. That would be wonderful."

"I'm Ray if you need anything else. I'm the owner, in case you hadn't guessed," she said, extending her hand. My eyes trailed to her well-manicured fingers, and I had to resist the urge to lean in for a cheek kiss.

"Isla. Thank you."

Ray nodded. "Please do help yourself to all the champagne you can drink. We've had a generous sponsor tonight." She shot me a sly wink, and I raised my glass.

"I might take you up on that."

I waited for Ray to walk away before I turned my attention back to the painting. I allowed myself to linger there. Sometimes the universe sends us signs, Luna had said. Was it a sign? Did I even believe in signs? The coincidence was all too great. Maybe there were no coincidences in life. Maybe it was all part of a well-constructed tapestry, and it was up to us to listen to what the world was telling us. I drained my champagne glass and set it down. I forced myself to turn away from the painting and wander the quarters of the gallery to take in the rest of the art. But I couldn't help glancing back. What was the universe telling me?

Luna finally found me, a bright expression on her face. "I sold three paintings!" she squealed.

I smiled back at her. "I'm so glad! You really deserve it."

"It's more than I could've imagined. That anyone would actually want to hang my work on their wall," she pressed her hand to her chest. "It's all too much. I think I'm going to cry. Oh! Can I have one of those?" She plucked a champagne flute from a passing server. "I need this."

"Honestly, I love the painting you did for me. I look at it all the time. And your last work on the Tenderloin was so beautiful it was almost painful to look at."

She smiled, her eyes glimmering. "You're a good friend, Isla. Thank you for being here tonight. It means a lot to me."

It meant a lot to me too, I thought. "Luna, do you really believe in signs?"

Luna chuckled. "I see your head is somewhere else."

I laughed lightly. "Yeah, I know. Just humor me for a second. You said yesterday in the coffee shop that the universe sends us signs. Do you really believe that?"

Luna looked around and shrugged. "I do. I think the universe talks to us in subtle ways. I don't necessarily believe that our fate is predetermined or anything like that. But I do think the universe tries to nudge us in certain directions. Give us some information to help us decide what to do. Then the rest is up to us."

I nodded, and my gaze trailed back to the painting of Mare Sereno. "Yeah, that makes a lot of sense."

Luna tilted her head and looked at me. "Is this about Italy?"

I pointed to the painting. "You see that one over there?"

Luna squinted. "Oh, yes. That's by Marie-Remi. I would love to have her brushstroke."

I nodded. "That painting is of Mare Sereno."

Luna swiveled her head back toward me. "The little town where you were all summer? Seriously?"

I nodded. "Seriously."

"I thought it was a tiny little village no one has ever heard of."

I chuckled. "It is. It really is."

A sly smirk crept up on Luna's face. "I'm beginning to see what you mean. And yes, I do believe in signs."

* * *

I returned to my rental that night feeling a sense of lightness. It was as though a curtain had been drawn back, and I could see things clearly now. I stood at the window, eyes trailing out over the city. I loved this little slice of land. I was born and raised here. But somehow, it just didn't feel like home anymore. So much had changed over the years—the geography, the development, the people, the economics. All these external things changing and growing and morphing as time marched on. And now here I was, thirty-two, homeless, single, and directionless. I half-laughed.

I had my career, but even the university didn't excite me anymore. The idea of going back there and teaching the same curriculum with the same colleagues—I just didn't know if I could get excited about it anymore. I felt an emptiness growing in me, like a smoky black haze that was spreading and clouding my judgment, blocking out the light. What was I doing? Where was my life going?

Maybe Luna was right. I did have more control over the situation than I had pretended. The universe was talking to me. And maybe all I had to do was take the step, that very first step, and listen. Was I brave enough? Whether or not I was, I had to be. Here I was in my life with nothing to hold me back. I could request a sabbatical and that would buy me some time to reassess. It wasn't the only university in the world, after all. Sure, the semester was only a few days away from starting, but it was worth a shot.

I pulled out my laptop and opened my Gmail. Before I could second-guess myself, I drafted an email to the dean of my department.

Dear Deb,

I would like to speak with you about a potential sabbatical for the fall semester. Can we please talk at your earliest convenience?

All the best,
Isla

Chapter Thirty-Eight

With a nearly depleted bread bowl of chowder in front of me on my outdoor cafe table at a tucked away spot in the Marina —a creamy, carby luxury I finally allowed myself—I pulled out my phone and mindlessly opened the photo app. I stared at the pictures—the glittering sea, the winding Italian coastline, the Riviera, and then, there was Enzo. His big brown eyes and a wily smile, one tooth slightly crooked, lent a charmingly imperfect touch to his smile. His skin was gilded, and his physique nicely chiseled from years of working outdoors under the natural sun. I swiped again, and there was Gianna, holding a glass of red wine, grinning with abandon, teeth a tinted light crimson. (Don't you dare filter that, Isla! she had said. I earned the stains). Everything about her was a testament to a life well lived under the sun, doing what she loved with the people she loved. Wasn't this how we were meant to live? Getting back to a truly natural state—sunshine, natural beauty, community, healthy food, daily walks along pristine cobblestones, admiring the beauty of both nature and art that thousands of years of humanity had created?

I knew I loved my home, but it didn't mean I was stuck

there. The life I had chosen until now didn't have to be forever. It was not my prison or my coffin. For the first time, I was grateful for what Ian had done. I was grateful for Miranda, with her little baby voice and her small bony hands, who came in and took what didn't belong to her. Because she showed me the cracks in my perfect life, the cracks in my seemingly perfect relationship, and the glaring flaws in Ian that I should have seen but was too numb to notice.

I closed my eyes and breathed in, imagining the sensations of sea salt and grapes filling my lungs. I opened my eyes and stared out at the choppy Bay. For the first time in my life, I thought I finally knew what I wanted.

My phone vibrated on the wooden coffee table, startling me. I glanced down at the screen and sucked in a breath. I exhaled and answered.

"Isla!" My boss's voice rang out over the other end of the line as I picked up my phone.

I took a deep breath, uncertain about what she was going to say to me. I'd been in a state of panic since I'd hit send on that email.

"Deb, hi. Thanks for calling."

Deb chuckled. "Well, I reviewed your proposal. I have to say I am shocked."

"Was it that bad?"

"The contrary. I'm shocked you would propose something like this. I don't mean that in a bad way. I just mean, well, let me be really blunt with you, Isla. This is a lot braver than I have ever given you credit for."

I laughed. "I know. And you're not the first person to express such surprise. So, what do you think? Do you think it will work?"

There was a pause, and then Deb exhaled audibly. "Well, I will be honest. The board wasn't exactly thrilled that you sprung this on us literally days before the semester is to commence."

"I know. I'm sorry, I should have thought it through better."

"Hey, I get it. Life isn't always perfect. You're lucky we have a parking structure under renovation, and the Dean is panicked about parking wars."

I laughed. It was true. The battle for a parking spot could be a gladiator sport on the best of days.

"The head of the Humanities School thinks it will be a refreshing addition to the curriculum. A hybrid model test case."

I exhaled a long breath I hadn't realized I'd been holding. When I'd proposed the elective track to do one month in-person and then move to online, with the opportunity to travel in person to the sites being studied, I figured they would think I'd lost my mind. But I prayed to the Mustache King someone else might see the benefit.

"We'll try it out for one semester. I don't know how many of the students will be able to travel all the way to Italy on short notice, but you might get a couple of takers. But the Dean loved your idea for a live Zoom directly from the ancient sites. Honestly, Isla. It's brilliant. And we can revisit how it all went in the spring. Although something tells me you're not going to come back."

I heard the mirth in her tone.

"And why do you say that?"

Deb chuckled. "Whether it's a man, the pesto, or the sea, I'm pretty sure you're in love."

I laughed. "You might be right. I think it might be a combination of all the above."

There was a moment of silence between us. In the years I'd been working for the University, Deb and I had grown close.

"I'll miss working with you. I know I've had my differences with the administration, but I do genuinely love the team there. And it's a wonderful school. I'll miss my students."

"I will miss you, too. The students love you. You always get fantastic evaluations at the end of the semester."

I chuckled. "I'm not sure the dean of the school felt the same way."

"He has a lot of respect for you. And he thinks you're an excellent teacher. You just don't always do what he asks."

I chuckled. "Who knew I was such a rebel?"

"I'm really proud of you. And I have to admit I'm a little jealous. I think you're doing this thing we all dream about."

"Thank you. Hey, maybe next time you have a break, you'll come to Italy. I'll take you to a place that has the best pesto in town."

She laughed. "Sounds like a plan. Watch your email for the paperwork. I'll see you next week."

I hung up the phone with a mixture of terror and resolve. It was done.

Chapter Thirty-Nine

"I'm sorry, you're doing what?" Ian asked with incredulity over the phone.

"You heard me. I'm taking a sabbatical. I'll be gone for six months."

"But—"

"But nothing, Ian. The only reason I'm telling you is so you'll know how to get in touch with me regarding the sale of the condo. Other than that, it's none of your business."

The line was silent for a few moments. I could practically hear his mind whirling, trying to come up with arguments about why I shouldn't do this. Even though it had literally nothing to do with him anymore. But that was Ian. He liked to control things, even things he had no right to control—like the trajectory of my life. But his reign of terror was over.

"Anyway, I'll leave you the forwarding address, so if there are any documents you need me to sign urgently. But you can always get in touch with me via phone or email. Do you have WhatsApp? That's the easiest way to reach me."

"Are you sure you know what you're doing?" Ian asked.

I took a deep breath before answering. "Yes, Ian. For the first time in my life, I think I know exactly what I'm doing."

There was a long pause. Ian's heavy breath came over the line. Finally, he spoke.

"I'll have the lawyer contact you with the buyout information soon. The market value has appreciated, so you're going to get a fair price. Don't worry."

"Thank you. Best of luck to you, Ian. I hope you find what you're looking for."

"You too, Isla. And you know what? I'm proud of you. What you're doing—it's brave."

I smiled into the phone. I didn't need his validation—not anymore. But it still felt good to hear.

Chapter Forty

The worst of summer had subsided. Small hints of an easy fall were all around, from the cooler nights to the changing topography. The colors were shifting from the vibrant jewel tones of summer to a gentler palette as autumn took over. I closed my eyes and breathed in the fresh air.

There was a gentle knock at the door. I walked over and opened it. Maria beamed up at me.

"Are you settled in? Do you have everything you need?"

I smiled. "I do, thank you. Everything is perfect, just like the last time."

Maria smiled warmly, her eyes crinkling at the corners. "We don't usually get repeat visitors so quickly. But we are so glad to have you back. You brought a certain something to this place."

"That's very kind of you to say. But I think it's this place that has a little something."

Maria chuckled. "All right, then. I will leave you to get settled. Will you be joining us for dinner?"

I nodded. "Yes, that would be lovely. I've been desperate for the food here. As it turns out, there's nothing like it anywhere in the world. And please tell me you have croissants for the morning."

Maria chuckled. "Never a day goes by without them. Do you still like the chocolate ones?"

"I dream of them. Night and day."

She nodded and then, with a smile, turned. "Welcome home, Isla."

It would probably take me a long time before I stopped second-guessing my every move. I think that was just ingrained in me since I was a child. I was so conditioned to be afraid of making the wrong move. But here I was, back in a place that felt like home in a way no place ever had. I stared out at the glittering sea. Everything around me smelled of citrus, sea salt, and wine. I closed my eyes and breathed in. I could bottle that scent up and use it as perfume. I turned and looked at my little room. It was as if I had never left it. Maria had been so generous in offering it to me as an indefinitely long-term stay. I thought I might just ask her if I could stay there forever. Maybe get a job behind the desk. Maybe even learn to cook. I smiled. Whatever happened, at least right now, I was happy. And that had to count for something. Because prior to the summer, I had never stopped and thought, yes, right now. This is the moment. This is all I'll ever need.

There was another knock at the door. It startled me from my reverie. But, although startled, I was no longer on edge, no longer nervous. I imagined it was Maria bringing me some afternoon refreshments or a tray of the aforementioned chocolate croissants. My belly grumbled at the thought of the flaky, buttery crust. I ran to the door and flung it open.

"Maria," I began before I had even registered who was standing in my doorway. I thought my heart would stop. My stomach turned over. His eyes were as bright and wild as the first day I saw him.

"I heard a rumor you had come back," Enzo said.

I nearly fell into the doorframe. "Who told you?"

He shrugged. "I have my sources. It is a small town. Very small indeed."

"Enzo, I, I owe you, I owe you—" I stuttered.

He took a step toward me. His hand touched my cheek. "You owe me nothing."

And then he kissed me. The hard, deep kiss of finally finding the thing at the end of your long journey that you'd thought you'd lost along the way.

When we finally untangled our lips, our eyes met.

"How long are you staying?" Enzo asked.

I smiled warmly. "I only bought a one-way ticket."

The look on Enzo's face was a mixture of relief and pure joy. That too, I wished I could bottle.

I stepped aside. "Well, I think maybe we deserve a celebratory drink."

Enzo grinned and reached behind his back. "I already thought of that."

He produced a bottle of limoncino.

Chapter Forty-One

As the sun sank low in the sky, casting a warm, golden, Instagram-filter-like light on the coast, I found myself sitting at an outdoor terrace table at Giovanni's restaurant, reveling in the laughter and chatter. The sea breeze, acting as an impromptu hairstylist, tousled my hair and generously spritzed my nostrils with the salty scent of the sea.

Our table was packed with Enzo's inner circle and Gianna all gathered to toast my latest life decision—moving to Italy permanently. I mean, who could resist the allure of a place where pasta is a diet staple?

Enzo, never one to shy away from drama, raised his glass in an ostentatious toast. "To new beginnings, and to Isla, who has braved the carbs and decided to make this beautiful, pasta-filled place her home."

"Ha-ha," I said sarcastically.

A symphony of glasses clinking together ensued as everyone echoed, "*Cin cin!*"

My cheeks flushed, likely due to the wine, but I attributed it to the overwhelming acceptance and love from these people. Then I locked eyes with Enzo. In his gaze, I saw a mix of pride and adoration—or was it just the wine? Either way, those butterflies were audacious, fluttering in my stomach.

Pushing back my chair, I stood. "Thank you all for being here, for welcoming me into your carb-filled lives, and for helping me come to terms with gaining a few extra pounds. This journey wouldn't have been the same without each of you."

I turned towards Enzo, attempting my best dramatic performance. "And Enzo, thank you for loving me, for battling over the last piece of pizza, and for showing me that sometimes the most unexpected paths lead to the best pasta."

"Ok, ok, enough with the pasta references. You're making me gain weight just by talking," Elena interjected with a mock scowl.

"I knew you would come back," Gio chimed in, grinning broadly.

I gave him an incredulous look. "Why is that? Because Enzo is too irresistible?"

"No, forget Enzo. You needed to come back for me," Gio responded, thumping his chest.

"You've got me. You figured out my secret motives," I said.

"Most people come back at least once," Elena added.

"It's the siren of Mare Sereno," Enzo said.

Gio groaned. "Don't start."

"Another legend?" I asked.

"Legend says the Sirens of Mare Sereno did not lure sailors to their death, but to their peace. They called them home," Enzo said.

Everyone came together in a collective patronizing smirk. Enzo winked at me, and I bit my lip. I think this legend might just have legs.

"Siren or not, it takes someone brave to come back permanently," Elena said.

I smiled. Was I brave? I wasn't sure. Was it bravery to

follow your heart, or was it just common sense that we often ignore? It didn't really matter. What mattered was that I was here, having followed a siren song back to where one person I loved more than anything originated. I was here to put down new roots, possibly to keep her memory alive. I felt her presence more strongly here than back home.

I looked at Enzo. And maybe let new love blossom as it should.

Elena turned to me. "How will you manage your work? Last time, you were concerned about visas and all those silly details."

I laughed. "Silly details indeed. I started at the university with a one-month in-person course that then transitioned to an online course for the rest of the fall semester. Luckily, there's a lot more demand for that these days, so the university was keen on my idea. I'm going to be doing some live classes from the historic sites we're studying. Some of my students are even flying out to do a two-week in-person intensive here."

"Brava! That's such a good idea," Elena said.

"Then—" I shrugged, "I'm not sure. I have some proposals out to take on some of the study abroad students in conjunction with the University of Genova. If approved, I could stay on in my current position for a while. Until—" I took a sip of my wine, "until I figure out the next adventure."

"You will have lots of time for limoncino breaks," Enzo added, a sly twinkle in his eyes.

"I think Enzo wants me tipsy and plump," I teased.

Laughter erupted around the table, and I felt Enzo's arm wrapping around my waist.

"I'll accept you in any form."

"You say that now," I said with a dramatic sigh. But there was something in his words that told me it wasn't a line, it wasn't seduction. It was real and raw and beautiful. Looking around at my new friends and my new love, I felt at home for the first time in my life.

"To a new life," Enzo proposed.

I smiled and raised my glass. "To a new life, then. To a new life together."

"What do you think of 'The History of Vespas' as an elective course?"

Enzo gave me an incredulous look tinged with excitement. "Don't tease me. That's just cruel."

I chuckled. "I'm not certain I can fill an entire semester's worth of content on that topic alone. But perhaps we could broaden it. 'Italian Vehicles'?"

Enzo dismissed the idea with a wave of his hand. "No, I could provide enough information on Vespas to last an entire year. Perhaps even enough for a full major."

I laughed. "'Vespa Studies,' the next hot master's degree."

Enzo pointed a resolute finger at me. "Now you're onto something."

I finished my espresso quickly and returned to my computer. I did need to devise a valuable proposal if I intended to continue teaching online courses into the spring. It had actually turned out quite well for everyone involved. I'd had three students come to the initial intensive in Genova, and they had raved about it. We toured ancient sites, saw precious artwork, and bonded over our shared nerdiness for Italian Renaissance and medieval history.

The university had been hesitant at first to keep it going, but then realized I could offer courses appealing to our students who were studying abroad, participating in exchange programs, on medical leave, or otherwise unable to attend class full-time. Online education had become significantly more flexible in light of recent events, of course.

Enzo approached from behind and nuzzled into my neck. “Can work wait? It’s a beautiful day. Maybe one of the last before Mother Nature gets angry. And speaking of Vespas, she’s just purring to be ridden along the coast.”

I shot him a look over my shoulder. “Sometimes, Enzo, you’re such a cliché.”

He shrugged. “That’s why you love me. I’m your very own archetype.”

I chuckled and closed my laptop. “Alright then. Where to?”

He shrugged. “Who needs a plan? Let’s rendezvous out front and see where the wind takes us.”

The End.

Did you enjoy Italian Rendezvous? It would mean the world to me if you would please leave a review!

Keep on traveling! Download Monte Carlo Mistake now.

Let's connect!

Don't miss a thing. Join June's Jet Setters on Facebook or find me on Instagram and TikTok at @junepatrickauthor and follow me on Amazon.

About June

June Patrick writes witty, escapist romance set in swoony far away places. She is obsessed with all things European and dreams of moving to the Riviera where she can run around all day like Grace Kelly.

A Northern California native, she now moves around the country like a nomad with her real-life hero of a husband and their toddler daughter. They currently call Colorado home, where they live in a giant country house and begrudgingly battle snow.

You can find her at junepatrick.com or connect on Instagram and TikTik: @junepatrickauthor.

Also by June Patrick

Italian Rendezvous

Monte Carlo Mistake

The French Inheritance (Summer 2023)

Printed in Great Britain
by Amazon